This written account

of Bill Morgan's life

is a gift to his

loving wife of

forty-three years

and their children

and grandchildren.

LIVING LONGER
THAN HATE

Living Longer
Than Hate

A Story of
Survival & Success

By
C.S. Ragsdale, Ph.D.

GanDale Associates
Houston

Typography and Printing by
D. Armstrong Book Printing Co., Inc.
Houston, Texas

AUTHOR'S NOTE

Twenty years of studying and lecturing on historical topics, coupled with my love of storytelling, guided me to accept Bill Morgan's offer to chronicle his life.

Mr. Morgan sought not only to leave a diary for his descendants and to release deep-seated emotions that had tormented him most of his life, but also to educate others in the lessons of tolerance. He hoped, too, that his life might serve as a guidepost for the belief that a person can create his or her own miracles; that, if a person wants something bad enough and is willing to work hard for it, there is no reason it cannot be achieved.

Through my research I recognized that, at some level, each of us has that hunger for success. I realized, too, that the essence of a human being lies in conflict. We are all in search of human understanding, wanting to penetrate our pain; sense our love and our worthiness.

In Mr. Morgan's biography I have woven the story around his life while adding a second dimension at the end of each chapter, which is drawn from more than fifty personal interviews I conducted for the research background. The interviews validated the historical events and gave breadth to the story while showing how our lives are separate, yet intertwined, and that memories are sacred to each as he or she views an event. Every effort was made to maintain the accuracy of the interview excerpts. However, minor revisions were made to adhere to historical fact or to accommodate the author's craft.

I would like to thank the many survivors I interviewed who individually have a profound story. My gratitude is extended also to the resource interviewees. Both groups include Harold Becker, Robert Berlin, A. Harrel Blackshear, Morris Blum, Howard Cohen, Wendy Morgan Cohen, William E.Dinerstein, Maria Devinki,

Vangy Mathis Elder, John Ely Jr., Teresa Chattaj-Cohen Fallas, Celina Izenberg Fein, Martin Fein, Melinda Etta Morgan Finger, Steve Finger, Sheldon Frisch, Henry Fracht, Jack Freeman, Alberta Gallagher, Warren Gary, Leonard M. Grob, Jenard Gross, Davida Handler, Leslie Hogan, Les Hollander, Phillis Hollander, Tanya Jablon, Max Jucker, Louis Kantor, Walter Kase, Joseph Krakauer, Linda Langston, Kathy L. Lamb, Billy Meyer, Edith Mincberg, Josef Mincberg, Michael Morgan, Marci Rosmarin Morgan, Patti Blum Morgan, Ronnie Morgan, Scott Morgan, Bill Orlin, Jon Pollock, Nick Russo, Bill Schwartz, Rabbi Jack Segal, Fred Sklar, Arthur Steinberg, Dr. David Thaler, Arkady Valgura, and Irene Vasileuskaya.

Photographs were furnished by Ronnie Morgan, Bob Berlin, Harold Becker, Cedar Rapids History Center, Phillis Hollander, Joe Krakauer as well as Shirley, Michael and Patti Morgan and Wendy and Howard Cohen.

Many thanks to draft readers Vicky Conley and Glynna Rogers, editors Judy King and Anne Hebert, and Pat Armstrong for print format.

Special thanks to Jenny Hughes, Bill Morgan's private secretary. She was my "anchor," transcribing more than one hundred hours of interview tapes, making follow-up calls, and willingly accepting whatever was asked of her.

Without the support of my husband, Ron Chess, Sr., my creative efforts would not have been possible.

TABLE OF CONTENTS

*This book is dedicated to the
seven hundred men, women and children
from my birth village, Czerniejow in the Ukraine,
who were brutally murdered only because they were Jews.
Since I am the sole survivor, I feel in my heart that God
must have guided me to be in the right place at the right time
and saved my life so I can be the spokesman
for those victims of hate.*

-Bill Morgan

PROLOGUE

The Ukraine, often referred to as the Russian "breadbasket," is located in southwestern USSR. It supplies the country with most of its wheat and rye, harvested from a belt of rich, black soil.

The area's origins trace to the ninth century and Kievan Russia. By the end of the sixteenth century the region's Jewish population had increased to more than forty percent of the total population.

Many Jews in the area were artisans and merchants. As they leased estates, they gained the right to collect taxes from the Polish aristocracy who lived in the Ukrainian region. This privilege placed them in a tenuous position between the nobility and their peasant subjects. Already a religious hostility existed against the Jews. Now they were viewed as economic as well as social competitors.

Subsequent rebellions in the seventeenth and eighteenth centuries promoted animosity against the Jews and resulted in the massacres of thousands of Jews as well as destruction of their communities.

In the eighteenth century the majority of the Jewish population lived in the western Ukraine, often making up at least half, sometimes the majority, of the populace. A small percentage of these made their living in agriculture.

During a 1905 revolution many Jews joined political parties, which led to an upsurge in anti-Semitism. One such party, the Hibbat Zion, a precursory to the Zionist movement, influenced and excited the Jewish communities of the Ukraine in the latter half of the nineteenth century.

With the onset of World War I, the Russian army conquered the area, releasing its Cossack units against the Jews in Eastern

Galicia. The western Ukraine became a battlefront in 1915, and the Jews were forced out of the region. Many escaped to other areas of the Ukraine, mostly the central and eastern parts.

After the war, the Russians attempted to strengthen their win by establishing boundaries, further crippling the defeated. It proved impossible, however, to draw perimeters that would include all people of one nationality under the same government. Thus approximately four million displaced Ukrainians were stranded in Poland as the "submerged minority." Even though outnumbering the Poles, the Ukrainians were forced to use the Polish language and culture. When that led to sometimes violent resistance, the League of Nations stepped in; however, the supposed protector of minority rights failed.

Adding to the problems of the Ukrainians were the Jewish refugees, a segment of the population who did not take sides in the Polish and Ukrainian issues. This made them enemies to both and tools of hate propaganda of one group against the other.

Jews were seen as people with strange religious customs, an unfamiliar language, an unusual way of dressing, and a reluctance to fight. This set them apart from their neighbors. Jews were finally able to get equal rights and national autonomy in 1917 as well as a Ministry for Jewish Affairs, but this victory was short-lived. The Germans seized most of the Ukraine in the spring of 1918 with the onset of a civil war; they soon surrendered and withdrew from the area.

Thousands of Jews were either disabled or murdered and Jewish homes and businesses taken or destroyed in the civil war that was led by units in the Directory, the Russian White Army, Poles, and armed gangs. This slaughter resulted in abandoned villages.

The Russian Bolsheviks gained control of most of the Ukraine in 1919 after a war with Poland. Under their regime the Communist Party instituted Jewish left-wing political parties as separate factions but soon nullified them and fabricated its own Jewish department. After a 1920 peace treaty, the area became a Soviet republic and a part of the USSR except for Volhynia and Eastern Galicia, which were annexed to Poland and Romania.

The vestiges of the defeated Ukrainian army remained in Poland and some of the western European countries. These remnants grouped into paramilitary nationalist groups in the late 1920s and gave rise in the 1930s to the Organization of Ukrainian Nationalists, which enticed young Ukrainians.

The Ukrainian population became disillusioned with the Soviet command after they were forced into collective agriculture, the deaths of millions of people, and Stalin's eradication of many Ukrainian intellectuals.

During the 1930s employed Jews in the Ukraine consisted of trained workers, office staff, professionals, and intellectuals, but with absorption into the work force many were ostracized from the Communist party, from diplomatic service, and some employment fields.

In the western Ukraine, Jews who lived under the rule and economic discrimination of the Poles and the Romanians experienced many vicious recurring anti-Semitic disruptions in their lives. Regardless, some led an active cultural and political lifestyle.

When the Soviet Union merged with the western Ukraine in the early fall of 1939, the Russians abolished Jewish institutions and organizations, exiling thousands of Jewish leaders and reformers. The Soviets incorporated the western Ukraine into the Soviet Union in 1939 and in 1940 absorbed neighboring Bukovina and Bessarabia.

The problems that had clouded the 1930s soon would be amplified. The Ukraine's Jewish population reached more than two million by 1941. Germany's Adolph Hitler wanted all the Ukraine, and he would not acquiesce to humane treatment of civilians.

1 Yossela's Decision

How could Yossela Margulies know this day would change his life forever? By habit, he awoke to the first morning light that found its way through the open door. He sat up from the floor pallet, stretching his body to relieve the cramps from sleeping on the hard mud floor, careful not to bump the pullout that served as a bed for his younger siblings.

As usual, he would need to remove his makeshift bed to provide space for eating the meager breakfast soon to be prepared. The ever pesky flies had already found the open door, buzzing at his head. The walls, made of mud and straw, held the summer heat, compressing the air and causing the youth to catch his breath. The stench of chicken droppings from the yard and stale cabbage from last night's supper filled the room.

This day would be no more unusual than the last. What claim could he make that it would not be like the others—filled with hard work and little to eat, a small existence scratched out of the dirt? It was the way he had lived his entire sixteen years. He knew nothing else.

Czerniejow, the village in which he was born, nestled in the rolling terrain of far southeastern Poland. Small farms dotted the countryside. Fertile soil and short growing seasons produced grains, potatoes, and less often, sugar beets for local farmers' consumption and for whatever small profit each could make. Small houses made of whitewashed wood or mud and straw clustered together to form small villages, and in nearby meadows an occasional cow or horse grazed.

Barefoot peasant women with loose-fitting skirts and sometimes a colorful babushka tied under the chin lugged sacks of produce or baskets of eggs, chickens, or other market goods as they walked along narrow dirt roads. Farmers in horse-drawn, four-wheel carts carried milk or animals to market, wagons leaning and jarring as they traveled the deeply rutted road.

It was his mother who had introduced Yossela to the market several years earlier. The younger children competed with each other to join Etta on her weekly trips to Stanislawów. They knew they might get ice cream if her sales went well. From the sale she could provide a traditional Jewish Friday dinner for her family and scanty meals for the week.

When Yossela, born Wolf Margulies, fourth in a family of seven children, reached the age for his bar mitzvah and graduated from the seventh grade, his mother had found him a job in a grocery store in Stanislawów. For room and board he delivered fresh bread and other groceries, swept the floors, and did whatever was demanded of him.

He had liked his new job, especially going to the city where he could venture into *der mahrk*. The marketplace attracted a mixture of nationalities—robust Ukrainians; tall, square-faced Poles; and less often now, the Jews in their unique stiff-brimmed hats and long black coats. He examined the line of tables and booths that displayed cloth, carvings, and foods. The hawkers—men and women shouting, coaxing buyers—fascinated him. Peddlers, often dirty, paraded their goods up and down the streets. The market was crowded with people—peasant women in colorful dress; stooped, baggy-clothed old men arguing; screeching children running and playing. Elderly Jews shuffled along the walk, hands behind their backs, heads lowered as though examining profound philosophy scribbled on the ground. Often gray-haired, skinny beggars held out their caps to passersby and were usually ignored.

It had been Yossela's first job away from home. Etta, a typical Jewish mother planning for her loved ones, had secured for each of the older children a place in the city to learn a trade. For years she had walked weekly to nearby Stanisławów, the district capital in the Polish province of Eastern Galicia. There she sold eggs, butter, or chickens. She made many friends among her customers, who sometimes gave her hand-me-downs for the children but, better still, often knew about job apprenticeships for Etta's older offspring.

"The children will be on loan," she said, "while they learn a trade. It will be *gut* for all. There is more good future in the city than in the village."

The children had learned trades and left fewer mouths to feed at home, where food and space were scarce. Yossela's sister Sarah, now married, worked as a seamstress; brother Solomon was a shoemaker; and brother Bunya, a typewriter repairman.

When Yitzhak Margulies' small store went bankrupt due to generous loans to those who could not pay, he helped his wife by staying home, cooking the sparse meals, and caring for the children and his elderly father. Following the Jewish tradition, Yitzhak spent much of his time praying and reading God's word.

Though Yossela had liked his new job, he treasured fond memories of his chores as a very young boy, sometimes missing them. Then he had taken the family's sole cow to the pasture to feed. The family owned a very small piece of land beyond the river, bordering Czerniejow. Depending on the time of year, he and the cow had easily crossed the river within an hour of home. In the spring when the snow melted, the river was cold and challenging, but Yossela always persevered.

To return home in time for a game of kickball or to play at the river's edge catching frogs, he sought out the tallest grass so the cow would fill up quickly. He found such grass in off-limits areas that separated neighboring parcels of land from his family's. It was not a large space in which to graze, and he had to be sure the cow did not damage a neighboring crop. Quietly he coaxed the animal to follow him into the plush grass to eat.

"*Gib zikh a shokl,*" he would say to the cow. "Go a little faster." He anxiously watched, waiting for the cow's stomach to bloat, a sign the animal was getting its fill. Once this was done, he could return home to play.

"You are a good boy," his father would say. "Always remember to work hard and the Lord will bless you."

Because his father told him this, he believed it. Doubt only came as he grew older and realized that circumstances had not improved regardless of his family's hard work.

Delivering groceries had given him a small amount of money, certainly not enough to equal the long hours and long walk the evenings he chose to go home, but he did not complain.

Then in September of 1939 the Soviets came, ending his short-lived delivery job. Etta wanted her fourteen-year-old son in the village near her, so he returned to the farm chores he knew so well.

She was right to remove her child from the unknown in Stanislawów. When the Soviets occupied the city, Jews were harshly treated—Jewish organizations prohibited, merchants imprisoned. Then in June 1941 the Germans and Soviets declared war against each other. A short time after the news reached Yossela's village, the Ukrainians became agitated and began harassing Jews who lived in and near the village. The laughing Ukrainians hurled slurs as well as sticks at the hapless Jews. The harassment was nothing new, but now more assertive, more frightening. The Hungarian army, a German ally who tried to stop the Ukrainian outbreaks, was not always successful and soon occupied nearby Stanislawów.

After the invasion, a heavy cloud of foreboding surrounded Yossela's village, where eighty-five Jewish families lived among the Ukrainians. Three families, including the Margulieses, lived on the outskirts of the village. The Jews could not understand the anti-Semitism of their neighbors but, knowing no solution, went about their daily chores as normally as possible.

Harvest time for the corn and potatoes had now arrived. Perhaps it was the summer heat that had caused Yossela not to sleep well, even after long hours in the field.

Had he dreamed the commotion he heard during the night? Probably so.

He had not heard his mother or father stir this morning, unusual for them, for both were early risers—his mother planning for market, his father preparing breakfast. The nights always seemed too short to the exhausted boy, who rose early for another full day of plowing and working the fields.

Stretching his arms behind his back, Yossela reached for the ceiling, trying to awaken his body. The absence of his parents' morning flurry troubled him.

He was putting away his pallet when his father and mother entered the doorway from the yard. The younger children had just awakened, sitting up in bed and rubbing their eyes. His mother, heavyset with thinning red hair, looked silently at him, eyes vacant, face stained with streaks of dirt.

Has she been crying? Yossela wondered.

His father moved slowly to the kitchen table, to the kerosene lamp. He reached above the stone stove and carefully chose a match from a box on the shelf. Striking it against the crude, handcrafted table, he lit the lamp. The flame sputtered, then caught, casting flickering shadows and kerosene fumes into the small, stuffy room.

Yitzhak picked up his prayer book that lay beside the lamp. He looked at Yossela and the smaller children, beckoning them to the table. Etta pulled out a chair, settling heavily into it. She motioned the youngest boy to her lap. The two other children sat on a bench nearby. Yitzhak's eyes followed his children as they moved about the room. His face, partially covered by his dark beard, revealed little emotion.

Yossela stood quietly, his heart pounding. His father's thin frame seemed more stooped than usual. Something was wrong— what did he see in his parents' eyes? He stood, waiting.

Finally Yitzhak put down the book. Looking dolefully at his wife and younger children, he turned to Yossela.

"Yossela, Grandfather is dead."

It was not until the moment the words were spoken that Yossela felt real fear. Never had the youth been so frightened, even when the neighborhood children taunted him as a child. It was not fear he felt when they yelled their racial slurs at him, chasing him, often throwing rocks at him.

"Dirty Christ Killer! Damn filthy Jew!"

He remembered feeling only bewildered by their cruelty. What had he done to cause them to be so vile? He worked very hard for acceptance, always trying to excel in his grades, in soccer. He had to surpass in order to be accepted by the Gentile children and to gain attention at home. His very strict father talked constantly about achievement, using other Jewish children as examples.

"Look at the Remoisha children! See how hard they work?"

Often his mother would interrupt, moving closer to stand beside Yossela.

Then his father's voice would become gentle. "That is the only way, son, you can lift yourself up."

The young Jew stood as though frozen in time. His younger siblings had said nothing and his parents sat motionless.

"Yossela?" asked his father. "Did you not hear what I said? Your grandfather is dead."

What did Father expect him to do, to say? Yossela's memory still plagued him. "Why do they still call me names?" he had asked his grandfather only last week.

"God will take care of you. You need not worry." That was always Grandfather's or Yitzhak's answer, and then one of them would pick up a prayer book and read more of God's word.

Yossela thought the years and his perseverance had somewhat softened the neighboring children's attitude. Now he stood in the bleak room—too shabby, too small, oppressive from the heat and his father's words—waiting for the truth.

"Yossela," said his father, "the Ukrainian militia came to the house during the night without our knowledge. They took Grandfather and other village elders—all Jews—to a nearby field."

The room was quiet, so quiet Yossela thought he could hear his heartbeat. Only the hissing of the lamp wick broke the silence. Even the younger children remained stone still, eyes wide, blood drained from their faces.

"We were told they shaved their beards and their heads, even cutting off the earlocks."

Yitzhak watched Yossela closely, anticipating his question. "We could have done nothing. What could we do, Yossela? They came quietly while we slept."

The boy did not answer. Had he heard them during the night? Was that the noise he thought he had heard?

"They called him names, filthy names. Those who saw said he never fought back."

Yossela remembered that Grandfather believed in nonviolence.

"Then they dragged him to the river."

The answer Yossela searched for registered in his memory. Through the years when he had asked, "Why? Why?" his grandfather always answered, "God will take care of you. You need not worry." Without emotion Grandfather would place his gnarled hand on the boy's head, repeating the same words each time the child questioned him.

"The Ukrainians dragged Grandfather to the river's edge and shoved him in. The men held his head under the water."

Yitzhak's voice caught.

"Those watching said he never spoke, even when they allowed his head to surface. He gasped and gave in."

Yossela stared into the space around his father.

"God will take care of you. You need not worry," echoed in Yossela's mind.

The boy did not understand why God allowed the children to call him names, but his grandfather must know the truth— because God had told him. God must have spoken to him as he sat in his unfinished room, separated from the rest of the small house by the chicken coops.

Alone in his room, once used as Yitzhak's store, Grandfather Margulies spent all of his time reading the Talmud or the prayer book. He stayed relatively isolated from the family since his entrance faced the street and theirs, the side alley that ran next to his daughter's home. He spoke to them only in parables, surely God's words, for Grandfather must be God's lieutenant on earth.

What were Grandfather's last thoughts? pondered Yossela. Did he wonder where God was? Was the truth double-edged? Would he and the rest of his family be next?

They buried Grandfather Margulies in the small Jewish cemetery at the edge of town.

In late July the Germans took over the administration of Stanislawów, appointing a council of Jewish leaders.

"It will be easier under the Germans," declared Yitzhak. "They are more civilized."

The Margulieses had lived a day-to-day existence during the Ukrainian outbursts of violence. Torn between his father's faith and the fear that clouded his days, Yossela went about his usual chores, but too soon his fears were realized.

Signs appeared in the village: *Jude frie*, free of Jews. Shortly after the signs went up with their deadline for Jewish removal, the invaders forced the Jewish families of Czerniejow to display an armband with the Star of David on it, designating their Jewishness. Soon the feared SS routed the Jews from their homes. Forced into the streets, they were given little chance to take more than the bare essentials.

The SS ordered the families to line up side by side in the streets while their Ukrainian neighbors jeered and taunted. These neighbors did not take long to confiscate what little property the Jews left behind.

Stanislawów was the destination of the Czerniejow Jews. By this time the Jewish population in the city had grown to forty thousand. The Germans designated an older sector of the city for their confinement. In late fall this area would be officially established as the ghetto. In actuality, it already was. Before long, more than one thousand Hungarian Jews were brought to the city and crowded into the allotted area. The goal of the German *Einsatzgruppen* was to rid Poland of the Jews—to move them from the countryside and localize them in ghettos within major cities. It was an elaborate plan to solve the "Jewish problem."

After an extensive search, the Margulies family found a corner in a building where many other families resided. Solomon, Bunya, and Sarah, without her husband, who fought with the Polish army, joined them there.

There was no sanitation and little food. Soon after their entry into the ghetto, Yossela and his older brothers decided to slip out

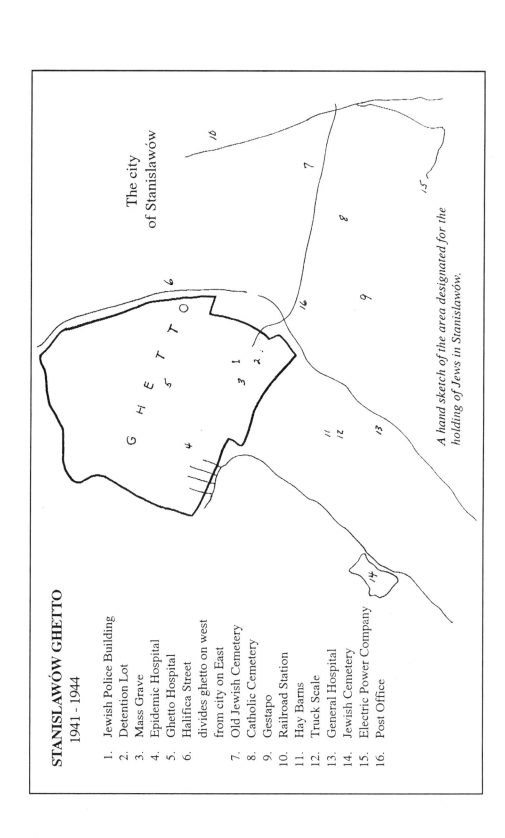

STANISLAWÓW GHETTO
1941 - 1944

1. Jewish Police Building
2. Detention Lot
3. Mass Grave
4. Epidemic Hospital
5. Ghetto Hospital
6. Halifica Street
   divides ghetto on west
   from city on East
7. Old Jewish Cemetery
8. Catholic Cemetery
9. Gestapo
10. Railroad Station
11. Hay Barns
12. Truck Scale
13. General Hospital
14. Jewish Cemetery
15. Electric Power Company
16. Post Office

The city
of Stanislawów

GHETTO

A hand sketch of the area designated for the
holding of Jews in Stanislawów.

under disguise of night, returning to their fields to dig potatoes to take back to their family.

When a former neighbor spotted them, he set his dogs upon them, snuffing future schemes. The boys knew the animals to be vicious and ran for their lives, losing their precious cargo.

Before they could try the venture again, a sorting of ghetto occupants took place. The Germans took the healthiest of each family for the labor force. Yossela and his older brothers and sister were chosen for work. Brother Solomon was selected for Jewish police duty, and Yossela had the good fortune to get farm work with a Polish farmer.

The man requested a skilled farmhand and Yossela volunteered. Not only did he know how to do farm chores, but he also spoke fluent Polish and Ukrainian, a talent which served him well. Because his work was deemed necessary for the economy, the Germans gave him a special permit that allowed him to leave the ghetto without marching with other laborers. When food deliveries from farm to city were necessary, they permitted him, under surveillance, to spend the night in the farmer's barn.

At first, having this particular job lifted Yossela's spirits for the Germans did not watch him closely. This allowed him to take every opportunity to smuggle food to the family members left behind in the ghetto. With each passing day, the danger of being caught—and probably killed—put great pressure on Yossela. Even greater was the demand from his kindred. Emotions always ran high when he returned to the family dwelling. They rushed at him, grabbing at him, searching his pockets, begging for something to eat.

Often his youngest brother waited inside the fence, ready to grab food from Yossela's pocket. This was dangerous, for a guard might see them.

The obligation that Yossela felt led to unwavering guilt. There was never enough food and not enough food smugglers to keep starvation at bay.

Yossela's bootlegging activities lasted only a short time before a guard spotted him.

"You blood-sucking Jude!" yelled the guard, pulling a potato from the youth's pocket. Red-faced, mouth quivering, the German grabbed Yossela by the shirt, pushing him against a nearby dwelling. "Drop them! Drop them all!" He slapped the young Jew's clothes, searching for further bounty.

Quickly Yossela helped him, reaching into the back of his shirt for three more small potatoes. He lifted his garment, and the contraband fell to the ground.

"Now get on with you and do not let me catch you doing that again!"

Yossela nodded his head, avoiding looking directly at the German. He knew he was lucky he had not been shot on the spot. He walked away, the precious potatoes left behind.

The youth watched his family deteriorate, the youngest brother growing more pale and thin by the day. The boy said little, his large doleful eyes speaking for him. His parents were helpless without the proper nourishment or medication. They had little money for the ration books needed to purchase from the meager food supply. The family members in the labor force supplied them with food as they could, living with the constant danger of being caught.

The constriction caused by overcrowding, little food, and no hope manifested itself in disease. Typhus took its evil toll. Epidemics followed. Corpses often lay in the streets and on sidewalks, sometimes for days waiting for the cemetery carts. Young Yossela moved through the crowded and cluttered streets, often stumbling over lifeless bodies. As he looked into the vacuous eyes of the bloated corpses, he prayed silently for the lives of his family.

On the farm Yossela worked hard, gaining the farmer's approval. He promised to put in a good word for Yossela if he ever got into trouble with the Germans. The boy thanked him, wondering after viewing the conquerors' "civilized" treatment of Jews, if anything would help.

Yossela soon met a Polish youth his own age who lived on the adjacent farm. The boys' chores often allowed them to visit each other. Gradually they began to talk, working as they visited. Occasionally between chores, they played kickball with an old soccer ball the Pole brought from home. Soon each began to appreciate the other's prowess at the game as well as the ability to do chores well. For the first time in a long time, Yossela found himself able to relieve some of the stress continuously surrounding him.

Taking respite from their chores, the two boys sat talking under a large oak tree surrounded by tall grass that edged the field between the two farms.

"Yossela, what is your dream?" The Pole flushed even as he asked the question.

"It is all right," answered Yossela. "I understand. My dream has always been to survive, to have as much food as I desired, to be accepted by others, to make something of myself." His eyes searched those of his new friend. "Do you understand?"

"I think so," said the boy. "I have lived in poverty all my life, but I am fortunate that I have not been treated poorly." He sighed, looking at Yossela. "I do not, did not, know any Jews in our village. The Ukrainians, even though they are not friendly, do not hurt me."

Yossela would have liked to answer, "We are no different from others," but he was not sure. All his life he had felt different. As a very young child he had begun to believe something was wrong with being Jewish. Was it his religion? He noticed more scorn toward the Jews during the Jewish high holidays than other times. When a drought ravaged the land or a baby died under mysterious circumstances, the villagers always blamed it on the Jews, though he never understood why.

The young Pole broke the silence. "You don't look like a Jew, at least the ones I've seen in Stanislawów."

A frown crossed Yossela's brow. "What does a Jew look like?"

"Well, I mean you aren't dark. Your hair and your eyes are light brown. My hair is darker than yours!" The Pole shrugged his shoulders. "You don't have those curls at your ears or wear strange clothes. You just don't look like a Jew. You look like me."

Yossela wanted to shout, "I wish I weren't a Jew!" but he remembered his grandfather's and father's teachings. The haunting refrain of their words would last a lifetime.

The two sat for a moment, silent.

Yossela looked long at the Pole, his mind reeling from the thoughts that trespassed more often now. Should he share them? Perhaps the Pole could help him. Finally he said, "You know, I think every day now about trying to escape."

The Pole looked at him, a frown creasing his brow.

"I just have to find a way."

Still the Pole did not answer.

"Do you think you could help me?" There, he had said it.

"How?"

"I've thought about it. We're about the same age, the same complexion. . . ."

"What could I do? I don't understand."

Yossela hesitated, then with a catch in his voice, quickly suggested, "Your . . . your birth certificate. I could buy it."

Even as he uttered the words, Yossela wondered how on earth he would get money to buy the document. Still he did not recant his suggestion.

His eyes wide, the Pole did not respond. He turned and walked away.

Now, fear swept over Yossela. Would the Pole tell?

Weeks passed as the Jew and the Pole worked side by side, neither mentioning the conversation. One day in early fall, the two were eating lunch when the young Pole turned suddenly to Yossela and asked, "Do you still want the birth certificate?"

Stunned, Yossela could not speak.

"Would you like to see what mine looks like?" Without waiting for an answer, the youth reached into his pocket and withdrew a folded piece of paper.

Yossela looked at the paper, then into the eyes of his friend. Could his friend ever realize what it was to be imprisoned by his birth?

The Pole pushed the certificate toward Yossela. "Here, look at it."

Frowning, he picked up the paper and unfolded it.

"If you speak Polish, you read Polish, right?"

"Sure."

"I'll bet I was born when you were."

Yossela looked closely for the date of birth. "Not quite. I'm a year older than you."

"You don't look it."

"What does it matter?"

"How much money can you give me?"

Caught off guard, Yossela answered, "I'm not sure. I don't have it immediately." Then, afraid his answer would destroy the deal, he said quickly, "I'll take it now and pay you as soon as I can."

"Soon?"

"Soon."

Yossela sat fingering the certificate as he watched the boy walk away. He knew he would not be able to find the money. Torn between guilt and relief, he folded the paper and put it in his pants pocket.

Each day death took its toll in the ghetto or countryside at the hands of the *Schutzstaffel*, who delighted in killing for the most trivial reason. This special guard detachment of the SS was created by Hitler and built into a police organization by Heinrich Himmler. Soon the Margulies family would suffer its first ghetto fatality.

Yossela came upon the hanging scene in the ghetto square as he returned from his job. The sun was just beginning to set. The wooden frame suspending multiple human figures and disguised by shadows of daylight reached to the sky. The bodies dangled from the hemp extending from the structure, necks stretched taut, heads limp on chests. The swaying had stopped. Now the bodies drooped silently.

The young boy would normally have avoided looking at the scene, but something compelled him forward. At first he did not identify Solomon hanging there among the others. Soon his eyes widened in recognition. Why would Solomon be there? Would he not be safe as a member of the Jewish police?

Suddenly Yossela could not breathe; tears welled in his eyes. As they dropped onto his cheeks, rage overwhelmed him.

Where is God now? He wanted to scream. What have any of us done to deserve this?

He heard no reply. After a while he turned from his brother's dangling corpse and ran toward his family's hovel.

Awake or asleep, Yossela saw Solomon's face. No matter how he tried, he could not release the image.

Mid-fall approached—the weather unusually warm, the circumstances worsening in the ghetto. Filth covered everything; the air was putrid. Overburdened facilities or the lack there of encumbered sanitation. The amount of food parceled out to Jews was meager and often not fit for human consumption even if they could obtain ration cards. For Jews, there was little hope. Rumors that Germans murdered about a thousand Jews in a forest near Stanislawów foreshadowed their destiny.

The three younger Margulies children were so weak, they lay silent, their eyes full of questions no one could answer. Both Yitzhak and Etta failed rapidly after learning of Solomon's death. Clothing drooped on their shrunken bodies. Their demeanor became more and more melancholy each day, their faces more jaundiced. Unfit for the work force, along with the younger children they survived on the scanty supply of food smuggled by the others, which became less and less each day.

On an October morning before sunrise, Yossela left for the farm. Sadness consumed him each day as he left his family. No matter how hard he worked, he could never smuggle enough food to them. His heart filled with dread for he never knew what he would find when he returned home in the evening.

As the youth approached the large cemetery on the outskirts of Stanislawów, he noticed several SS officers. They were stopping laborers—Jews, tagged by the Star of David armband, and Poles. Yossela's heart beat out of his chest, but he had no place to run.

"You, Jew boy, come here!"

The German looked no more than twenty, tall and thin, his uniform freshly pressed with shining buttons.

"Sir?" Yossela asked in Polish, approaching him.

Pointing to the cemetery entrance, the guard said, "Get a shovel from over there."

"Sir, the farmer is expecting me for work."

The young officer looked intently at Yossela, who held his breath, thinking perhaps that he had sounded impertinent.

"Do as you are told, Jude! Today you are in this labor force. Understand?"

Yossela nodded and started toward the stack of shovels. Soon others joined the shovel crew. The SS ordered them to begin digging and not to stop until told to. Each man dug in an open area within the existing cemetery. By noon the individual digs became a large hole. The Germans ordered them to keep digging in areas adjacent to a huge ditch. They were still digging when the first trucks arrived in the afternoon, loaded with Jews.

From his position at the rear of the hole, Yossela watched as the SS troopers herded the men, women, and children from the back of the trucks. Shouting and cursing, the SS ordered them to undress and put their clothing in the back of the vehicles.

The Jews complied, passively. Occasionally Yossela heard a child whimpering or a mother trying to convince the child that all was well. A few of the men quoted scripture. Following orders, the people began undressing and lined up at the edge of the freshly dug ditch.

When the first machine gun blast sounded, Yossela almost dropped his shovel. He looked up in horror as the captives fell into the hole. Bodies tumbled like rag dolls into the pit, moans rising from the hole.

Yossela watched as the troopers brought more to the edge, guns poised. The boy darted behind a tombstone, quietly putting down the shovel. Flattening himself against the back of the stone, he leaned against it, his heart in his throat, terrified. He was afraid to breathe lest the noise bring the Germans running.

From his hiding place behind the stone, he heard more trucks approach and the same orders given by the SS. Yossela became the stone that sheltered him, a mute at the grave of his fellow Jews.

As evening approached and the slaughter continued, Yossela decided to risk moving from his hiding place. Quietly he dropped to his hands and knees and crawled away from the murder scene. Occasionally he paused behind another stone, waiting to see if the Germans had found him.

This is too easy, he thought. Surely they will notice, but the slaughter had consumed them.

By the time he returned to the ghetto, it was dark. He approached the fence where he had previously discovered a loose board. Unnoticed, he crawled through the hole left by the defective slat and returned to his family.

Yitzhak leaned over a box toward the shallow light cast by a small kerosene lamp. As his son entered the room, he looked up from his prayer book he had managed to save. Nearby, Etta sat on a stool and quietly rocked back and forth, holding one of the boys. Yossela's ten-year-old brother lay moaning on the floor. Sarah and Bunya had not returned from the work force.

Yossela stood for a moment, his mind racing with his heart. Then he blurted out, "I am leaving. Now!"

His parents looked blankly at Yossela. No one spoke.

"I will not stay and die like a dog as I have just seen others do." Yossela reached inward for the courage he needed. "I would rather die escaping."

His brother, lying on the floor, raised up on his elbow, looking somberly at Yossela, his eyes glistening with tears. His mother's eyes said more. They cried, "You cannot leave. Where will we get food?" She spoke not a word.

After what seemed a lifetime to Yossela, his father motioned him to approach. Yossela obeyed as Yitzhak rose slowly from his stool, his wasted body trembling with the effort. Yossela knelt before his father, who placed a large, bony hand on his son's head. The young Jew sensed the tremble as he felt the weight of the hand.

"The Lord go with you, my son. We will meet in heaven. Say a kaddish for us."

Yossela struggled to hold back his tears. He looked at his mother. If she sensed his newfound bravery, her face did not show it. She said nothing, but her eyes consumed him as though to memorize him forever.

It was the most difficult thing Yossela would ever do. He turned away, moving slowly to the door. There he stopped and looked back over his shoulder. No one spoke, but their eyes followed him as though to escape with him.

Yossela made his decision. Now he must remember his father's blessing and use it for the strength to survive.

"God loves the persecuted and hates the persecutors."

That was the teaching of God and the great scholars, according to his father and grandfather.

Henry

I was twenty-one when I was in the ghetto, studying to become a lawyer at Stanislawów University. The war started in June, and the Germans moved in—the Hungarians right along with them. In a couple of months, maybe three, the Stanislawów ghetto was already established. They closed off an area in the older part of the city for it, a very long street called Halifica, a boulevard, two to three miles long. One side was in the ghetto and the other side was out of the ghetto.

A tall, wooden fence was put up, with certain wires electrified along the top. They had dogs outside the fence. Still some—not many—crawled under the fence, unnoticed.

They picked a section of the city that was mainly Jewish for the ghetto. If there was a Polish or Ukrainian family, they moved them out. My house happened to be in the ghetto, but we could stay in it only a short time. The more people they killed, the smaller the ghetto became. They narrowed it down by simply moving the fences. This was not a problem. They had cheap workers, Jews who were forced to work for nothing. In the beginning, I would say the ghetto was, in square mileage, around two miles, maybe a little better.

Even when the ghetto grew smaller in dimensions, there was no such thing as asking for permission where to live. You just moved into wherever you could. And people moved in, sometimes together. It took about a year for those two square miles to narrow.

Between August and November, Jews were put in the ghetto not only from Stanislawów and the surrounding villages but also from Hungary, Romania, and Czechoslovakia.

My older sister and brother-in-law lived with me. She was in her thirties with no children. My mother was in a different city. My father had already passed.

The minute they marched in, I was chosen for the labor forces. There were one or two exit gates for the laborers. Every day they took out the groups in the morning to work, thirty to thirty-five people through those gates.

I was assigned to work in the *Hauptzollant*, where very big buildings served as control centers for the whole area from the Ukraine and Poland. That was like the United States' customs on the borders where they check for alcohol and tobacco. They were mainly checking to tax whatever valuables people were bringing in.

The Germans took over the factories too. We were cleaning up the offices. There were nine of us in the work crew. We didn't get paid anything. One of the headmen was a very tough guy. As a matter of fact, his name was the same name as the chief from the Gestapo—Krueger.

I spoke perfect German, so I could communicate with them. I always came to work clean-dressed. I was the leader of this group. The Ukrainian bishop's palace was just two houses away, taken over by the Germans, and there were large stables. When we had to stay overnight to work, we slept in the hay.

I was stopped one day on my way to work by a Jewish policeman, someone I knew personally. He insisted I dig graves. The next day they were going to have a big *Aktion*, but I didn't know that at the time. They grabbed people from the streets and those people never came back after they dug those graves.

I told him, "I'm not going to go. I am working on a job and I'm going to go to it."

He said, "No, you're going to go where I tell you to!"

When they had an order to get two or three hundred people to dig the ditches, they had to do it or they got shot too. They grabbed anybody they could.

I refused, saying I had my work to go to. He would not let up. I refused, finally breaking away and running. If he hadn't been distracted, he might have caught me.

The next day the Germans had an *Aktion*, and the day after that some Jewish policemen were hung.

Most of the mass graves used were connected to a Jewish cemetery. I remember one *Aktion*, not sure when, but it was still hot. That day alone they killed eight to twelve thousand Jews at a Jewish cemetery on the outskirts of town.

There were trips to Belzec death camp as early as 1942, but a lot of people were killed right there in the ghetto. The food rations were very little in the ghetto. You were given cards for bread and very weak cabbage soup. People died in the streets from starvation. Children, old, young—there was no choice.

I also worked in a camp with Russian soldiers, war prisoners. This was in Stanislawów where the Polish military stayed. The Russian prisoners were not treated badly at that time. The chief of the camp was an Austrian and he was a very nice man. I stayed in the labor force a year and a half until the ghetto was liquidated.

One of the Jews had earlier built a mill in Stanislawów to make flour. He never finished it, but the skeleton of the big, tall building still stood. The Germans used it as a slaughterhouse. The rooms had cement floors. They would take in, every day, two hundred, and sometimes four hundred people, whomever they caught. They called it an *Aktion*. It's like you see, sometimes in a picture, a bunch of hunters surrounding a bunch of wild animals. That's how this looked.

The day before an *Aktion* graves were dug. Often they killed people right there in that mill. From there they loaded them on trucks and took them where the mass graves were dug.

You could feel the ghetto getting smaller and smaller. I had a choice—stay and be killed or try to escape. Before I could get away, another *Aktion* was about to take place.

Most all the Jews had already been removed from the ghetto. They were still using the mill as a slaughterhouse even though people lived there. They rounded up the last Jews from Hungary and Czechoslovakia and brought them to the mill one day. I was the only one left inside when they came. It was the first place I found to hide. I had no other choice. There was no time to find a safer place. No one knew I was there. Two closets, armoires, still stood. I hid behind one of them. It was large and close to the wall with just enough space for me to hide behind, a very narrow space.

I heard every word they said. The Germans drove in with truckloads of Gestapo, and they started shooting wild. They shot right in front of those closets that I was standing behind. They were like wild animals, shooting everyone.

I was like stone. I could not move. I couldn't cry then, but I can cry today.

They finished the slaughter, loaded the bodies on trucks, and drove out the main gate, locking the gate behind them. That was the end of the ghetto. It was 1943. I was the last Jew there, locked in.

Lenny*

The tales of Stanislav (Stanislawów) had a tragic ending. Sometime between 1941 and 1943, Nazi killing squads, the notorious *Einsatzgruppen*, put my father's entire family, the Grobs, along with approximately thirty thousand other Jews of Stanislav, to death. The destruction of his family cast a pall over my father's telling of Stanislav stories; an ineffable sadness haunted his being. Later I would come to realize how alone he must have felt in America. Surrounded by his family, by numerous relatives on my mother's side, and by friends, my father remained—in some significant sense—a solitary being. At age forty he led an orphaned existence.

As he recounted the little he had come to know of these tragic years, my father's eyes would fill with tears. Frightened by this display of sorrow, I withdrew further into thoughts of friends and baseball. And if the subject of the Holocaust emerged in my mother's presence, it was instantly and firmly rejected: my mother decided the children were to be protected at all costs from stories of Nazi atrocities half a world away.

My father's failure to learn the precise time and place of his family's murder added to a sense of grim mystery surrounding his "other" life. The Jews of Stanislav, roughly one-third of the city's 1939 population, were killed in a number of Nazi *Aktions*. The major actions are well documented. One thousand of the intelligentsia were killed in August 1941, twelve thousand Jews were killed at the cemetery on October 12th of that year, and ten thousand were deported to the Belzec death camp in the spring and fall of 1942. Many thousands were killed on the ghetto streets on the Jewish New Year of 1942, and the remaining Jews were killed and the ghetto liquidated in February 1943. The exact circumstances of his family's death remained unknown. The constant stream of letters from parents, sisters, and brothers simply stopped.

*Edited excerpts from "Good-bye, Father: A Journey to the USSR," by Leonard M. Grob, Ph.D., reprinted by permission from *Judaism*, vol. 39, no. 2, copyright, spring 1990, American Jewish Congress.

2 STEFAN

THE YOUNG JEW WATCHED HIS SHADOW CAST ON THE TRAIN WINDOW BY the compartment lights.

Is that me? he wondered.

The dark silhouette seemed to belong to another being, a stranger looking in at the boy inside the train, fenced in. Who was this Jew among Gentiles, lost in the confused landscape?

Fear of the unknown threatened to overtake Yossela. The huge vehicle that transported him creaked and cracked as it wafted from side to side, its wheels clanking loudly against the metal rail guiding it to its unknown destination. Finally the train's quivering rocked the youth to sleep, his head resting against the window.

Startled by a loud screech, Yossela sat straight up. Daylight streamed through the window as the train pulled to a stop, letting passengers on and off.

He rubbed his eyes and shook his body, trying to erase the sleep.

"You slept well," remarked the man who sat across from him.

"Like a hard-working farm boy," answered the person sitting beside the speaker.

The Ukrainian farmers smiled at the boy who smiled back at them.

"Yes, I did." He would have to be on guard and speak Ukrainian or Polish and not accidentally slip into Yiddish.

Yossela had lost track of time since he had gotten on the train in Stanislawów. Once he slipped through his secret loose fence board, he removed the armband that marked him as a Jew and walked briskly toward the train station, leaving the ghetto behind. There he found large numbers of Ukrainian farmers waiting to catch a train. He moved in and out among them, listening to the conversations. He would need help in knowing what to do; after all, he was a poor, uneducated farm boy who had never been away from home. What did he know of catching trains?

Throughout the crowd the conversation was the same. The men told of leaving the area in which they lived due to heavy flooding and the lack of jobs. Stanislawów was a stopping place for them, a transfer to another train, one that could take them into areas with promises of farm work.

When Yossela saw an SS guard move into the crowd, he struck up a conversation with two of the farmers nearest him. Watching the German out of the corner of his eye, he put his hand to his shirt pocket, making sure the false birth certificate was still there. He avoided the officer's eyes, speaking in Ukrainian with the two men. The German moved past them, ignoring the three dirty-looking farmers, focused on finding a Jew.

When it was time to board, Yossela tried to attach himself to the two men, following close behind them. Smaller than most of the men, he was soon lost in the crowd. He did not know it, but this factor would allow him to blend in and move onto the train without notice of the ticket taker. How would the youth have known he would need a ticket? He had never ridden a train. Once aboard, he managed to reclaim the two farmers, finding a seat which faced them. He smiled at them as he slid next to the window.

"What is your name?" asked one of the farmers as they settled in for the ride.

"Ah, Zgeslow, sir. Zgeslow Chesnofski." The youth silently thanked his Polish friend for the name and the birth certificate.

"A Pole?"

"Yes, sir." Yossela looked away from the man, glancing out the window, hoping the man would not ask too many questions.

Suddenly the train jerked, moved forward slightly and jerked again, the wheels squealing loudly. The boy did not know whether to feel relief at leaving or be overpowered by the need to cry, from fear and sadness. His decision to leave had been difficult, but it was made—and he would make the best of it. He would have to, for he promised his family he would survive. He did not know where the train was going, only that it carried him away from a hellhole. Someday when all of this was past, he would return and find his family.

A whole night passed. He could not believe he slept through it. He tried to forget his hunger. Perhaps it would not be long until they reached a suitable destination.

The train traveled east, southeast further into the Ukraine. As it picked up speed, the countryside rolled by. Small farms, occasionally interrupted by a stream or a forest, dotted the landscape.

For two days and two nights they rode. Weakened by the lack of food, Yossela sat motionless, often napping.

It was late afternoon when the train pulled into a small village.

"We will get off here."

"Do you know this place?" asked the young Jew.

"No," answered one of the farmers, "but I have heard there is much farming here. That means a possible job."

The youth sat for a moment watching the men prepare to exit the train car.

"I'll go with you," he said, following them.

This place is as good as any, thought Yossela.

As they walked from the station, they passed houses that fronted small acreage. Because it was late afternoon, they found people in several of the yards. Each time the farmers with whom he traveled used a common Ukrainian courtesy as a greeting.

"*Bog v pom-mich.*"

"God bless you, too." It was the same response each time to the farmers' greetings.

At each house they inquired about temporary work and each time they were rejected.

The three had not gone far when they saw a tall, heavy-set lady with a wooden leg about to enter her home.

The farmers gave the usual greeting, and she responded in kind.

"If you're looking for temporary work like the others that have come by," she said, "I'm not interested. I need someone full-time."

Yossela could not believe his ears. "I need a full-time job," he answered quickly.

"Oh?" Her eyes narrowed as she looked him over. "You know farm work?"

"All my life."

"Then you'll have a chance to prove it. We're harvesting, and I need a full-time farmhand."

Pleased with himself, Yossela looked at his farmer friends, a smile stretching across his face. "I got a job!"

Smiling, both replied, "*Shch-us-tya vum.*"

"*D'uck-oo-you vum,*" the boy answered. "Thank you. I wish both of you good luck also." He watched them walk away, a small knot forming in his stomach.

Can I do this alone?

"Come on in and we'll talk about your chores over supper," said the woman.

He would not let his doubt rule. I can do this alone. I have to, he thought.

He slept that night in the barn, his belly finally full but his mind racing with new fears. "How will I fit in? How soon will they find me out?"

Each day Yossela tried harder to fit into his surroundings. The day he left the ghetto he decided to pretend to be a Christian because that was the only way he could survive. Only if he seemed to become a part of the lives of these people could he continue to triumph over his enemies.

The first few months after leaving the ghetto were frightening because he was afraid of revealing Jewish habits or the emotions enveloping him, sadness pervading most of his time. He soon became a very good actor.

Yossela's first visit to a Christian church was traumatic. He entered the building, looking for a seat on the last row. When the service began, he watched the others, copying what they did, mumbling words, incoherent only to him. He prayed for the service to end.

Later as he walked home, his fears had subsided somewhat. They had not found him out. Perhaps the disguise would work after all.

Weeks passed and Yossela was very busy. It was a big farm, and he worked hard all day, collapsing exhausted on the hay at night. The lady was alone, her husband and children away. Yossela believed they were in the service, but never questioned. It was not his place to do so. She was bossy, and he earned no money, but he had plenty of food and a place to stay.

Not long after he arrived, he met his employer's male friend, a local farmer. Yossela always knew when he came to visit. If the boy was near the house, he could hear the man cough, deep hacking sounds that seemed to erupt from his soul.

At first the friend ignored the boy, but after a while he began to ask questions. It made Yossela very uncomfortable. He did not trust the man, especially now that German soldiers had been seen in the area.

One day while running an errand for the lady farmer, a German patrol, combing the village for young, able-bodied men to send to Germany to work, stopped him. He went with them quietly to a schoolhouse. In the basement he joined other young men, many school-age Polish boys too young to leave home. Soon the small room became crowded. The Germans ordered the boys to undress and prepare for a physical examination.

Yossela was sure someone would hear his heart beat. He knew this could be the end of his disguise, for surely he would be unlike the others, the circumcision giving him away.

He waited patiently for an opportunity to escape. He looked around the room, seeking any kind of exit. A number of open windows at street level lined the back wall. One, he noticed, was just above a table.

Perfect, he thought. All I need is a distraction and a little luck.

As the commotion of undressing began, he edged his way toward the back, watching the Germans closely. By the time the doctor entered the room, Yossela was sitting on the table conveniently under the window. The soldiers' attention turned to readying the recruits for the lineup. Using the confusion to his advantage, Yossela quickly climbed through the opening and made his way back to the farm.

He had already considered leaving his job because of the lady's male friend but had not known where he would go or how easy it would be to get employment. The more the boy avoided the man's questions, the more suspicious the man acted. This, coupled with the incident at the school, made him decide he would look for the first opportunity to leave the area.

As it happened, one day the woman sent Yossela to pick up some medicine in a nearby village. While he waited for it, a farmer came and sat beside him. He was a tall, thin Ukrainian with dark hair. He looked stern but spoke a friendly greeting to the boy.

Soon the conversation led to farming and the man's desire to hire a farmhand to do the fieldwork and take care of the horses. He was without help because two of his boys were off fighting in the war and a third taught school a distance away.

Yossela could not believe his luck. Even before the medicine arrived, they had finalized plans for the young Jew to leave his current job and move to Jezierzany, a nearby village where the farmer had acreage and his home.

It was the winter of 1941 when Yossela went to live among the Ukrainians in Jezierzany. When the farmer told him he was welcome to spend the nights in his house, Yossela declined as he had done with the lady. His greatest fear was being found out. Sometimes he slept restlessly, threatening dreams disturbing his sleep, and sometimes he cried out in Yiddish. What if that happened while he slept in the house? He could not—would not—allow it to happen.

The farmer gave Yossela warm clothes—his son's—and blankets. Food was abundant and the hard work kept his mind occupied and made his body strong.

Each evening the youth had supper with the farmer and his wife, and occasionally the farmer's daughter and son-in-law who lived next door supped with them. Often their conversation turned to the war and the Jews. The son-in-law was particularly bitter toward the Jews, his conversation filled with hate.

"Swine! That's what they are. All damned Jews are pigs!" His face would turn red as his words continued to explode, "Bloodsucking Christ killers! I hope they get what's coming to them."

Yossela could never distance himself from the words. They stung too badly. Every fiber in his being wanted to lash out at the bigot. During these tirades he avoided looking directly at the man for fear his emotions would show. Instead he concentrated on picking at the food on his plate. As quickly as he finished his meal, he excused himself, explaining the need to retire early.

Alone in his makeshift bedroom, he felt tears welling up as he remembered the words. They hurt, just like they had in childhood. Creeping guilt filled his mind, and he silently repeated over and over, "God, forgive me that I do not speak in defense! God, forgive me!" If only his family could hear his words and understand.

The Jew's hard work pleased the farmer, who had nicknamed him Stefan.

"You should see the work Stefan does," he would say to his neighbors. "He is a good worker and is no problem."

Yossela, who now called himself Stefan, wanted to please the farmer. He wanted him to stay happy. He did not want him to become suspicious. If the farmer let him go, where would he go? He had plenty to eat and a place to put his head at night, and the hard work was a blessing, preventing his mind from giving in to his fears about his family or being caught.

A few Poles lived in the village, and he became a friend with one of the boys his age who worked on an adjacent farm. It was the Polish youth who took him to his first Christian church service in Jezierzany. One Catholic Church served the large Ukrainian population as well as the few Poles who lived in the area. He watched his friend closely, mimicking his movements. He even pretended to sing, mouthing the strange sounds.

The politics of the Greek Catholic Church were unknown to him. Had he known or even understood, he would have been puzzled that the church's head in southeast Poland, a man by the name of Andrei Steptylsky, as well as other church clerics sympathized with the Ukrainian nationalist movement in Poland. In fact, Steptylsky's diversity in attitude would have shocked him, for while he was friendly toward the Jews, he played politics with the Germans hoping this would benefit Ukrainian nationalism.

Soon Stefan was invited to join the youth activities of the church. He complied, even singing Christmas carols during the holiday season and going to confession. He was a good listener. The priest did all the talking. It was strange and he never stopped feeling guilty. What would his Jewish family think?

Stefan's resolve to remain anonymous would soon be tested further. One day as he worked in the yard, some ragged and dirty men approached the gate. When the farmer saw them, he quickly moved to Stefan.

Maxim and Anna Gayauska with whom Yossela lived as "Stefan," a Polish farmhand from 1941-1945.

This barn which sat behind the farmer's house was Stefan's sleeping quarters.

"Get an ax," he whispered. "Damn, dirty Jews think they're going to get anything they've left here, they can think again."

"What do you want me to do with an ax?"

"I want you to get the damn Jews," spurted the farmer. "Don't let them get away. Kill them before they hide in the forest again."

The farmer shoved Stefan toward the barn, looking anxiously over his shoulder to see if the Jews were still at the front gate. Obviously they had not heard the conversation between Stefan and the farmer for they stood quietly.

Stefan moved quickly to the barn. He could feel his heart beat in his ears, pounding so wildly he thought his eardrums would burst.

What do I do? he thought. What can I do?

He picked up the ax and walked toward the house, avoiding the side where the farmer stood quietly watching the Jews. As Stefan rounded the opposite corner of the house, he stumbled against some tools lying on the ground causing him to drop his weapon. The clatter startled the Jews, and seeing the boy reach for the ax, they fled into the forest.

The farmer yelled, "Stefan, get them! Get them!"

Stefan ran into the forest, ax in hand. Once under cover of vegetation, he slowed, stomping his feet to make plenty of noise.

When he returned to the house, the farmer said nothing, but his eyes were full of questions.

"I'm sorry, sir," said Stefan. "They got clean away. Those dirty Jews got clean away."

The farmer sighed and turned back to his work, and Stefan walked to the barn to put up the ax, a broad smile stretching across his face, crinkling the corners of his eyes. He would later learn that the Jews were local and had left some belongings with the farmer for safekeeping.

Stefan had become a fixture in Jezierzany, so much so the villagers included him in their vigilante activities. One winter day two local Ukrainian militiamen came to the house.

"Stefan, get a horse!" one yelled. "We're gonna go hunt Jews."

"Yeah," said the other one, "we are going to kill those Christ killers and get their clothes."

Stefan wondered why anyone would want the clothes. Heaven knows by now they would probably be rags.

He got a horse and followed them into the woods, silently praying, "Run! Run, Jews."

The trip into the forest revealed no hiding Jews and the men returned to the village, cursing loudly. Stefan followed, smiling inside. He thanked God once again for not allowing him to be a part of the disgrace of killing his fellows to save his own life. He did not know how much more guilt he could take.

The boy had no way of knowing if the hidden Jews were partisans, trying their underground activities, or frightened families seeking refuge among the trees. Forty thousand Jews hid throughout the forests of German-occupied countries during the war. Most of them would not survive.

Every spring, every fall, and every winter, it was the same—work, hard work. Stefan survived in disguise, but the too frequent nightmares plagued him.

The awful illusions worsened after the ax and the hunt for Jews. Often in the coldest night Stefan would awaken, his body clammy with sweat, his heart beating rapidly.

In one of the dreams, Stefan, deep in the dark forest, grabbed a runaway Jew by the back of his shirt. The Ukrainians stood near, axes raised. "Kill him, Stefan! Kill him!" they yelled.

Stefan raised his own ax just as the man turned and faced him. It was Solomon, his brother.

Too frequently Stefan dreamed of digging the mass grave—only this time, a German SS demanded Stefan strip off his clothes and move close to the edge. He stood there, naked before all. As he looked into the pit, vacuous eyes of men, women, and little children stared up at him. He wanted to run. His legs would not move. Then he would hear the gunshot. The gunshot always awakened him.

Sometimes in his dreams tall, people-like shadows moved slowly toward him. They had no faces, no gender. The thin phantom creatures crowded around him, staring. He wanted to awaken from the dream, but he could not force himself to do so. He stood there in the vision like a stone while the shadows seemed to beckon.

Suddenly a small figure moved from behind the others. Faintly Stefan could see eyes where the face should have been. The stare possessed him. Thoughts of his ten-year-old brother left behind ravaged him. Even as he slept, the lucid questions came to him.

Could I have saved him? Should I have given him a chance to survive? Will I ever forget the look in his eyes the last time I saw him? What if I had taken him, and he accidentally revealed we were Jewish, a slip of the tongue, a gesture?

The questions, those in his dreams and those he lived with daily, haunted him. He existed from day to day, living with the guilt and struggling with the fear of being found out.

In 1943 rumors spread through the village that the Russians had outlasted a third German assault in the Soviet Union. The Red Army hammered away at the German front line, using consolidated military equipment—tanks, artillery, even the new Stormovik plane, which could swoop low in its attack. With the use of these weapons, the Red Army reversed the German offensive, killing thousands of Nazis. History would document that the American lend-lease program, called an "arsenal of democracy" by President Roosevelt, aided significantly in providing the equipment Russia, as well as Great Britain, needed to push back the Germans.

Large Russian fighting units as well as guerrilla forces, containing not only men but also women, aided the enemy pursuit. The Russian armies used the victory to chase the Nazis from Russia, tracking them westward.

Could it be, thought Stefan, the Germans will lose? And if they do, can I give up my disguise? Will I be able to trust the Russians?

And what about the *Banderovytsi*? The Ukrainian underground does not like Poles or Jews. I am one of those while living as the other. What if Germany wins the war? Will I have to marry and be a part of the Ukrainian or Polish culture? Can I live as a fake the rest of my life?

One fear always replaced another.

It was mid-fall 1944 when Stefan heard the first guns in the distance and saw planes flying above the fields covered with a light, early-season snow. Soon the sounds of dropped bombs, exploding in the distance, shook the ground. The cannon blasts continued all through the night. Each time an explosion sounded, it seemed closer.

When Stefan walked to the furthermost field the morning after a night of bombing, he saw soldiers lying face down, their bodies partially covered by frost. The death scene brought back the memory of Solomon dangling from the rope, of the Jews falling into the pit, and corpses in the streets of the ghetto. Stefan wondered if he would be killed as a Christian, not a Jew, in the middle of the war.

After a while the bombing stopped, and the Russians marched into the village. It was then the villagers learned that the Germans were losing, being pushed back across Poland.

Immediately the Russians drafted all able-bodied men, Stefan and his Polish friend among the recruits. The Russian strategy was to create a Polish army under their command. By 1945 the Russians would have carved out two Polish armies.

After the young men gathered in the village and registered, the Russians loaded them on trains. The trip proved to be dangerous, for the Germans had regrouped and attempted to bomb the trains. Each time a German plane appeared on the horizon, the train stopped and the draftees ran for shelter in a field adjacent to the tracks.

After weeks of transport they finally arrived in Moscow for basic training. At the completion of the schooling to use guns and other ammunition, the Russians gave them a short course in specialty areas. Stefan and his friend were fortunate to get into a supply unit. There Stefan learned to drive a truck.

After a relatively short time Stefan's unit was shipped to Katowice, Poland, where they remained as a reserve unit for Warsaw's front line. Since August the Red Army had camped across the Vistula River from Warsaw. Fighting was still heavy.

It was only a matter of time until the Russian command called the reserves to the front line. The new soldiers stayed in makeshift barracks, waiting for their orders to serve as night patrols or reserve troops for casualty replacements.

Shortly after their arrival a number of rumors spread among the Polish troops fighting under the Red Army command. The first rumor said that the Polish civilians resisted reparation. The reluctance to leave the land, given to them in the Treaty of Versailles that followed World War I, should have been no surprise. The treaty had established an independent Poland carved out of land formerly owned by several countries including Russia.

Further commentary centered on the fact that the Poles resisted Communism. This may have provided a motive for the Russians' lack of help in the Polish armed resistance to the Nazis. When the British requested use of behind-the-lines airfields to airlift supplies for the resistance, the Russians refused.

Was Poland prey for its neighbors? Was it true what some Poles suggested—that the Russians wanted the Germans to kill the Poles in order for them to expand Communism more freely and to weaken capitalist countries?

All this talk made Stefan and his Polish friend nervous. After all, they served in a Polish army commanded by the Russians. They felt caught in the middle of two ideologies, that of the conquering Germans and that of the liberating Russians. Would they be killed by the Germans or by the Russians?

A curfew had been placed on Katowice civilians, not only to keep them out of danger, but also to diminish the possibility of

Germans slipping through the lines. Soon after Stefan and his Polish friend from Jezierzany arrived in Katowice, they had patrol duty. Dressed in their uniforms and carrying rifles, they walked the dark streets of Katowice, preparing to ask for a password if they saw someone suspicious.

As he walked, Stefan pondered his future. He could live or die fighting at the front or be murdered by the Russians. His instincts were correct, yet he had no way of knowing that. A year earlier the Soviets had slaughtered eight thousand Polish officers, their mass grave later discovered by the Germans.

It was an easy choice. Stefan had not survived this long to be killed as a Polish soldier.

"My friend," he said to his soldier partner, "I am looking for a way out, a way to save myself. How about you?"

"You think it looks like we are going to get killed?"

"Let's put it this way—we have a chance of going to the front. You know they are replacing casualties daily from the recruits at the barracks."

"It is only a matter of time until they take us?"

"Yes. I think we should desert."

"When? How?"

"Now, tonight. While we are patrolling, we'll find out what trains are leaving."

"What about our uniforms, our guns?"

"A disguise. Who will question two soldiers on duty?"

Once the decision was made, the two walked briskly to the train station where they asked if a train was scheduled to go near Jezierzany. The answer was what they were looking for. They boarded the next available train headed east.

The ride was long. The two had money for food and the uniforms actually kept them incognito. They would use "discharged for medical reasons" as an excuse for returning home before the war's end. The Pole volunteered to create false discharge papers once they arrived, just in case someone questioned their appearance in the village. Shortly before the train reached its destination and in cover of night, they threw their weapons off the train. It would be hard to explain keeping them.

Upon his arrival in the village, Stefan went immediately to the farmer's house where he could reclaim his clothes and his job. He was happy to see the house again. Though he still had his old fears, he realized he was relatively safe there. The farmer opened the door to Stefan's knock.

The old man looked at him, his eyes wide. "Stefan! What are you doing here?"

"I've been discharged."

"Come in! Come in out of the cold!" The man's eyes followed Stefan, questioning.

"*D'uck-oo-you vum.* Thank you, sir."

"How can this be? My sons have been gone longer, and they have not returned. I do not understand."

Stefan had not expected the comparison. He moved quickly to his lie. "I was discharged for medical reasons. The papers will be coming soon."

The farmer looked intently at him. Stefan held his breath, hoping his story rang true.

Suddenly the old man slapped the youth on the shoulder. "Well, welcome back! I am amazed, but I am glad to see you! I need help badly." The farmer looked closely at Stefan. "You are up to doing the work?"

"Yes!" Stefan quickly responded. He hoped he would not be questioned further.

The young Jew had been back only a few days when late one night a pounding noise sounded on the door. Since his return, Stefan had slept in the farmer's living room. He awoke immediately, quietly rising from his pallet. Instinctively he sensed danger was near. He whispered to the farmer who had entered the darkened living room, "Don't open the door! Ignore it."

Stefan moved quickly to the attic stairway, praying silently the farmer would heed his advice. In the dark recesses of the attic space, Stefan heard the knocking continue, then stop suddenly. His heart in his throat, he prayed softly, "Dear God, keep me from harm!" Tears welled as he thought of his father's blessing, remembering the trembling hand on his head.

"The Lord go with you, my son."

Even after the silence came from downstairs, Stefan could not find the courage to return to his bed. He stayed crouched in his hiding place the rest of the night, shivering from the cold.

The farmer sat at the table eating breakfast when Stefan entered the kitchen the next morning. He looked up at the boy. He said nothing but motioned for Stefan to sit.

"Rumor has it that your Polish friend is dead."

Stunned, Stefan looked at the farmer. The old man did not look up from his food. His face showed no emotion. Stefan, heart in his throat, did not respond.

"The *Banderovytsi* killed several Polish families last night." The old man spoke with little feeling. "At your friend's house, villagers found that each member of the family had been taken to a separate corner of the house and shot."

Fear swept over the youth. He tried not to show it in his face. Stefan had heard the farmer and his son-in-law speak of the Ukrainian underground. They spoke as though the covert organization was an ally to Germany. The conversation as well as one he recently overheard had confused the young Jew.

"Now is the time," the farmer had remarked, "for an all-out effort to build an independent Ukrainian state—now while the Germans and the Russians are tired from fighting each other."

The son-in-law had agreed.

Had the farmer not earlier praised the work of the *Banderovytsi*?

He too had pressured Stefan to go hunt the Jews. He too praised the militia effort to gain independence by whatever means necessary. They wanted the Poles to leave the Ukrainian villages and go deep into designated Poland, and they wanted them to go now. The Ukrainians had killed his friend and his friend's family in cold blood. Stefan could not help but wonder if he was next.

He and the farmer ate in silence. As soon as he had finished, the boy took his jacket from the knob that hung next to the door and headed for the barn. He went about his work, numb from the cold and this new knowledge.

Around midmorning he lay down the hay rake he was using, stood for a moment looking around him, and then walked resolutely out of the barn. He walked past the house, never looking back. Soon he came to the street that led out of the village.

Celina

He lived in fear. I know, because I know what it is like to live in disguise.

Fear was the main emotion that he felt all the time. He had to pretend, had to act, watch what he said, what he did. Even when he was sleeping, he was afraid he would betray himself. Pretending is very difficult when you are in pain.

I am sure it was a torturous life. However, as every human being has the instinct to survive, nothing was too much to overcome. Though all the circumstances made life extremely difficult, the determination to survive was so strong that he managed to triumph over seemingly impossible obstacles.

Though I too lived in disguise, it was a different situation. I was slightly more confident in some respects. The family I lived with was financially secure as they were in business. I really didn't believe that they could discover my identity. It was so impossible to imagine a Jewish girl could come and live among them. They could not think that this was a possibility, especially since their daughter sent me to them.

It happened this way—I was in the Warsaw ghetto and my sister-in-law's brother secretly lived on the Aryan side as a member of the police. He met a German nurse who didn't know he was Jewish. During their conversation she mentioned to him that her family lived in Germany and that they were looking for a girl to help them in their restaurant and butcher shop.

"Oh! I know of such a girl," he said. "She would be perfect! Just give me a few days and I will contact her and she will come introduce herself."

He sent a message to me in the ghetto, saying he met the nurse and an opportunity to escape awaited me. He said I should quickly get false papers stating I was Christian and introduce myself to the nurse. At that time I was fifteen.

My oldest sister was married and had twin boys. Her husband was a brilliant businessman. They were quite comfortable financially. Even in the ghetto, he managed this. So as soon as my sister heard of this great opportunity for me, she contacted the underground. I am not sure if it was a Jewish or Polish underground, but she paid them a large sum of money, and within one day I got false identification papers with my picture on them. My fingerprints were on it, with a false name, birthplace, age, everything.

My new name was Anna Cakczewska, and the papers were a ticket to my new life.

I looked Aryan with my light blonde hair. I was a very pretty girl; that greatly helped. I went for two years to a Polish gymnacium where I studied German, so I spoke the language well.

I got the papers and introduced myself to the nurse. She provided me with a train ticket, and I traveled to meet her family. Naturally since their daughter sent me, they couldn't suspect that I was coming from 'hell'! Why would they suspect a Jewish girl would come into Germany to hide?

The family that I went to work for consisted of a mother and four daughters. They were Nazis. The son was away in the army, and they had no father. A big portrait of Hitler hung in their living room. And the first thing I heard was, "You see this man in the portrait? This is the savior of the world."

I wanted to kill them all. After I was there awhile and I felt somewhat secure that they would not discover me, I looked at the mother with such hatred in my eyes that she felt it.

"I wonder why Anna is looking at me like this?" she asked her daughters.

When they burned down the ghetto in the 1943 uprising in Warsaw, a soldier came to the restaurant and told them what the Germans had done. She became jubilant! "Anna! Anna! Can you imagine finally we are going to get rid of the Jews!"

I said to her, "You know the Jews are humans too."

She was shocked. "I thought you would be pleased because you are Polish."

I never worried about my statement giving me away. Sometimes I felt no matter what they did to me, I didn't care.

They had a Gestapo office in that city and other Polish girls, the real ones, were coming to work for the Germans. The family I worked for was prominent in the city, well known. When I came, I spoke German so well that the Germans used me as their interpreter for the other Polish girls. Every time they called me, I thought they had found me out and it was the end of my life.

These were my most fearful times. But the most comical moment came when I first arrived. Every Polish girl arriving for the purpose of working for the Germans had to go first to the Gestapo office, where they had to fill out a form. Among other questions was one that asked if we had Jewish ancestors or anyone Jewish in our families.

When I hesitated, one of the officers looked me over and said, "You don't have to fill this out. That's impossible!"

Impossible that I would have Jewish ancestors?

I was giggling inside! In the Gestapo office you kept your mouth shut, but I thought of my father. He would have laughed out loud!

After I was there a few months, I realized my greatest victory was hiding in the mouth of the lion.

3 AFTERMATH

"STEFAN" ANSWERED THE ADVERTISEMENT IN THE PAPER FOR A TRUCK driver, silently thanking the Russians for the training he received in Moscow.

Once he reached the nearest reparation center to Jezierzany, it had taken several days for the necessary papers and train accommodations to come through. Finally he was able to travel to internal Poland. The choice of destination was not his, and ironically he ended up in Katowice.

The young Jew, now almost twenty years old, lived as a Polish refugee, not concerned that the Russians would discover their missing soldier. The Russians had taken Warsaw from the Germans in January 1945 and were concentrating on how to keep the areas of East Central Europe under their control. He would not feel completely safe until the war was over. Until then he would work and plan his next move.

At the truck depot he met brothers by the name of Moshe and Haim. One of the brothers, along with a military officer, came to the depot to hire a truck and a driver. Stefan was that driver.

Four years living among the Ukrainians had taught Stefan to be skeptical, noncommittal. Without a word he followed the destination directions the two Poles gave him, never questioning the distance or the cargo to be picked up.

As they traveled, he listened to the casual chatter between the two men who shared the truck cab with him. When they slipped into Yiddish, Stefan almost lost control of the wheel. He could not believe he heard the familiar language. Stefan thought he might be the only Jew alive. One of the men cursed him in Yiddish for driving so poorly. Stefan could not yet risk revealing he was Jewish, nor was he ready to accept the surprise of Jews walking freely in Poland. He kept quiet.

From the Yiddish conversation Stefan learned they were going to recently liberated Rotslov to buy contraband goods and transport them back to Katowice. Stefan realized the purpose of the military officer was to act as a decoy in case they were stopped at any of the checkpoints along the way. Had he not understood Yiddish, he would not have known what was happening.

Stefan worked as their truck driver for several jobs, never revealing he understood their Yiddish conversations. He wondered if they were really Jews and, if not, why they spoke in Yiddish.

As they returned to Katowice from another of their trips, the two again spoke in Yiddish.

"This dumb driver doesn't know what we have been doing," remarked the civilian.

"He's fired as soon as we get back to Katowice anyway. We don't need him anymore."

"You're right. These trips are no longer profitable."

"Another transaction or two, and we'll use the Russian driver."

"Right."

Silently Stefan analyzed his situation. By now he believed they really were Jews. Living in disguise the rest of his life was not what he wanted to do. He could be brave and reveal he was a Jew. Too much was at stake to lose contact with the only Jews he had run across.

As the vehicle rolled to a stop at the truck depot, Stefan turned to the men and spoke in Yiddish. "I want you to know I am a Jew, and I understood everything you said."

Startled they looked at each other. Stefan did not give them a chance to respond. "I survived with Christian papers. I didn't know other Jews survived. I thought I would have to stay a Christian all my life."

"Stop!" said one of the men. "How do we know you are not an impostor? How do we know you are a Jew?"

Before Stefan could answer, the man said, "Get out of the truck."

Stefan obeyed. Once out, the man directed him to the rear of truck, away from the street and passersby.

"Drop your pants!" he demanded.

Without hesitation Stefan did as he was told.

For a brief moment the men observed Stefan's evidence, then turned and smiled at each other. Quickly each held out a hand to Stefan. The young Jew jerked up his pants, holding them in place with one hand while he hurriedly reached out the other.

It was the beginning of a new life for him. Now there were people with whom he could be himself, with whom he could be a Jew. Little did he realize how difficult it would be.

From Moshe and Haim he learned of the camps and the number of Jews killed. His heart ached, for now it seemed even more unlikely he would ever find his family. The men told him there was danger in going back to his village because Jews were still being killed by Ukrainians.

"Don't take the chance," they warned.

The brothers told him they could arrange for him to leave through some leaders in the city. Those people helped post-war "leftovers," Jewish survivors, go through the Czechoslovakian and Polish borders into Germany to a camp for displaced persons.

"The safest way to go across the borders," said one of the brothers, "is to go as a recruit of the Jewish underground. The organization helps Jews immigrate to Israel. Once you get across the borders into the American zone, you can decide what you want to do."

The young Jew could hardly wait for the opportunity to distance himself from his holding existence. Soon the chance came.

Stefan decided he would use a new name the moment he reached Germany. As he waited to cross the border, the idea permeated his thoughts. Disbelief that he was completely safe led him to the decision. Perhaps his security lay in a German name just as it had with a Polish name. He named himself Willie Weisberg.

It was easier than he expected to cross to the American zone. Willie arrived in Regensburg in the early fall of 1945. There the Red Cross assigned him a room with the Reimbachs, a German family, who lived in a three-room apartment. The husband had one eye, the other supposedly lost in the war. Willie was not sure whether it was the Second World War or the first. He wondered if the man was a Nazi. It would be a very difficult thing to overcome, living with a killer of Jews.

The German couple treated him well, if not totally warm. Still he could not relax from his apprehension that the man was a Nazi. Torn between his apprehension and the idea that the liberators forced him on them, Willie felt uneasy.

After a while Willie came to believe that the wife was a nice person. When the husband was not there, she cooked for Willie—potatoes and other delicious foods. Still he was reluctant to accept eating a meal with them. Willie had learned to be self-conscious, still seeing himself as an uneducated farm boy, raised in poverty with one wooden spoon and one bowl to his name. He was an uncivilized Jew without knowledge of proper manners, even the proper use of a knife and fork.

Being a Jew again was not as easy as he had assumed it would be. Willie tried to find a way to be like the others, to be accepted. Each morning he went to the Jewish Community Center. There, and in a little cafe on one of the side streets, Jewish refugees gathered where they told stories about the camps.

Willie listened carefully to the tales, hoping for the smallest tidbit that would help him know what happened to his own family. Some of the camp refugees seemed strange and rough to him, and after hearing some of the stories, he understood why.

He learned of the liquidation of not only the ghettos, but also the camps. The news of the death toll shattered the hope that he would find a single member of his family alive. He had not been confined in a camp, nor did he go hungry. He simply survived as an innocent farm boy. Now, as he confronted concentration camp survivors who actually walked over their dead relatives and fellow campmates, a new sense of guilt swept over him.

The memory of taking up the ax to go find the Jews in the forest almost overwhelmed him when he met some of the people who survived as partisans. Slowly he learned the fate of the majority of the Jews in Europe. No one knew the numbers for sure, but the combined stories painted a picture of little hope that many had survived.

Once again Yossela, now Willie, questioned being Jewish. What could the Jews have possibly done that was so wrong that millions would be put to death? He lived with this knowledge— sad, alone, and apprehensive about his future.

The others registered for sponsorship and the chance to start a new life in another country. From what Willie could see, the American GI lived clean, with plenty of chocolates. Willie heard of the luxury in the United States, milk and honey, and no hate. He had nothing to live for in Europe. He was single and had no one. He felt very much like he did not belong. He did not trust his intelligence to create a new life in Europe among his enemies so he followed the crowd and registered for a sponsor and transportation to the United States. He did not want to be the only one left behind. Gradually excitement replaced the fear of leaving the familiar behind to live in America.

While he waited, he needed to find work. He did not know how long the wait would be. The subsidized clothing and food could not sustain him. Within a short time he learned there were too few jobs for the number of survivors looking for jobs.

Meeting other Jews at the Jewish Community Center provided him with the opportunity to see the brothers he met in Katowice and their associates, Bolek and Henry from Waldenburg. He met Josef and others and was thankful for the new friendships. Eventually he participated on a soccer team as a goalie, met girls, and learned the craft of trading.

Willie did not understand girls. Not many Jewish girls had survived, and he could not get close to a German girl. His friends tried to fix him up with a girlfriend, once with a Czech, a girl they met during a business transaction.

He went out, sometimes to a German movie with subtitles. Learning a new language was not a problem. Conversing with a female was. Often his date was as shy as he was.

His friends teased him about the girls and nicknamed him "Rybciu," which meant "slick like a fish."

If they only knew how clumsy I feel, thought the innocent farm boy.

If he was shy in aspects of his social life, he was not when it came to learning a new trade. The one thing Willie had going was his experience in driving, and his friends needed a chauffeur. He would learn how to buy and sell, learn how to mark up the price.

Willie watched and learned from good teachers, his sophisticated friends. They were experienced in trading, some already experts in business, especially in dealing in German marks. They knew value and how to buy and sell.

One of his first business trips took him back across the Czech border to Prague. In a car loaded with hidden cigarettes, he and Josef, followed by a second car loaded with clandestine cigarettes, headed for the border. At the border a military patrol stopped them,

Regensburg: Liberation 1945-49 "the Soccer Team."
Willie, front row middle; Bolek, back row 3rd from left;
Josef, back row 7th from left.

Regensburg 1945-49—Willie,
front row right with pals .

Willie and friend—Regensburg.

searched, and found the contraband. The two remained in jail three weeks before their Prague business contact pulled strings to have them released.

Willie gradually became more experienced in the world of trade, making enough pocket money to buy the clothes and food he needed. Occasionally he splurged to buy a meal in a restaurant. Sometimes he felt rich, especially when he bought a new pair of pants.

Willie had four years in which to analyze his life, to get direction, and to try to erase the hurt in his heart.

Am I a good person for surviving? Did my parents deserve to die?

He never got an answer. As he matured, he began to think in terms of why he survived. These thoughts brought him memories of his father's last blessing. Maybe God saved him so he could understand how precious life is.

Some of Willie's friends decided, early on, to go to Israel to fight in the underground. Willie pondered doing so himself, but each time he was reminded that it would have been fruitless for him to survive for his family and be killed fighting. He struggled with the decision to fight for Israel or to continue to survive and carve out a new existence.

He matured considerably during those four years he waited to emigrate. His life was as normal as it was going to be. He lived in a house with Germans; he had friends— more sophisticated than he—whom he loved, and the poverty he once knew as a child was replaced by another kind. Sometimes the fear of living independently in another country where he did not understand the language nearly overwhelmed him. He was afraid to stay in Europe, afraid to go to Israel, and afraid to go to the United States. The decision seemed staggering to the once naive farm boy, turning into an adult without the guidance of his family.

Hardened by circumstance, he learned self-defense, to push

*Willie, as a promising entreprenuer
in Regensburg, wearing his first suit .*

his way out of any environment in which he felt trapped. That was how he survived, the only way he knew.

Though he still tried to find surviving members of his family, Willie's hope began to fade. He looked for four long years. They were the hardest four years of his life, searching with little hope and living among the people who killed his family.

Once his decision was made to emigrate to the United States, he began to think in future terms, his thoughts centering on starting a new life. Perhaps he would marry and have children. Perhaps somewhere else he could heal the wound in his heart. In 1949 he had that chance.

Josef

Rybciu. That's what the others called him. I think it means fish. I'm not sure. Don't know why they called him that. After I got to know him, I called him Haidz; I think it means cowboy or country boy. I never knew what his Polish name was. Later when I found out he was Jewish, I learned his last name was Margulies.

Anyway I met him in 1945—June or July. We did some business with some people in Katowice, Poland. He was driving the truck. We didn't know who he was. We thought he was a Pole or a Ukrainian, just the chauffeur.

We were more interested in the other people, the brothers. They were going to help us transport and sell the goods we got because they had more experience in the black market. We were young. I was only eighteen.

We brought them some black market merchandise from a camp in Waldenburg and were looking for someone to transport it.

I had been a prisoner in the camp, and when the Russians liberated it, I lived there. Several of us took over the escaping German's apartments. There were five of us refugees, all from one camp. We were very close, like brothers, and we lived together.

We did business between the camp and Katowice. We had, how would I say this, the instinct to survive; we had to find ways to do it. We made acquaintances with some Russian soldiers, officers who had to survive in their own way. They had more experience; we had the shrewdness—I mean, the shrewdness to manipulate things because of our backgrounds in the camps.

At that time the business was whatever we could get our hands on. We found out there was a deserted factory not far away where we could get some items and a camp where we could get cotton thread.

We got with these Russians, who were in it for the money too, and with their help, we got into the camp. We took out the thread and whatever we could. Then we went to Katowice where we met the two brothers. We made a couple of trips over there, once with a load of matches, cigarettes later.

Poland didn't have anything, and the goods didn't cost us anything. They were left in the factory and the camp when the Germans left. We just took it and sold it. We got Polish money for it, but we didn't know what to do with it. All the survivors knew where we lived, and they came to buy from us. That was our headquarters for the goods, the trades with the brothers.

It wasn't until we went to Germany that I saw Haidz again. He was with them, the brothers. I don't know how he got there. He had his way and we had our way.

We found a way to sneak out of Poland when things got bad with the new Russian recruits. They were real bullies, attacking the women and everything. We wanted to have more of a life and knew the only future was to go to the American zone in Germany. From there most of us wanted to go to another country—Israel or the United States.

We arranged for a truck with the Russians and paid them to take us to Czechoslovakia to the American border. No one bothered us because we were in an army truck.

Then when we got to Germany, we found out we could make money selling cigarettes in Czechoslovakia, and we needed a driver. That's when Haidz became a partner too. Well, let's put it this way. I split the fifty percent of the profit with the other four guys I had worked with in Poland, the ones from the camp with me. The other fifty percent went to Haidz. He was a big negotiator, even then.

He was tight with his money too. He had no girlfriend, nobody to spend the money on. Even when I wanted to buy something for a girlfriend, he wouldn't let me. We were very close to each other.

He was looking all the time for news of his family. Always asking about his parents and things like that. We knew he was by himself. We knew who he was, and we liked him. He was with us now.

We knew a guy who had a uniform from an organization that worked with displaced persons. It looked like an American uniform, and he had some kind of papers. So Haidz, the guy with the uniform, and I went to the border with cigarettes we got there in Germany and slipped into Czechoslovakia. An acquaintance there sold the goods for us.

We had pulled out all the springs in the truck to pack the cigarettes so they shouldn't be visible at the border checkpoints. We used our friends, the girls we knew, to help pack. We had a whole assembly line of all our friends. We took out the springs from the truck seat and hid the cigarettes there.

Haidz and I came along all right. He spoke some Russian and I spoke Czech. We crossed the border several times, shipping whatever we could find that didn't cost us anything—alcohol, cigarettes. We got to be good friends, very close. We were always together, business and fun.

One time we were out driving and I said to Haidz, "I want to
learn to drive."

"Not yet," he said.

"It's time already."

"Oh, no!"

"It's a straight road to Prague. Let me drive already!"

He still refused.

I begged him, even told him I would kiss him if he wouldn't
teach me. I think he changed his mind because he thought I might
really do it, kiss him if he didn't. So he taught me.

Anyway, that was the way I learned how to drive. I became
a cowboy, more than him, later on. I drove wild. My wife says I still
drive too fast, even today. I always tell her, "It's Haidz's fault. He
taught me."

Then one day Haidz and I got caught smuggling. As we were
coming to the Czechoslovakian border, I saw a black cat crossing
the road.

"Haidz, go back!"

"*Zuruck geht a kose.* It's a Jewish saying—'The only one who
goes back is a goat '"

So I said, "All right."

We went on, and we got caught.

The Czech border police told us to stop the car at the check-
point. We didn't know why they stopped us. Maybe somebody
squealed.

Haidz argued with them, but it didn't do any good at first.
Then, for some reason, they changed their minds. The man in
charge ordered one of the soldiers to climb into the back seat and
told us to drive to Prague.

So we came to the city and to the border patrol headquarters
just as we were directed. We thought we could give away some
loose cigarettes, a bribe. It didn't work. They searched the truck

and found all the cigarettes, and they put us in jail. They had named the jail "the Gestapo" because the SS had used it as an office during the war.

We were in different cells, but we saw each other on the hour walk each day. We got our stories straight so we would know what the other one said when they questioned each of us.

"We were just drivers," we told them. "We didn't know what we had. If you sit on the seat, and you drive and you worry about the traffic, do you know what you're sitting on? It was comfortable sitting. We didn't know what was in there."

We were sitting, all right, twenty-one days in the jail. Nobody knew where we were except when I failed to show up for the soccer game I was supposed to play. We had a friend by the name of Helm, a Czech soldier through the war, and married to a friend's sister. Somehow he found out where we were. He probably paid them off, the border patrol people, because we got free. We lost everything, the truck, the cigarettes. We didn't even get the money.

After that we didn't smuggle to Czechoslovakia; we smuggled to Poland.

Bolek

The first time I saw the Pole, he was sitting in the back of a Russian military truck. It was a Studebaker, an American-made vehicle. The Russians received a lot of them during the war. This was September or October of '45 as I remember. I had just completed, along with my friend Henry, a business transaction.

We had been liberated in Waldenburg, a German city that the Poles were now occupying as compensation for their losses. The Germans and Russians took their eastern borders, so the Poles took the western. Anyway the Russians liberated us. The post-World War period left devastated cities, and the economy was in ruins. It was tough to make a living as a refugee. We had no family. We had no income. We did what we could to survive.

My friend and I made connections with Russian officers who were trying to make some pocket money also. That's how we met this Russian captain, and we became very friendly. We negotiated to exchange some fuel, some barrels of grease, for matches, which were in short supply. The barrels were to be delivered by the captain, who used his authority to get the goods from a plant the Polish military had occupied. We were to use the merchandise to exchange for a truckload of matches—about two hundred thousand boxes, large boxes.

I had friends, Moshe and Haim, who lived in Katowice at the time. We contacted them and made a deal to deliver and sell the entire truckload of matches. This was the way we had to conduct business in order to survive.

So we had a Russian military officer and a Russian chauffeur. My friend Henry and I rode in the back of the truck with the cartons full of matches. There was a canvas to cover the back so nobody would see us, and if we were stopped by the military and questioned, the Russians seated in the cab would handle it. The captain, of course, was exempt.

We sat quietly, not making any noise in case they stopped us. Civilians caught dealing with the military would have been put in jail, if you were lucky, or put against the wall and executed. This was Stalin's regime. No telling what would have happened to the Russian officer and driver.

When we reached Katowice, we turned over the merchandise to my friends. We stayed at Moshe and Haim's apartment and played a little poker with the captain while the two brothers, along with the Russian driver, took the truck to a warehouse. There they unloaded the cargo of matches. The completed transaction gave us eight hundred thousand Zloty, four Zloty per box of matches, eight thousand dollars in American money, which was a lot of money after the war. We gave the Russian captain three hundred thousand Zloty, equivalent to three thousand dollars. He split the money with a major, his boss. This was a fortune for them because they got hundreds of thousands of Zloty, which at the time were two hundred thousand Russian rubles.

The captain later told me what happened when he went back to his headquarters.

The major asked, "Where's the money?"

"I left it there with Bolek and my friends," answered the captain. "We will get it tomorrow."

He said the major was going crazy.

"You've never seen the money? Why did you not take the money with you?"

The captain explained the major was nervous because Russians don't trust people and the Russian officers were risking their lives. If they were found dealing with civilians, they would be in big trouble. They would wind up in jail, the civilians shot.

The captain said, "But I trust my friends."

When the captain finally gave the major his part of the money, the major kept it in a money belt, which looked fat with all the money in it. When he went to the bathroom, he had it on him too, afraid that someone would steal it even there. Under the circumstances they wound up becoming rich people.

Shortly after Moshe and Haim returned, we got paid and started back home. When we lifted the canvas to crawl in, we saw this stranger sitting there. I guessed the two brothers hired him to help the Russian driver load and unload. We didn't know he was Jewish at the time. I don't remember the name he went by. Stefan sounds familiar. I know he changed his name to Weisberg later in Germany, but we called him Rybciu, a Polish nickname that means fish.

So this stranger rode with us to Waldenburg. We were kind of making jokes because we thought this was a Polack and he couldn't understand Yiddish. We made certain remarks about him, like we were businesspeople and he was the poor, dumb Polack. I don't remember Jews having sympathy for the Poles at that time. We just knew he didn't understand a word we were saying. I don't remember the way we found out he was Jewish, but the usual way you found out was to ask the suspect to drop his pants.

We didn't see him again until we all got to the American zone in Germany. Each of us had a different way of getting there, trying to get away from the Poles and the Russians. There was a group of us who lived together in a vacated Nazi apartment in Waldenburg— five couples, friends, sisters, and cousins. We kind of took care of each other.

When we decided to leave for Regensburg in Germany, we hired a Russian chauffeur with a military truck because we had thirteen people. We decided to get away from there before they drafted us into the Polish army.

We hired the Russians and we smuggled over the border, the Polish Czech border also patrolled by the Russians. We hid under the canvas in the back of the truck, and they dropped us off at nighttime near the border. We were caught by the Czech military police as we walked in the dark along trails leading to the border. They took us into their headquarters where they told us to empty our suitcases, to take the clothes but leave the cases. We had suitcases with double decks, a regular case with a disguised compartment. That's how we hid most of our assets, whatever we had left from our transactions.

We also had marmalade cans. In the bottom of each can we laid various pieces of gold and stuff we were able to get from the retreating Germans after the war. On top of the hidden goods, we put marmalade, spreading it neatly and placing the top on it.

They let us keep the cans, but they took the suitcases, suspicious that we might be smuggling goods in the disguised second deck of the case. They were right and they took everything we had hidden. Somebody must have informed them that people were using double suitcases to smuggle goods out of the country. We lost a lot of our valuables.

Strangely enough, I think they knew we were Jews. At that time Jews were trying to get out of Eastern Europe and into the American zone in Germany, many trying to get to Palestine. The British would not permit us in there because Palestine was under British occupation at the time and there were already eight hundred thousand Jews under the British mandate.

The Jewish Zionists were there on the border trying to help Jews cross the borders and get to Israel illegally. We suspected they made some kind of deal, a bribe with the Czech border police. The Czechs would let the Jews who wanted to get to Palestine cross easily, but businesspeople like us would be searched and valuables taken. Even though we were upset that we were the victims and lost our accumulated goods, we understood.

I remember another deal we made before we left Poland. It also had to do with a Russian officer, a lieutenant, who was desperately in need of getting food supplies for the Russian officers' club where he was in charge. With a requisition signed by the Russian military, a Russian military truck with a driver, and a list of Nazi farmers given to us by the local mayor, we were able to confiscate about twenty cows.

What did I know about livestock? I chose the fat ones. We were fortunate that we had the requisition order. The military police came, and I showed them the paper. They saluted us, clicked their feet together, and walked away.

We took one cow as commission, gave it to the butcher, and filled the attic full of salami. We were the richest people in town because we had all that food. A lot of Jews ended up in trouble, just trying to catch a chicken for food, and we had an entire cow. Many people came to see us. We gave a big party on June 8, 1945, my birthday, one month after the official end of the war in Europe.

Once we arrived in Regensburg in November or December of '45, we looked for housing. Moshe, now the president of the Jewish Committee in Regensburg, secured for us a ten-room apartment with a grand piano. We donated about ten thousand German marks to the Jewish committee. The apartment, once owned by a German family, served our needs well, all of us.

It was at the Jewish Community Center we ran into Rybciu, the Polish truck driver who worked for Moshe and Haim in Katowice. By now we knew he was Jewish, going by the name of Willie, and we included him in our business transactions because we needed another driver.

When we learned we could make money smuggling cigarettes across the Czech border, we prepared for the deal. Through contacts we bought cigarettes. At the time we had two cars and lived in a different style, you know, quite different from what we did during the war. With the cars parked in the garage out of sight, we took out the springs of the car seats and packed them with cartons of cigarettes. And we stuffed the sides with single packs of cartons upon cartons.

By now we had "adopted" a younger Jew by the name of Josef. The plan was for Rybciu to go with my friend Josef in one car with Rybciu driving while my cousin and brother-in-law, Julek, and his wife, Didka, went in the second car. The two vehicles loaded with cigarettes, once they crossed the Czech border, were to head for Prague where my other brother-in-law, a businessman, lived. The load was to be dropped off with him. He had people who would buy it.

Julek and Didka knew Rybciu and Josef had a problem when they saw the Czech border patrol detain them. Somehow Julek was able to take off and get away to return home. We notified my brother-in-law in Prague, a Czech soldier and the husband of my wife's third sister. He was able to get them out of jail.

Rybciu became one of us. He was young and handsome. I think there was some romance between him and a tall Czech girl, a contact person for smuggling cigarettes across the border. She would come to visit us in our apartment in Regensburg. We all did what we could to survive and we made fast friendships. In February of '46 four of the couples who were very close friends were married in a huge ceremony in Regensburg. Our friend Josef became engaged at the wedding.

The next year, my wife and I came to the United States on the *Marine Flasher*, a military boat. It would be several years before we saw Rybciu again, in a new place with a new name.

Max

My brothers and I met the Polack when he was driving a truck for us. During the summer of 1945, after liberation, we were working in a munition factory in Ludwigsdorf. We stayed there, I don't know, a week, two weeks. He was driving this truck between Poland and Ludwigsdorf, going back and forth between occupied Germany. My two brothers and I bought him some gasoline, and he took us to Prague.

I don't remember what name he used. He used a Polish name. My brother learned he was Jewish from this girl named Laura, who lived near our hometown. She was in a camp with my sister. I don't know how she found out. Anyway she told us. Otherwise we would not have known he was Jewish.

We knew the people he was driving for. My brother-in-law was involved with those people. That's how we met him. I think the Russians trained him to be a driver or a mechanic. He would tell us stories about how he survived.

We met him again in Regensburg, Bavaria. In 1946 my

brother-in-law took over a Nazi bakery. My two brothers and I ran the bakery. This truck driver used to come into the bakery, and we became friends. This went on until 1949 when we came to the United States on separate ships. We came on the *U.S. Marine Jumper*, an old 1934 model, I think. It was a nice ship though. I would guess at least thirteen hundred came over on that boat. It took us about seven days. That was May. I think the Polack driver came over later in the summer. It was a number of years before I saw him again.

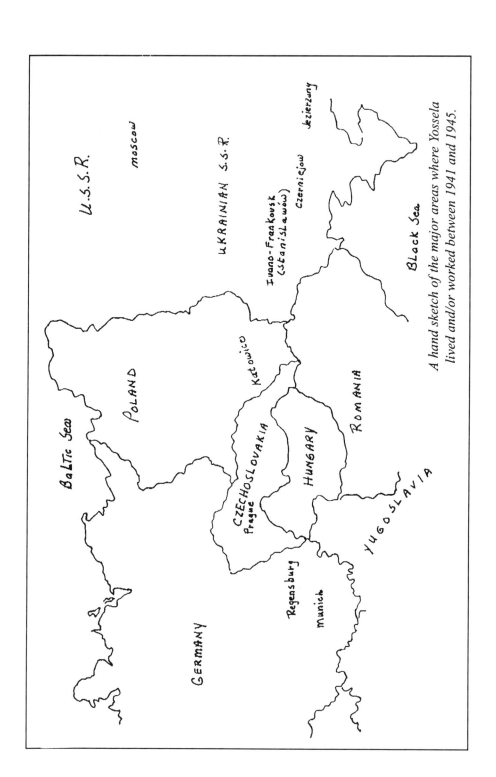

A hand sketch of the major areas where Yossela lived and/or worked between 1941 and 1945.

4 COMING TO AMERICA

THE LONG JOURNEY IN JULY 1949 HAD AT LAST ENDED. AS THE *SS Holbrook*—an old military vessel—creaked slowly through the dark into New York harbor, Willie came out from the bowels of the ship finally to breathe the fresh air. He had found himself alone in what seemed like endless days and nights. The young immigrant lost track of time early on, struggling in self-made isolation with seasickness.

God, where do I go from here?

Those were Willie's first thoughts as he stood at the rail looking at the sight in front of him—tall, endlessly tall structures consuming the sky and small glittering lights flashing like tiny beacons. Willie turned briefly to observe his immigrant kinsmen, standing as he was, waiting to disembark into the alien land. Many of his fellows stood mute, bewildered at the prospect of the unfamiliar. Children clung to bedraggled mothers and others leaned heavily on any support they could find, too weak to stand alone. Some cried with the sudden reality of survival. Soon others began silently exiting from below.

Until now all of these creatures had seemed faceless to Willie, lost in his own agony and relief. One moment the fact he survived fortified him; the next he admonished himself for feeling safe and happy to be alive. In those moments when he rebuked himself, great waves of guilt threatened to glut the very breath that sustained him. The eyes of his younger siblings, dull and vacant from the pain of hunger, peered at him from every corner of his memory. He had endured deprivation. They had not. Then his father's words would sweep over the thoughts threatening to castrate his hope, "The Lord go with you, my son."

Once again he could feel the weight of his father's hand on his head and the strength of his father's words. The fact was he did survive, and it was his destiny and obligation to leave his lost family the gift of life through his legacy.

If he thought there were long lines in Germany, he was mistaken. The ones in America were endless. After the processing, Yiddish-speaking guides directed the immigrants into small groups and onto buses. From the docks they rode through streets crammed with dirty tenements. Both strange and familiar scents drifted through the open bus windows, and horns blared from the automobiles that crowded the narrow streets.

After what seemed an eternity, Willie found himself standing in the center of a small lobby waiting with the others for a room. He would later learn that a worldwide Jewish organization called HIAS maintained this shelter on Lafayette Street for protégés arriving as displaced persons. The American president, Harry Truman, issued a directive for its formation in December of 1945 as a part of the Joint Distribution Committee.

Willie, unaware that he looked unkempt—a stubble darkening his face and his hair hanging dirty and limp— stood clutching an old metal suitcase, his only possession. It contained a change of clothes. He had between four and six dollars in his pocket.

It was late when Willie settled into a small, sparse room he shared with two other men. He fell exhausted onto the small bed. Much later he lay sleepless, listening to the others snore, wet from his own sweat. The air, still and oppressive, sucked at him.

Surely this must be hell, he thought. Have I made a mistake?

The odor of decaying trash drifted through the open window from the noisy street below, and a newsboy hawked *The New York Times*, "Read all about it. Big Fourth of July celebration in Central Park."

The irony of two occurrences coinciding—the Americans celebrating Independence Day and a young immigrant gaining his freedom to build his future—was lost on him. It would be years before Willie could look back and be eternally grateful for having arrived on the shores of a country that would give him so much.

Now Willie was apprehensive. New York was like an over-grown jungle, thick and oppressing. Would he ever see the gentle countryside again?

He could not stand the heat any longer. He crawled out of bed and went quietly into the hall. A door with a lighted sign over it stood across the way. He opened it and found staircases leading up and down. Following a series of these upward, he found himself on the roof, high away from the noise and the stench. There he lay on the cement, looking at the sky, searching for a breeze. On the roof of the Lafayette House, Willie finally fell asleep.

In two days the young man was on a train. Having received directions in Yiddish, he knew he traveled to a town called Chicago, Illinois, and from there he was to take another train to a town called Cedar Rapids, Iowa.

How can I survive in a place where I don't understand the language?

This thought hounded Willie even though he followed the guide's instruction, robot-like. Too often his doubting the decision to emigrate to a foreign nation almost smothered his common sense.

When Willie arrived in Cedar Rapids, he was surprised. He thought he would land in another huge city like New York or Chicago, but instead he found a quiet little town nestled in rich farmland. For the first time since arriving in the United States, he felt a ray of hope. Large pastures with bales of hay and fat cows grazing alongside horses bordered the town. Occasionally thickets of trees dotted the countryside. He thought of Czerniejow, and his heart warmed.

The first person he saw when he disembarked at the Chicago and Northwestern Railroad depot at Fourth Avenue in Cedar Rapids was a short, rotund man with a cigarette hanging from his mouth.

"Name's Sam. Sam Cohen."

Willie took the large man's hand and returned the shake, though he did not know what the man had said. Another man—tall, handsome, and smartly dressed—stepped forward, introducing himself partly in English, partly in faulty Yiddish.

Did these people think he understood and spoke English? Was either of them Jewish? The man with the bad Yiddish said his name was Wolf. That was one of the words Willie understood. Later he would learn that Zig Wolf owned a local dress store.

The two men directed Willie to a big car sitting at a nearby curb, where a third man waited. Again Willie took the offered hand, not understanding what the man said. Many years later he would learn the third man's name was Becker and his Jewish family owned a number of grocery stores in the Cedar Rapids area.

A short distance from the railroad station, they pulled to the curb in front of a three-story building with large letters on the front, YMCA. This is where Willie would live.

It seemed like a clean place compared to some he had seen and it had an elevator. Once Willie checked in, Sam Cohen followed him and the clerk upstairs.

A single, metal bed stood in the small room. A printed spread and a pillow adorned the bed. In a corner stood a small dresser, worn with age. Below one window was a radiator.

Willie glanced around. The clerk motioned toward a small door, walking over and opening it to reveal a tiny closet. Willie placed his suitcase there. Though no outward sign showed his approval, he felt rich having this room.

Sam took Willie downstairs, and as they approached the door to another room, delicious aromas permeated the entry and they smiled at each other.

Willie had forgotten hunger, simultaneously excited and fearful of all that was happening.

Sam introduced Willie to a man behind the counter, a tall, slim man who had dark hair and wore glasses. From a peephole into the kitchen, a graying man with a large mustache and dark eyes smiled. The man behind the counter shook Willie's hand and the other one waved. The man at the counter spoke very fast. Willie did not think he sounded like the others.

It was at times like this that Willie became exasperated. He knew five languages, some learned from the streets, but did not understand the language of the country to which he immigrated. Little did he know that the two Greeks, father and son, who owned the restaurant, were also immigrants and spoke broken English.

Arrangements had been made for Willie to take his meals free at the cafe and stay free at the "Y" until he could make enough money to pay his own way.

For the first few weeks in Cedar Rapids, Willie ate with the Greeks. They gave him breakfast and lunch. He always sat at the counter, avoiding the tables. It seemed easier. It was obvious to the Greeks Willie could not read the menu when he chose his order from the menu pictures. Once Willie learned to order soup, stew, and French fries, he consistently ate the same thing.

The fries did not taste like any of the potato dishes his mother had made. He wondered why Americans coated everything with ketchup. When he tried to order a hamburger for breakfast, the Greeks laughed. He did not drink coffee, considered a luxury in Europe. The first time he ordered tea, they gave it to him with ice. He did not like it, but did not want to seem unappreciative.

He ordered little food, for he was afraid it was costly, and he did not want to impose on the friendly men at the restaurant.

Sam picked up Willie and took him to his new job only a day after arriving in Cedar Rapids. The Big Shoe Store, owned by Schiff Company, was several blocks away from the "Y," which meant Willie could walk to work. The railroad tracks served as his benchmark. The small building, crammed between two larger ones, featured a display window covering most of its front. Sam was a district manager for the shoe company and made the Cedar Rapids store his headquarters.

It was Willie's job to keep the basement area in proper order. His responsibility was to arrange in numerical order shoes stored there. With his ignorance of the language, confusion delayed learning the job. Willie determined to make knowledge of the English language his immediate goal.

He found an unlikely teacher in Skinny, the shoeshine person who used the back of the store for his independent business. Skinny was the only person who paid attention to him, except for Sam, who was often too busy to help his new employee.

Immediately Skinny took Willie under his wing, pointing to the various pieces of equipment the young man needed for his chores and distinctly pronouncing each word. He gave Willie a pencil and paper, and each time Skinny gave the name "mop," "broom," or "dusting," he directed Willie how to print the word. Willie was a good pupil. He taped the individual pieces of paper on the wall for further use.

Every day Willie felt more comfortable with the Black man whose ever present smile stretched across his entire face, exposing shiny white teeth and crinkling the corners of his eyes. The Jew had a new friend.

Soon the young immigrant learned new words such as "polish" and "galoshes." He was pleased with himself. Once he learned a little English, he enrolled in the night classes Sam suggested.

When winter came to Cedar Rapids, it struck Willie as hard

in its bitter cold as the New York City summer was hot. Unprepared for the drastic change in weather, Willie was forced to use one of his week's paychecks, eighteen dollars, to buy a coat.

By now he was paying for his food and rent. Not much was left from the eighteen dollars, but he saved as much as he could. He took a part-time job in a nearby cafeteria, where he cleaned tables after the shoe store closed. For his efforts, he was allowed to eat there. Soon he was able to save twelve dollars from every check.

If the shoe store had an overflow of customers on the weekend, Willie came up to the floor. He had an instinct for what people wanted and could use a measuring stick for size. In school he had been good in arithmetic. Sometimes he made several trips to the basement to get the correct size.

Customers came in with shoes wet from the snow and Willie gave them a little extra service, wiping the slush from their shoes. It would be awhile before he learned to write a ticket. He did not say much—he could not—but he smiled a lot. He tried hard to please everybody. Often Sam's gruffness and demands made him a little afraid, but for the most part, he knew Sam was a good person.

Willie was always the first person waiting outside the shop each morning and the last to leave. Finally Sam gave him the key to the place. The other salesmen, often late to work, also left early. When Sam was not around, they talked on the phone to girlfriends. They liked to tease Willie, but Willie did not let it bother him.

Sam took Willie under his direction for part of his social life. He invited him to meals at his home, especially on the weekends when his daughter, Phillis, was home from college. When Sam saw Willie eating a bologna sandwich for lunch for the third day in a row, he said, "I'll treat you today," and off they went to the American Legion club where Sam was commander. That treat got to be a habit.

Sam was very involved in community activities and was well respected. He had fought in World War I and was the instigator for helping American fighting men during World War II. He gave every soldier who left Cedar Rapids for the service a going away present and originated the "Keep 'Em Smoking" campaign for supplying servicemen with cigarettes. He was called the "official town leader" in the local newspaper. When Willie finally understood this, he was amazed. Sam was a big guy locally, and he was a Jew.

Within a couple of months Willie felt comfortable with his surroundings. By now he had met the rabbi at Temple Judah, who on several Fridays had already invited Willie to have dinner with him and his family. They had come to the states in 1938 from Germany.

Willie had questioned his Jewish background since 1941. When the local rabbi invited him to a synagogue in Cedar Rapids, he accepted but for other than religious reasons. He welcomed the familiar Yiddish and the opportunity to be among his own kind, socializing and being accepted. These feelings led to a gradual rise in self-respect.

In Germany he associated mostly with refugees, having little to do with civilians. Now he was finally in a country where people appeared to lead normal lives in an intelligent, respectful way. They seemed so wealthy. Being Jewish didn't make any difference. He realized how big the world really was and how some people were luckier than others.

Though he sometimes felt sorry for himself, he realized that common sense acquired through hard work and the effort to survive helped him with the problems confronting him. Little did he know that this philosophy would guide him significantly in the future.

Still all his thoughts were in Polish, Yiddish, or German. Those European habits were difficult to change.

Never did thoughts of his family leave him. He dealt almost nightly with frightening dreams. Willie depended on hard work to help him banish them, falling into bed each night exhausted.

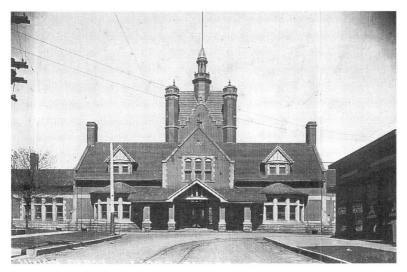

Union Station in Cedar Rapids covered an entire city block. The Chicago &
Northwestern passenger depot was a part of the station and located at 326
4th Avenue. Willie arrived here in July, 1949.

Courtesy of the Cedar Rapids History Center .

Sam Cohen and Family. (left to right) Sam's daughter, Phillis;
his son, Stanley; Sam, and Mother Cohen. Sam sponsored
Willie for immigration to the U.S. and Cedar Rapids, Iowa.

Source: Schiff Shu Nus Newsletter, July 1947.

Sam treated Willie to lunch at the American Legion luncheon—held in the basement of the Guaranty Building on Third Ave. and Third Street S.E.

Willie's first place of employment, the Big Shoe Store, managed by Sam Cohen. Here Skinny taught English to Willie.

Cedar Rapids YMCA—Willie's first home in the U.S., 1949.

Willie's evening English class celebrates graduation. Willie-back row fifth from left.

The Peoples Groceries & Market located at 119 3rd Avenue, SE where Willie purchased bologna for his sparse meals. The store was owned by Orrie and Anne Becker.

The young immigrant completed night school, and Sam allowed him to work on the main floor more often. He had become Sam's prize salesman. In later years he would consider Sam, along with Skinny, his first professional mentors.

Willie believed Sam was one of the best businessmen he had ever known. From him he learned how to finagle a deal. Sam was tough with his salesmen, chastising them if they let a customer walk out of the store without buying a pair of shoes. He demanded hard work and got it. Those salesmen who misused the system when Sam was not there to supervise were eventually found out and dismissed.

Willie was certain Skinny was one of the reasons he succeeded in integrating into the American system so quickly. His patience with the young immigrant's broken language and his constant barrage of vocabulary lessons kept Willie on the cutting edge of his learning.

Only six months after Willie arrived in Cedar Rapids, Sam promoted him to manager of a Schiff store in Kansas City, Missouri. When Willie confessed his fear, Sam patted him on the shoulder. "It'll be the experience you need to move forward," he said. "You have to learn to take risks in life. Grab your chances, work hard, and use your common sense."

It was a lesson Willie would not forget. As he reflected on Sam's words, he could not help but compare them to his father's last blessing. Had he not used that blessing to survive? More and more, he believed his father somehow knew that, if anyone could survive, Yossela would. Had he not pushed him as a young boy to imitate those who succeeded, like the neighbor's children?

Soon Willie found himself in Kansas City during the winter of 1950. He got a room in a local boarding house within walking distance of the store, met his new area boss, and quickly discovered he had become a virtual slave.

Willie alone ran the store—the sole salesman, window trimmer, stock boy, marketing person, and whatever else was needed. And the shoe business competition was fierce. Willie worked day and night, but it was not the hard work he minded.

On rare occasions he attended activities at the local Jewish Community Center, meeting another immigrant with whom he would become a lifelong friend.

Willie understood the need to work hard, but also realized he could never build a private life on thirty-eight dollars a week, with no free time to meet a girl and start a family. Instinctively Willie knew his future lay elsewhere.

He took the money he saved in Cedar Rapids and Kansas City and bought a used four-door Pontiac for one hundred fifty dollars. He liked the cow horn on the hood.

With his meager possessions in the trunk, he headed west. He had always wanted to see where movies were made.

Edith

It was 1949 when an army transporter called the *SS Holbrook* brought Joe and me to the United States.

My first American experience was donuts, the first ones I ever had. They were cake donuts, and I fell in love with them.

Some lovely ladies walked through the crowd of arriving passengers with baskets of donuts. I think the ladies were from HIAS, the Hebrew Immigrant Aid Society, that met us at the boat.

When I got on that boat, it was the first time I was ever on such a big ship. The first night was wonderful. There was a big dining hall and a wonderful meal. Let me tell you, it was just great. The food was delicious to us. The first time I saw Jell-O, I didn't know what that was. It was red. I was going through the line, cafeteria style, and we were saying to each other, "Look at this. They're eating jam with meat! What is that red thing on the plate?" We liked it. We had cabbage too. Listen, we went for seconds because it was so good. That was the last meal we had.

The trip itself was the most miserable trip on earth, not because of the people around us. They could not have been nicer. We were so seasick, and we just had to wait it out as did so many others.

Besides the sickness, the men and women were separated, even husbands and wives. Joe and I were only six months married. Women were in one section, and women with children were able to sleep on the lower bunks.

It was one big hall with rows of cots double and triple decked. I remember I was all the way up on top, and my husband was somewhere else. The trip took ten days and I only saw Joe toward the end.

After the first meal I just lay there sick. A man came to me at one point and he said to me, "Did you know that your husband is sick?"

"Well," I said, "you go right back to him and tell him I can't move. I am sick too."

Toward the end of the trip we got together on deck, Joe and me, and took photographs of each other.

The people on the boat got wind that I knew English, and they needed tea and sent me downstairs to the galley to get some tea bags. It was the funniest thing. These Chinese were down in the galley preparing the food or whatever. They didn't understand me and I didn't understand them. They were just smiling. I was just smiling and pointing. I ended up with sweater pockets stuffed with tea bags.

We arrived in New York July 2. I laugh so much about it now because I see all these immigrant movies, and they show you how people are moved when they see the Statue of Liberty. We did not see it. We came at night.

My first sight was these blinking lights, a lot of blinking lights like a highway or something, car lights. You see it was the Fourth of July weekend. Traffic was bumper to bumper. We didn't see any fireworks though. I don't know how we would have reacted to that.

On the boat there was a lot of commotion as we were coming and a lot of gossip. Rumors, rumors, rumors. We did not know whether we were even going to be able to land. Some feared they might send us back because there was some kind of holiday nobody knew about. We thought the port would be closed and who knew what would happen to us?

We came to New York through the regular port, not Ellis Island. We didn't know what the future was going to hold for us. I finally felt safe though.

When we got off the boat, we were glad and everything went in a very orderly fashion. We had to go through customs, the usual things. One man talked to me and he was surprised I knew English. He said, "How come you know English?" I guess they were used to the old immigrants who didn't know English.

There were these long tables, and they were asking us questions, taking our papers, and telling us they knew we were going to Houston, but we would have to spend the night there in New York.

We went to this little hotel. I don't know where it was. It was not very luxurious. When we looked out the window of our room, we saw nothing but adjacent big walls. We said how happy we would be to leave.

The thing I remember about New York was stalls and stalls of fruit on the street, and the men tending the stalls wore big flowery shirts they let hang out of their trousers. We never saw men in Poland or Germany wearing flowery prints.

It took a long time to get to the States. Everybody wanted to leave Europe. It was a God forsaken place.

Joe and I met in 1948 in a displaced person place where we came to visit. We got married in 1949 in Munich, applied for immigration, and moved to Stuttgart, where Joe had lived before we were married. We waited six months there for emigration.

At that time you couldn't get work. You worked for a Jewish organization or something like that if you were lucky. We got some rations from UNRRA, a relief organization.

Once you got your visa and everything allowed emigrating to the US, you immediately had to leave where you were living in Germany and go to the Bremerhaven port. It was like a big enclosure, like a camp, but not like a Nazi camp. Once you got there, you couldn't leave. We were sitting two weeks in Bremerhaven waiting to get on the boat.

One thing I remember, we were trying to find a library to find out where we were going to settle down. We knew it was a place called Houston, Texas, but we didn't know anything about it.

We found out, in a big way, when we came to Houston and got off the train. We thought we were going to die, it was so hot! We were still dressed in the same clothes we were wearing in New York because everything was packed. We weren't dressed for July in New York or Houston. We had never, never felt such a heat. The summers in Poland and Germany were not that hot.

It wasn't until many years later that Joe and I learned that a young man named Willie came over on the same ship with us in 1949. By the time we met him, he'd changed his name.

It's a small world. We all ended up in the same city.

Harold

We had the Jewish Federation at that time in Cedar Rapids. In fact, we founded it in the 1930s as well as the Jewish Welfare Fund. Then in the '40s we had it designated as a 501(3)C charity. We founded it in order to help people who were having trouble paying their rent, not surviving in their business, or who needed groceries. We still have it. I'm a trustee for thirty, forty years. We've brought about ninety families to Cedar Rapids.

Willie was probably brought over by the United Jewish Appeal for HIAS, an outfit out of New York. Its official name is the Hebrew Immigrant Aid Society. They brought immigrants into this country, then asked communities to sponsor people. The United Jewish Appeals Association sent some of their money to HIAS.

I think somebody, probably my father, called Sam Cohen and asked if he would take Willie in, help him get a job, sponsor him. Back in the '40s you needed a sponsor to get in this country because you didn't have any money and nowhere to go.

In today's society it's a little different. With the government system the way it is, an immigrant, within a short period of time, gets medical treatment, Social Security, and everything. Back then that didn't happen. Somebody had to sponsor you.

Sam Cohen was a very fine man, a good friend of mine, a good friend of my father. He has an extremely interesting history of his own. He was in World War I as a soldier, and he fought in France. He ended up marrying a French Jewish woman, and they came here and raised a family, a son and a daughter. His daughter still lives here. Her name's Phillis.

Sam had a big heart, and he was a people-oriented man. He and another man, who wasn't Jewish, wanted to form a club for the servicemen coming back from the war in 1945. They felt the men needed a place to relax and enjoy themselves.

He came to my father, who at that time owned this bank building we're in now. My father said, "Look, I'll give you the basement, free of charge. You can have it for two years, no rent. You can fix it up, make a place for the soldiers and sailors coming back."

It ended up becoming the American Legion Club, and Sam Cohen and this other man did it single-handed. They went out and raised money to build this club room in the basement. The Legion was not known to be a very liberal organization. Its policies were just a little right-wing for me. Sam Cohen was very active in it.

Sam wanted very much to be the commander for the American Legion here in Cedar Rapids. He wanted to be the elected president. There was a man at the time going around campaigning saying, "You don't want a damn Jew to be the head of the American Legion." A couple of my friends, who were not Jewish, came to me and said, "We fought in this war, and we're not going to tolerate that kind of garbage in Cedar Rapids."

They asked if I could help them. We went out and raised money on a campaign and we got Sam Cohen elected and got the bigot thrown out. It was a triumph for justice.

There were three Greek immigrant brothers—Mike, George, and Gus. I think they ran that restaurant in the YMCA. The Greeks at that time had a great empathy for the Jewish community of Cedar Rapids because of their respective immigrant backgrounds. They have all passed on now. They were probably the ones who fed Willie when he first came to Cedar Rapids. There was someone else who had a night school for immigrants at that time. The Jewish Welfare Fund paid for it, most likely, or Sam went around and got handouts.

We had a grocery down the street called People's Grocery Market. I suspect that's where Willie bought his bologna. It was a short distance from the Big Shoe Store, where he worked for Sam.

Phillis

Skinny was good to people. He helped Willie, this new guy, some guy from Europe who dressed real funny. When I was home from college one time, I asked Skinny if Willie had bad kidneys. I thought that because he was always going downstairs.

Skinny said, "No, that's where your father wants him to work."

I don't remember my father doing anything like that before. I guess he probably wanted him to learn how to speak English before he came up and dealt with the customers.

I'm sure Skinny thought it was remarkable that this young guy, "punk" he probably called him silently, was trying to learn English. Skinny would say to me, as though I didn't understand how hard it was, "Are you learning another language?"

I'm sure he praised Willie to his face. Skinny would kid around and fool around and make you laugh, but he was sincere. He wanted you to succeed in what you did. I could just hear him say, "I never got a chance to pursue what I wanted to do in life. Why should Willie suffer?"

He always encouraged me to improve. "You can do it," he said. And yet it's ironic what happened to Skinny.

He was going to law school when he met a white girl, fell in love, and married her. After that the law school wouldn't accept him back, so he shined shoes at my dad's store. He was just like you and me, didn't speak with an accent, no Negro dialect. He was a very intelligent man and what a comic! Whatever he said or did, he put a little bit of humor into it.

He would tease me, and he took up for me when others did. One of the guys at the store would always call me a silly last name, Irish sounding. I had red hair and I didn't look Jewish, and Skinny would come up to me and say, "Don't let him bother you. He's just jealous because he's not Irish."

When I went into the store, I'd go back and see him sitting at his shoeshine stand.

"Come here. Your shoes are dirty," he'd say.

"I've been waiting for my shoes to get dirty," I'd say. "I don't like shoes."

"Get up here," he'd say with a gruff voice, but a twinkle in his eye.

He would make my shoes spotless. I'd tease him and say, "I'm going to have to go stand out in a mud puddle, I guess."

He'd look at me and squint his eyes. "I'll just clean them up again."

Skinny would have a customer whom he knew very well and I would come in from school and sit down. He would say, with a frown on his face, "What are you doing here now?"

"Skinny," I'd say, "we just got out of school."

Mind you, he's cleaning someone's shoes, and he would stop and talk to me.

I would tease back. "Skinny, just finish the shoes."

"Hey, don't tell me what to do," he'd say. "This gentleman will wait until I'm ready to do his shoes." The customer would smile and listen to what we were saying. And believe me, Skinny always had something to say about any given subject, made no difference what it was.

As a child, I was always down at the store, and when I got older, I worked there before I went to college. When my father moved from the small store downtown out to the malls, Skinny didn't follow him. Skinny liked my father, but he said dad was too hard on people. Said he couldn't be hard on him because he was independent from the shoe store. He was his own boss.

Skinny wasn't real tall, but he was really, really skinny. He looked like a displaced person. Never in all the years that I went in and talked to him did he ever mention his wife, but he talked about his children. Adolf Wilson was his real name and he had the kind of smile that, if you were sad, he would smile and you had to smile back. His teeth were white, straight, and made a great smile. There was always a twinkle in his eye.

I remember one time I went into the store right after a dancing lesson and Skinny was talking to some guy standing there, and when I walked in, he asked, "Would you like to meet Bill Robinson?"

I said, "Oh, come on, Skinny. I know you know lots of people, but you don't know Bill Robinson."

"All right, turn around."

I think my mouth must have fallen down to the basement when I realized the man he'd been talking to was Bill Robinson.

Mr. Robinson said, "Which steps did you just learn in dancing class?"

I was so nervous, I really was, because I knew what a great dancer he was. I sort of showed him a step or two, and he said, "Is that how you did it in class?"

"No."

"How did you do it?"

Suddenly Skinny took out a harmonica that he had in his jacket and started playing music. Bill Robinson asked, "What's the name of that step?"

I told him. He said, "OK, now show me how you do it."

All the time Skinny was playing that harmonica.

So I was showing him this step I learned. He said, "That's good." Then he started doing it. And we danced together.

I couldn't believe I was dancing with a movie star, a person who had actually danced with Shirley Temple. Even now, once in awhile, I'll see old Shirley Temple movies and there's Bill Robinson.

It's true Skinny practically raised me. He probably started working in that store when I was five or six years old. I'm sixty-five now. He died sometime in the 1950s. I never thought they were all like Skinny and I loved him.

5 SEEKING THE DREAM

WHERE WERE THE COWBOYS AND INDIANS? SINCE DETOURING south on his way to California, Willie saw only large areas of open fields with few towns. Occasionally cows or horses grazed in nearby pastures. The further he moved south, the flatter the land became.

His car broke down in Texas, on the outskirts of Houston, a comparatively large town, not like New York or Chicago, of course, but large compared to Kansas City and Cedar Rapids. Bill wondered how one found a landmark in the middle of this flat land without even a hill as a guide.

The repair work completed, Willie realized he would not be traveling to California, at least for awhile. The money he had left in his pocket would find him a place to live while he looked for a job.

He got a room in the YMCA on Louisiana Street, and within a day or two he was selling shoes in a large department store called Foley's in downtown Houston.

Selling shoes was a familiar trade though not what he wanted to do. Nevertheless, it would have to suffice until he could do better.

Rapidly Willie learned that, in order to get the customer and thus the commission, the salesman must be aggressive. Soon he was making good money, enough to give up his "Y" room and rent a room with a Jewish family on Almeda Street.

The one thing he really resented about the job was the manager. Just when Willie got a good footing for successful sales, the manager had other thoughts, other chores in the stockroom. That did not suit Willie. He knew he was a good salesman, a big producer, and the highest paid man on the floor.

Willie always started work early, stayed late, and never took long lunches. When he tried to reason with his supervisor that he had taken his turn in the stockroom and did not want to miss the chance of making a commission, the manager became angry, shouting at him.

He was surprised when the man fired him, his most successful salesman. Willie did not feel good about being discharged especially when he had worked so hard. His anger led him to the decision he would not work for anybody else again. He would be his own boss.

In Germany he had heard the stories about opportunities for success and "making it" in America, an assumption that the "American dream" of success could be realized through hard work and determination. He certainly had experience in those categories. What was to deter him but himself? After all, this was America, there were no conquerors to stop him, and the luck was there for the taking.

Often his father had compared him to the neighbor's children, "You see, Yossela, if you work hard, put your all into it, you can be just like the best of them."

Willie's goal was to make his father proud of him and be the best, whatever it was. Above all, he needed to be accepted.

Immediately after the dismissal from Foley's, he picked up a newspaper and began to search the ads, still struggling with English words. One ad attracted him. It indicated he could buy a cafe for a small amount of money. It sounded like the right chance. He had saved what he considered a large sum of money, between two and four hundred dollars. He called the listed number and a man with a heavy accent answered. Willie explained that he was not a native American and that he was looking for an opportunity to run his own business. When Willie told him how much he had to invest, the man laughed.

Willie refused to be disheartened, insisting he could make his dollars work to obtain the business. Convinced by Willie's argument, the man met Willie and took him to meet the owner of the cafe.

It was late 1952. Willie changed his name to Bill Weisberg, and with his savings in hand from the Foley's job, he negotiated the purchase of a small cafe near the corner of Texas and Caroline Streets, not far from the Foley's store. If he could learn about the shoe business, he could learn about the restaurant business. He decided the risk was worth losing a few hundred dollars. What had Sam Cohen said? "You gotta take a risk to get anywhere." The common sense behind this thinking would serve him well as he searched for the "American dream."

A part of buying Kwik Snak Cafe was keeping on the payroll two Black women who worked there, Freddie and Bula. Bula worked the counter and washed dishes, and Freddie cooked.

Freddie was his "ace in the hole." She made the house specialty—Irish stew. The previous owner indicated it was a favorite among the customers. Bill quickly reasoned, if she left, the specialty disappeared. She was the key to his success in the restaurant business.

Freddie was an asset to Bill in more ways than one. His relationship with Skinny back in Cedar Rapids taught him to rely on his instincts for new mentors. Freddie was just that, his new teacher.

"Mr. Bill," she'd say, "yo' can't make coffee worth a hoot. Yo' go on over to dat cash register and let me make da coffee."

Kwik Snak Cafe, near the corner of Texas and Caroline, 1953. Willie's first business. Willie, now Bill Weisberg, mans the cash register while Bula tends the counter.

Bill did as he was told.

The new cafe owner had a few other things to learn. America had some faults. The first time he asked Freddie and Bula's friends and relatives why they used the back door instead of the front, teacher Freddie was there to explain.

"I know yo' don't understand. Yo're a furiner. Now, I say yo're da best white man I ever did know, but Black folk don't come in da front dor. Dey use da back."

When Bill protested, Freddie explained, "Yo' let dose Black folk come in da front dor, yo' may not have any white folk comin' in. Might hurt yo' business."

Finally Bill conceded, but not without experiencing great disappointment. He thought he had left discrimination behind in Europe. How could he ever understand this attitude in a land where so much opportunity existed? Did it not exist for all people? Would he find out that it might not exist for the Jew either? He would have to make sure that it did.

On January 1, 1953, he officially and legally changed his name to William Jacob Morgan, an American-sounding name. Hidden in its sound was the Jew in Bill—William for Wolf, his birth name; Morgan for Margulies; and Jacob, a common Jewish name and concealed by the other two.

Bill took in only eighty-five dollars a day and paid out sixty-five. In order to make his cafe business a success, he abandoned his rented room on Almeda to sleep on the kitchen floor of the cafe. To save on food, he ate leftovers even though Freddie's cooking did not seem like leftovers. He ate well.

He was single, had no dependents. He could learn everything he needed in order to run the place. What did he have to lose? He was twenty-eight years old and already an American entrepreneur.

Seeking ways to save money, he tended a parking lot near the restaurant and in return received free rent for his eatery. He awakened at four o'clock in the morning in order to get the day's supplies for the cafe and maintain the parking lot for people who did business downtown.

Plus keeping the cafe clean, he made the menus and did the accounting. He also cleaned the grease trap himself because he did not have the money to pay someone else to do it.

He served hamburgers, sandwiches, eggs, soup, and the famous Irish stew. Each day at three o'clock, the restaurant was through with what was called a noon rush hour.

A year after he purchased Kwik Snak, Bill had a chance to sell it at a profit and did not hesitate. He was anxious about wasting time with his life. He did not have time to date, and he did not see any big money in the business.

The same man who sold the cafe to him brought by another buyer. Bill sold out for almost two thousand dollars in profit, big money then.

Good-byes were difficult.

"Mr. Bill," said Freddie. "Yo' been lak family. I say 'dere go my brother.' Yo' loaned me money when I needed it, and listened to my problems." Eyes glistening, she took his hand. "Don't think I ever been treated with so much respect nor work for anybody dat worked so hard, right 'long side me."

Bill would not forget the large, heavyset woman with the bowed legs who knew every customer by name. When things got tough, her sense of humor made her boss smile.

The first thing Bill did was to buy a new car. He fancied the one with double cow horns the moment he saw it. It would take him to California for a much needed vacation. He drove straight through, sleeping in the car to save money.

When he arrived in Los Angeles, he got a room in a boarding house. If he liked Los Angeles, he would make his home there, but first he had to get a job. It was easy.

Selling used cars was a new experience in sales techniques. The sales manager was an Irishman, tall and mean. He supervised a big lot with many salesmen who talked fast. Bill knew he could not come close to talking as fast nor be as conniving and "slick" as they, but he gave it a try. Three months later he had sold only two cars.

Back in Houston again, Bill rented a room from a Mr. and Mrs. Berger at the corner of Blodgett and Almeda. The woman and her husband, who worked for a grocery supply company, were friendly to their new renter. Renting the extra room would supplement the husband's salary.

While Bill had worked at the car dealership in Los Angeles, he had learned the manager was buying his used cars in Texas, where they were cheaper. Bill decided he would learn about buying and exporting used cars. He began attending car auctions, watching carefully how it was done. He decided to make the plunge, buy two used cars, take them to Los Angeles, and run them through the auction there.

He hooked them together and drove to California. Bill made three trips in all, returning each time to Texas by train. He made enough money to encourage him to try it a fourth time. It was the wrong decision. He bought a lemon, and he lost money.

Until he could find a business with a promising future, he got a job working at Oshman's selling clothes, all the while looking for ads that shouted, "opportunity." Finally he saw one that said he could be independently wealthy. He was excited and immediately went to the promoter to purchase the merchandise.

Between shifts at Oshman's, Bill sold door-to-door to businesses with restrooms. He pushed the product that would make customers want to return to the establishment just because of sweet-smelling restrooms. Actually, on close examination, the touted merchandise was just a piece of soap and a fan.

Soon Bill found his soap customers unwilling to pay the monthly cost of keeping their restroom smelling sweet. He got few to renew the contract. When he went to collect, they told him it was no good and to take it out.

Disheartened by the waste of time, Bill ended up leaving containers in the restrooms. He relied on his Oshman's job but continued to look for the right break to help him reach his goals. If he was not finding his niche in business, he was surely finding what he did not want to do.

That is when he decided he would learn the meat business. The idea had filtered through his mind several times while he tinkered with the used cars. When he was in the restaurant business, he met a man who had a packing house called Kay Packing Company. When he picked up meat for the cafe, he saw a large number of people coming in. Business seemed brisk for hot dogs and salami.

With a plan in mind to buy meat from the packing company and resell it, he went to the man who managed the meat house. Bill bought two boxes of hot dogs and a few salamis, loading the meat in the trunk of his new car. Having bought a book with carbon paper for orders, he drove by small concerns, grocery stores, and cafes. Door to door, he pushed the meat, and within two hours he had sold out. He made two dollar's profit.

With the extra two dollars added to some of his savings, he returned to the meat packing company and bought a little more inventory. Once again, he sold out quickly.

Even he was surprised at how quickly he became an experienced meat salesman. Some of his original customers became regulars. At the same time he realized the car was too small for his inventory, he learned it was illegal to haul meat in a nonrefrigerated vehicle. Afraid the Health Department would stop his promising business, he decided to invest in a used truck and found a mechanic who could refrigerate it.

Bill could not believe his good fortune. Not only was he making money, but also he had some freedom to meet friends and attend functions at the Jewish Community Center.

Bill had come a long way, and each day life seemed more precious. How quickly he had grown from that sixteen-year-old who walked out of the ghetto! His life virtually stood still as he lived among the Ukrainians those four years disguised as a Polish farmhand. Again in Germany Bill felt his life was held in custody as he waited another four years for emigration.

Fearfully Bill grabbed hold of hope for his future when he arrived in the United States. Within the next year he learned English and experienced a trade.

He took the risk and moved on, first to Kansas City, then to Houston. His base knowledge grew, and the more it expanded, the more he determined life was passing him by. Would he ever, at the rate he was going, not only achieve material comfort, but also defeat the loneliness that haunted him?

Intermittently the nightmares of wartime Europe and the panic of future life left Bill sleepless and concerned. Sometimes during the night he sat straight up in bed, perspiration streaming from his body, his heart beating rapidly. Strangely enough the underlying panic created a mindset that drove him to attack furiously each task he created. His life centered on work, spending long hours at the tasks. Anxiety guided him to crave learning new skills. The same apprehension guided him to date, sensing it was time to focus on a another goal—finding a wife and starting a family. It was then he met Shirley.

Bill S.

Willie was a happy-go-lucky kind of fellow. He was very friendly, had a good personality.

I had been working at Foley's for a while when he came in to get a job. From the very first I got along with him very well as a co-worker. We all worked on commission. Even though Willie was new to Foley's, he worked hard. He was right there in the middle

of the salesmen, going forward and trying to get those first customers.

I saw him, from the very beginning, as a person with strong
ambition. I really enjoyed working with him and liked him a lot. His
other co-workers felt so-so about him. I wasn't sure why they were
reluctant toward him. I think they misunderstood him, or maybe
they put him in another category because he was a foreigner. He had
a thick accent.

I understood his drive, where he came from. He handled the
public well, but he didn't get along too well with the manager who
was kind of hard to deal with. The manager was a perfectionist, and
if things didn't go exactly the way he wanted, he was not bashful
about jumping someone right there in public, screaming at them
right on the sales floor.

I never did understand if Willie was fired or if he just left.
Anyway his leaving was probably the best thing that could have
happened to him.

Bernard

My retail store was on the southeast corner of Texas and
Austin in downtown Houston, adjoining the Greyhound bus station.
I was in the menswear business—Leeds Menswear, it was called.

Catty-cornered across the street was a big, wholesale, dry
goods company called Hogan-Allnoch. In those days it was a very
reputable company and well known throughout the area. Hogan-
Allnoch serviced a lot of the dry goods stores throughout Texas and
this area.

Also in the same block, around the corner and on the north half
of the lot, was the Cotton Exchange Building, which in those days

was a very important building. All the area cotton brokers were in there. Three structures—Hogan-Allnoch, a small cafe, and a bank—were on the south half of the lot. Directly across was the Petroleum Building, at that time called Houston Natural Gas, Arco.

So it was a good, active area. On occasion I would go across the street to the small cafe sandwiched in between Hogan-Allnoch on the east and on the west the Federal Reserve Bank building, a huge building with guards all around. It was two blocks from Union Station, so the hamburger stand would get some of the traveling people who were looking for a quick snack.

That's how I met Willie Weisberg. I ate hamburgers there and I got to know him. At that time his command of the English language was not that great. He looked rough, very immigrant, a little uncouth, not polished.

Willie acted as the cashier and counterman. I heard his story of being a refugee from the Holocaust. He didn't go into too many details. Of course, he knew I was Jewish because of my name.

I was particularly interested in the subject because I was in Europe during the war. The last few days when the war was over and I was on my way down from north central Germany—where I was stationed—to the Riviera, I went through Dachau. There were still some inmates or refugees, so I always had a strong feeling and compassion for what was going on.

I never did ask him or question him how he was able to escape going to the camps. As a matter of fact, I didn't know until years later the details of his survival.

I can't recall how long Willie was there in the little cafe. I was there from 1948 to 1958 when I sold my stores and went into the real estate business.

I sort of lost track of him for a number of years. Then all of a sudden I hear about this man named Bill Morgan, and I put two and two together. I felt very proud of the fact that he pulled himself up by the bootstraps and went and got a successful business—with or without polish.

Bill O.

I remember the time Bill, known as Bill Weisberg then, and I went fishing in Kemah, down toward Galveston. I think he probably knew as much about fishing as I did, and I knew nothing. We rented a rowboat and went over to some little island. We stayed there probably a total of thirty minutes.

Shortly after we got there, he said, "Nothing is biting. Let's go back."

All of a sudden as we were rowing back, this huge freighter was coming at us. We're trying to get out of the way, and it's almost running over us. Finally we pulled away, but the waves from the large ship caused me to fall off the boat. Lucky for me, I fell right next to the pier.

I remember thinking, "Oh, oh, here I go. I'm dead."

I went straight down. I was five feet seven, five foot eight, and the water was about six feet. I hit bottom and I popped up and grabbed onto the boat. Bill pulled me in the boat. That's the last time we went fishing.

I met Bill about the time he bought the cafe. I had just come from Canada in December of 1951, last two days of 1951.

I think we met at the Jewish Community Center on Herman Drive. I worked downtown then, on Prairie and Fannin, and I was talking about looking for a place to have lunch downtown, and he said, "Why don't you come by and have lunch with me at my place?"

The name of his place was Kwik Snak Cafe. After we met, I used to go over there and have lunch every day. I think his specialty was chicken and dumplings, which cost seventy-five or eighty-five cents. The place was on Texas and Caroline in a little building.

I still remember one of the ladies who worked for him, kind of a heavyset Black lady. I don't remember her name. She was a jolly kind of a woman. I think she was the cook. He was the "PR" man. That's how he got started.

When I first met him, his name was Weisberg. His English was pretty good. He looked like someone who had a hard life, tired, deep-set eyes. I think he was balding, even then.

Then I got to know him socially. He was single. He never talked to me about his family. At that time I was young, about twenty, and I think he was a number of years older than I was, maybe twenty-eight or twenty-nine years old.

He was the person who took me under his wing when I got here. I came here, I had no car, I didn't know a soul, I wasn't even a citizen of the United States. I had come from Poland to Canada in 1948 at the age of sixteen, lucky to escape the war. He was my mentor.

After we got to know each other, we double-dated a few times. We met the girls at the Center. He'd been in Houston a little longer than me, so he was introducing me to the area and some girls because I didn't know anyone.

He worked hard, but he tried to find time for a social life. When I first met him, he was very fond of one particular girl. I can't remember her first name. I got to be friends with the girl's sister through him.

We even went on a couple of trips together, three of us in a new car he bought at Burkett Motors downtown, a four-door Dodge, I think. He worked hard, but he had learned he needed fun too.

I think he lived in a place on Southmore and Almeda. I only visited him there one time. As time went on, I was working, and he was working, but I would go see him and have lunch with him occasionally.

A friend of his from Kansas City, by the name of Walter, lived on Bellefontaine and Buffalo Speedway, he and his wife. We all used to come to their apartment because they were actually the only married couple we knew at that time. And I remember one New Year's Eve we had a big party at their house. In fact it was New

Year's Eve, 1952. I have a picture of all of us. At that time Bill was dating someone. He wasn't with Shirley yet.

Then I was drafted into the armed forces of the United States on April 5, 1953. I was stationed in Europe, in Germany. I corresponded with Bill, nothing earth-shattering. He did write saying he had met this most wonderful girl, and he said he didn't have to go far to look for her. She was his next-door neighbor.

I think he lived on Blodgett at the time, at the end of 1953 or the beginning of 1954. That's when he met Shirley. She had been engaged to someone else, but then nothing happened. He happened to be there at the right time and right place.

You know he changed his name about the time he met Shirley. I asked him one day, "How did you come up with a name like Morgan? I mean, it's not a Jewish name and it's not a Polish name."

I never knew for sure why. You know Morgan in German is *Morgen* and it means "tomorrow." Kind of fits someone who is trying to change his life, doesn't it?

Nick

Bill came to the store soliciting business. We had a fairly nice store named Save U Supermarket. It was between the University of Houston and Texas Seven on Holman Street, corner of Holman and Sampson.

My wife and I used to laugh about Bill. Both of us said, "This guy's got to become very rich one day."

He didn't have an office, didn't have an adding machine, didn't have a telephone. He didn't even have scratch paper. He used to come in my store and use it as an office. He would sit at the courtesy booth and call different stores.

He would give my bill to me on a piece of scratch paper, and

I'd say, "Bill, you gotta be rich. You have no overhead. The only thing you have to do is buy gasoline for that vehicle you drive. When are you going to buy an adding machine?"

I remember him delivering out of his car when we first met him. I thought that was really something. This guy is selling meat out of the trunk of his car. So when he graduated to that pickup, he was in high cotton.

He dressed like a real working man. I think he wore khaki just like I wore, a common work shirt. I guess that's why we got along so good. He dressed just like I dressed.

He was a super salesman, good personality. I don't think his English impaired him at all. He worked harder than anyone I ever knew. Bill would work probably eighteen hours a day and think nothing of it. He would never stay still. He was always trying to make things happen. And he could do that. He was a terrific negotiator. I believe he could have sold ice to Eskimos.

He would come into my store and help us as much as we helped him. He would say, "Hey, I've got five hundred pounds of bologna. You want to put it on special?"

We just sat back and watched him work.

"I'll sell it to you for X number of dollars per pound."

"Sure, that's fine," I'd say.

So we would advertise it that weekend and Bill would bring us five hundred pounds of bologna.

That's how it started, our business together. He would find things for us. The grocery business was real competitive. To market it, we'd put on specials to draw customers in. That's why I say he was a big help to us.

Mostly he would bring whatever he had to offer you at that particular time or the next day. He probably went around to packing companies and found things they wanted to more or less unload. They might have been overstocked with bologna, or liver, or anything.

Bill would say, "I'll take it all."

Then he'd come to my store and several other stores and sell it. It worked real good for both of us.

My wife and I had been in business since 1938, and I think he kind of admired us because we worked hard in the store. Like I said, it worked both ways. He liked what we were doing, and we loved what he was doing.

I probably did business with Bill for five years—until we sold our business and retired. I felt, from the beginning, he had to be successful because he would not let any grass grow under his feet. Every time he made a move, it was for the best.

I knew he wanted to become wealthy. You could just tell, and we would have bet our lives that he would be a successful person. He was just a terrific guy, earned everything he made.

Bill said he arrived in New York broke. He had to have been smart. Now, where he got his education from, God only knows. Maybe it was a gift from God. I feel like the good Lord had something for Bill to do. God works in strange ways.

6   A SENSE OF BELONGING

"GOD," HE SAID, "WHAT DO I DO NOW? WHERE DO I GO FROM HERE?"

This had been Yossela's first thought as he stood on the ship deck, looking at the skyline of New York.

"Plan your future, Yossela. Make a better life away from the farm."

The words of his parents echoed in his mind. They truly wanted a better future for their children.

His older siblings sought a new beginning, each leaving the farm and learning a trade in the city. Bill had just begun his efforts to find that future when the Germans invaded in 1941.

From the moment he decided to leave the ghetto, he had a calculated plan to stay alive and return to his family. In braving the dangers surrounding him, he learned the essence of life, but more importantly, he learned that it was each person's right to claim that life.

When he came to America, he saw people living a normal life and wondered, "How can I create this kind of existence? I bring no common language, no money."

Sometimes he thought the faith of his father and grandfather held up to him as a child had diminished. Trying to hang on to those tenets, he wondered if effort and planning grounded his father's and grandfather's belief in miracles. He would never know now.

Surviving the destruction around him gave him new insight. No question about it, Bill now lived with the certainty that life granted no guarantees of easily found success. Perhaps he would have to make his own miracles.

Whether it was intuition or a deep sense of loneliness, Bill knew it was time to rebuild the family he lost. His confidence wavered. How could he build both a profession and a family with such deficiencies—no education, no one close with whom he could confide or who could guide him as he grew into manhood? He was totally alone. The one thing he knew he had was a capacity for diligence, whether it was escaping danger or using his hands in menial labor.

He did not know his capability as a businessman, nor did he have the money to educate himself. Common sense and a willingness to struggle would have to supplement his inadequacies.

It was time to raise a family, to reclaim a sense of belonging, yet he had not settled in an established trade. An underlying fear that "time does not wait" ate at him, pushing him. He was twenty-eight years old. Since arriving in the States, he had had no opportunity to find a Jewish girl with whom he could form a serious relationship.

Time was at a premium. Learning the meat business consumed much of his time. How would he find a girl who understood his poor English and his empty pockets? Where could he find a girl able to see through him and find his assets without wanting immediate gratification?

He first saw Shirley sitting on the porch next door to the room he rented on Blodgett Street. He saw her again waiting at the bus stop and at the Jewish Community Center. One evening at the Center he finally got up the courage to start a conversation. Struggling with confidence, Bill maneuvered until he stood next to her.

Shirley's home–next door to Bill.

Bill's room (lower right) he rented from Mrs. Berger at Blodgett and Almeda Streets, 1954.

"I've seen you next door," he said.

Embarrassed by his own awkwardness, Bill blushed, wondering if he should have approached her. What if she ignored him? He was about to turn and walk away when she smiled. He thought it was the most beautiful smile he had ever seen, crinkles forming at her large brown eyes as the grin spread across her face. She tilted her head slightly, causing her auburn hair to fall softly onto one cheek.

Yes, he thought, she is definitely beautiful.

"You rent a room next door to us."

Her voice was soft. His heart and his mind seemed to race each other, and he could not find a voice to answer her.

She interceded. "I noticed your car pass the bus stop."

Bill stood silently, wondering what he should say next. When he finally gathered his wits, he selected a safe topic—her family. He learned she had several brothers and sisters. This he had suspected since he noticed frequent movement from the house and assumed a large family lived there. Because of high holiday observance, he believed they were Jews, but the dark complexion puzzled him. The more Bill and Shirley talked, the easier the dialogue came.

Bill knew she was younger, perhaps as much as nine to ten years, but he found himself going to the Center more often, offering Shirley and her girlfriend a ride at every opportunity.

He wondered about its significance the first time Bill noticed the huge diamond on her finger. She saw him staring at it and explained.

His heart sank when he learned she was engaged. For a while he tried to date her friend who drove in from Galveston, but Shirley remained on his mind. Even if she was free to think seriously about him, what did he have to offer? He did not have dating finesse or suave approaches. Where would he have gotten fine manners— from feeding the cows and hogs and fighting for his life? As a youngster, his only worldly travels took him to nearby Stanisławów.

While in Germany he observed his well-educated friends from big cities. Watching their expertise and hearing their smooth lines made him feel less than competent in handling a dating situation. Not to be outdone by the others and to cover his personality flaws, he kidded with many of the girls in their crowd.

Secretly he would not have known how to manage any serious relationship. Furthermore, he did not want to get involved with anybody until he settled in America. It was easier for only one person to obtain passage.

Bill knew he still looked the immigrant, owning only two pairs of pants and one pair of shoes. Clothes were the least of his worries as he struggled to find a trade with only a grade-school education. He certainly could not support a mate for long on his salary. It was hard enough to maintain a lifestyle for him.

Shirley's engagement disappointed him, but the friendship continued because she asked him regularly for rides to the Center. He gladly provided them. Their conversations became more comfortable, with a kidding and teasing atmosphere. He even expressed to her his innermost wishes, the desire to marry and build a family.

Finally Bill got the nerve to ask her about her betrothed. Her fiancé was a Syrian from Dallas and already established in a trade.

Surprised to find she was not particularly happy with the match, Bill wondered if he might have a chance to win her.

"If you will give back the ring, I will buy you a bigger one."

Even as he uttered the words, he chastised himself. How could he say that? He did not have any money, certainly not the kind to match or better the ring she had. She would think him a fool.

She took him seriously.

Astounded at the turn of events, he was both overwhelmed with joy and paralyzed with fear. This was his chance to gain a family and to build his own, but could he do it? Did he have what it took to overcome his past?

He had never experienced courtship. Would he know what to do? She really didn't know what she was getting into. She was only twenty. Could she handle it?

Sometimes he felt his feelings were so trampled, he would never regain them. He had an inferiority complex from the day he first went to school.

"No-good Jew," they had yelled at him, and they threw stones.

He grew up with it. Dehumanized, he carried the weight of being a European Jew, always hearing he was no good. Then suddenly he did not have the right to live, and he found himself running, changing his name, trying to blend into a society that did not want him.

When he came to the States, he understood that people viewed him as an immigrant, an uneducated foreigner. When he told people he came to America because of the economic situation and to build a better life, they had no way of knowing the depth of the statement. Sometimes he mentioned he was a survivor who lost his family, but never did he tell the details or talk of the pain.

How could they understand? Could he overcome the past, the tortured feelings, and the guilt of leaving his family? Would he learn to express happiness, to unlock the cavern of hurt?

In years to come he would not remember the exact moment he asked Shirley to marry him, but he finally got the courage. Her willingness to accept the proposal stunned him.

The short-lived courtship lasted only five to six months. Bill did not have time for dating, nor did he have money to go to fancy places.

Bill started going to her home, but he had difficulty conversing with her family. Already self-conscious about his rapport with Americans, he felt his lack of proper English and his foreign personal habits put him at a disadvantage. When the family invited him to dinner, he made excuses not to sit down with them. He felt out of place, concerned with whether or not Shirley's family approved of him.

If Shirley's mother disapproved, she set it aside to prepare for the wedding.

It was a simple wedding at Temple Emanuel synagogue. On his wedding day Bill reflected on where he came from and what he had done. He never anticipated even being alive, much less getting married and living in a great country.

For him it was a heavenly day and a day of regret, one mixed with joy and pain. He was dressed up for the first time in his life. He had a beautiful bride, friends, and a new family—but felt really alone.

Being by himself was difficult, the question always hovering in the back of his mind, "Why can't my parents be here to see this achievement in my life?"

He was frightened, nervous about the unknown, and afraid of the responsibility of having his own family. Everything he experienced after leaving the ghetto was new. He always planned a way out, just in case. His "just in case" was working hard.

"I'll learn as I go," he said.

He knew he needed and wanted to get married because marriage meant acquiring a family. He needed to belong. If something happened to him, someone would cry or care for him. He missed the belonging.

He wanted to savor being a "normal person," stepping out and doing things that a human being is supposed to do. He was permitted to grasp the American dream, to marry a beautiful girl, to gain a family.

"I'll make this work too," he said silently as he allowed the good feelings to envelop him, feelings of bliss, like winning a prize.

Bill and Shirley Morgan
1954

Teresa

Shirley's mom thought her daughter was committing the biggest mistake. Who was this Bill Morgan? He was not a Sephardic Jew. Where was his mother, his father? She and her husband were very much against Shirley's marrying him.

At the time Shirley met Bill, she was going with this very handsome, very, very handsome man. We're talking about tall, dark, handsome, educated, and rich. I believe he was in the grocery store business, big business. She met him through the grapevine, through family friends. You know all of the families of the Jewish community at that particular time knew each other. He was a Sephardic Jew and lived in Fort Worth. So now he's getting ready to be married, and he needs to choose a wife. There's not much choice in Fort Worth or Dallas, so he goes to Houston.

It used to be that Sephardic Jews contracted for marriage or at least the parents pretty much chose the wife for the son. This was obviously a very long time ago, but the tradition of marrying in the same culture guided him to try to meet some of the girls in Houston. At that particular time there were maybe twelve Sephardic/Syrian Jewish families in Houston.

They were very isolated from the rest of the Ashkenazic Jewish community. At that time Houston was a small town, and the people did not readily accept those from the Middle East. These were not Jewish people to them; their backgrounds were completely different. The Texas Sephardic Jews were not as well known because their main community was in New York.

The Sephardic Jew is typically the Spanish Jew, or Turkish, Greek, or Italian. The Sephardic Jews go back to the time of the Spanish Inquisition. They have their own culture and tradition, absorbing the customs of the countries in which they lived. Sometimes at our tables during the Seder, the Passover table, the Sephardic Jews ate many of the foods that the Ashkenazic Jews did not. You eat what your country produces, and it becomes your main meal. The European countries did not necessarily have the same agriculture or products as in the Mediterranean countries.

The Spanish Sephardic Jew spoke Latino, a mixture of Ladino-origin languages, unlike the Ashkenazic Jew who spoke Yiddish, a remnant of German, Russian, and Polish dialects. So they are very different in makeup, in looks, in customs—different in almost every way.

Then you have what you call the Syrian Jews, my ancestors as well as Shirley's. They kind of coattail the Sephardic Jews because they are very similar in cultural background. Obviously all Syrian Jews are not born in Syria. Some of them come from Lebanon, Morocco, or Egypt, from all of the Mediterranean Arab countries. But we have very much the same customs as the lower part of Europe and of the Asian nature, meaning Pakistan, India, and so forth. It's like when you call someone a Mexican-American, but he or she is really a Hispanic-American from countries such as Guatemala, El Salvador, Nicaragua, Costa Rica, or Brazil.

Like the Sephardic Jew, we speak Arabic, which has different dialects in different countries, a very difficult language.

The Ashkenazic or European Jew, Bill's heritage, are usually the people born throughout the upper northern part of Europe, such as Poland, Czechoslovakia, Austria, the Netherlands, and Germany.

A friend of Shirley's family introduced the young man from Fort Worth to her. Her family was very impressed with the young man. Both her mother and father were very pleased when they became engaged, and at first Shirley was very happy. She was just a youngster, maybe eighteen, and she was smitten. This was her very first encounter with someone reasonably serious about a relationship.

Her fiancé was definitely serious about their relationship. He gave her a gorgeous two-carat, pear-shaped diamond ring.

I don't think he was that old, maybe five years older than she was. And he came from a very nice background, a very lovely family.

I came to Shirley's family in 1951 and immediately was able to fit in. Even though I was from a different country with a Spanish background, my customs were very much the same.

There were eight children in the family, three girls and five boys. When my husband and I married, he was living at home. All the children had what they considered to be a normal childhood, well educated and good mannered.

I felt very close to all of them but especially close to Shirley, who was like a sister to me. She had some of the warmth from her father, who was a very jolly person. I've known her to always give without any reservations and not demand anything back. I believe when you do that, you receive blessings back in ways you never understand.

I too wasn't sure why she chose Bill Morgan. The courtship was too quick. I had not gotten to know him. Shirley and I did not talk on the phone much. I was already married with a couple of children, and she was a young schoolgirl.

Her whole family thought she was too independent, too smart for her britches. The children were noncommunicative. None was outstanding in a social setting, always waiting for others to start the conversation. Not Shirley. She was a whirlwind in everything she did.

When she was a young schoolgirl, she worked for her father, a merchant. Each weekend the children went with their parents to Galveston to help in his store, a man's clothing store, a very ordinary one. They were middle-class people, not wealthy.

The mother was always very demure, quiet and conservative, not a showy woman but extremely bright, well read, well educated. Not only did she have common sense, she was just plain intelligent, devouring books.

The father worked as a peddler for many, many years. He was a good provider, but she was the pillar of the household, very strong. She knew what she wanted even though she was very submissive, typical of those times. She raised the five boys and the three girls.

Shirley's dad worked very hard, but I don't think he had enough education to be completely successful. He was always trying different things. He was a good provider as far as food and clothing, household things.

Shirley was almost seventeen when I met her. I thought she was extremely independent, to put it bluntly—excelled in being very independent. She did not always obey her parents and experimented a bit more than the others.

She got her streak of independence and smarts from her mother, who had a very good education for being a child from Alepo, a very small town in Syria. She came to Houston at the tender age of one with a very young mother, recently widowed. Her mother remarried and she and her husband had ten kids.

My mother-in-law's lifestyle was a little bit harsh because she was the stepdaughter, older than the new children. She always had to help her mom. But she did finish high school.

My father-in-law came to this country, also from Alepo, at the age of thirteen. He met his future wife in New York. Their parents paired them, and so the two were married and began to have their children.

The only reason they came to Texas was because my mother-in-law wanted to get away from New York. She did not like the pompous society, not wanting to do the things society dictated in order to be accepted.

"Tootsie"—that's what I called Shirley—used to live on Blodgett Street in the Riverside area, a very elite Jewish neighborhood at that time. She had a best friend living in Galveston who came every weekend to see her. They used to go to the Jewish

Community Center, where Shirley enjoyed lots of friends, more girlfriends than boyfriends. They hitched a ride with Bill, who rented a room from a Mr. and Mrs. Berger next door to Shirley's family.

That's how it started between Shirley and Bill. I'll tell you what Shirley told me when she chose Bill over the guy in Fort Worth. She said they often sat in Bill's car talking. Evidently he was telling her what he planned for the future, what kind of life he wanted, and what he planned to do about it. As Shirley listened to him, she thought he was such a bright man and had a good long-range plan.

She felt very attracted to him and his plans. That was it. She probably did a mental evaluation of both men because the other one already came from a very nice family. The man from Fort Worth was not aggressive, not a man who had planned his own future, but rather a man who allowed his parents to plan it. She saw him following the typical tradition, which was very much what her brothers were doing. She thought independence was the stronger quality of the two.

She knew Bill was an immigrant, a refugee who came from Poland. She saw in him someone who felt so strong about his future that he was going to be successful or die trying. He was a challenge for her, an independent thinker like her. She saw in him an attitude she did not see in her own family.

I admired Shirley's mother, who was independent, but in a very sad way as she probably never realized her dreams. Maybe that's why she came to love Bill. She did—gradually. The more she knew him, the more she respected him, growing to love him like a son.

It was easy to see that Bill Morgan was a hard-working man and a man of family values. She understood that. When the children were born, she sensed the caring that went out to those children. She relished his moderate success as he struggled through the years, never giving up.

Bill's mother-in-law gloried in the fact that he made her his confidante in business matters, sometimes discussing things with her he couldn't discuss with her husband. I sensed that Bill didn't want to demean his father-in-law by asking him questions he could not answer. Bill realized that he came to this country as a poor youngster, accepting many responsibilities that may have blocked the achievement he sought.

Shirley's dad wanted to be very sociable. People did like him, but sometimes he wanted to do things more showy than with substance. Family values were more important to his wife than social climbing. She was a very strong woman and didn't want to be in a rat race. She wanted a normal life.

If Shirley had been seeking wealth, wanting to be rich for social reasons, she would have married the other man. He and his family were socially settled in the Fort Worth area, handsome and prominent people, yet she said "no" to life served on a silver platter—"no" in order to go out with Bill Morgan who had nothing to offer.

She decided one day that the betrothed relationship was going nowhere, that she did not want to be married to a man who showed no independence but followed in his mother's shadow. Remember, she was very independent. She gave back the ring and started going out with Bill, a man who offered her something different, an agenda, an objective for life.

Shirley wasn't even sure where they would live or how they would be able to make it financially, but she had a very strong feeling that this young man would find a way to provide for her, and she was going to help him do that.

The wedding was a typical Jewish wedding, not too large but very nice. She borrowed my gown. He rented his tuxedo.

Walter

Bill asked me to be the best man at his wedding because we were good friends and he knew I wasn't a fly-by-night. I already had a wife and a child.

The wedding was a very religious wedding, a gala event. Bill was not nervous. It was his first step on the way to where he wanted to be.

Bill had never been one for dating. He was too busy, but he also was not one of these guys who really chased women. That was not his goal.

When he met Shirley, he felt she was a solid person, someone he could trust with his life, his work, and his means. That was the most important thing to him because he had lost everyone. I know because it was the most important thing to me too.

It was good she came from a large family who didn't have any scandals or divorces. Divorce was something that we are not familiar with in the old country. It showed a lack of stability.

Bill wanted a companion. And it worked out. He got to love his companion and they've had a very good life together.

I was probably the only survivor he knew very well, at least that he was close to. I was married and had a child by the time he met Shirley. At one time we contemplated being partners.

Bill used to call me when he was single.

"Can I come over to your house and make dinner?"

He would come to my house because he lived in a room while I had an apartment. He was running a little hamburger joint then, working very hard. On Sundays when he was closed, he used to come to my apartment. He loved home cooking. In fact he loved to cook. I understand he did much of the cooking when he married Shirley. He used to love to make salads, so my wife would let him.

I first met him in Kansas City. I came to the States in 1946 with an organization out of New York called the Four Hundred. A group from the organization called the United States Children's Committee had as its goal to bring four hundred Jewish children to the United States. I was fortunate to be chosen out of many, many thousands of applicants.

I was in the group that came to United States ninety days after being selected. Eighty or ninety kids like myself came over on an old army transport ship called the *Ernie Pyle*. I was not quite eighteen years old.

Before the war I lived in Lodz, Poland, where I was born. When I arrived in New York, I didn't know any English. I moved into a Polish neighborhood instead of a Jewish one because I spoke very little Yiddish. Being Jewish was like a real big shock to me for a while.

"The children immigrants" had guardians in New York. My guardian was a lady who told me, "Go west, young man," an expression I later learned from United States history.

Well, I didn't know where west was, so I asked, "What do you mean 'west'?"

She says, "Well, west is the new part of the United States. If you stay in New York, you will always be a refugee. If you go into Middle America, you will become an American."

She had train tickets for Cleveland, Ohio, or Hartford, Connecticut, and a plane ticket to Kansas City, Missouri. As a child in Poland, I always read a lot of western stories by Max Brand, so Kansas City meant cowboys and Indians. After I chose to go there, she paired me with another young man so we wouldn't feel alone. I had never flown before.

Actually, in the mind of every young child raised in prewar Poland was the premise that the United States had three distinct things—Wall Street, where every building was one hundred stories high; Hollywood; and everything else was cowboys and Indians. So I chose cowboys and Indians.

In Kansas City I lived with four other young survivors, most of whom were learning a trade. My goal was to go to high school and college. My family had made their livelihood using their brains or their professions and this was a great influence on me. I knew I didn't want to become a tradesman.

The only place in Kansas City we could afford for entertainment was the Jewish Community Center that was right down the street from where we lived. At the Center I met Bill, known then as Willie. I think his real last name was Margulies, but he didn't go by that. Later he changed his name to Bill Weisberg, then to Morgan.

Willie had a job working in a shoe store as a manager. He was a little older than the rest of us, maybe twenty-four, so he was like on the fringe of our little clique. If we did something larger in scope, then he was a part of it.

I went many times to the shoe store where he worked. If I'm not mistaken, it was on 31st and Troost Streets in downtown Kansas City. It was like a popular-priced shoe store. Most of the time Willie would be there by himself. He would open and close the store. I was amazed at this— he had been in the United States only a short time and here he was already running a store. He was a hard worker.

We fellows, when we weren't working or going to school, met at the Center and played table tennis or poker or we would go swimming. We were very limited. First of all we had no money and we had no cars. There was not even a television set then.

We used to go to dances at the Jewish Community Center, which had a mixer every week. I don't remember Willie being "the Romeo" at the mixers. First of all he was always busy in the shoe store and couldn't come to a lot of things, but even when he came, he was a little timid with strangers.

I got married in Kansas City and was drafted into the army. After I came out of the service, I moved to Houston, and that's when I ran into Willie again, under a new name. We became very close friends, lifelong friends.

Bill is one of the very few people I know who laid out a plan and made it happen, and everything he planned to do has happened. He did it all. That is an accomplishment in itself.

7 PROMISES KEPT

FROM THE "MUD FLATS OF 1836" THE CITY OF HOUSTON EMERGED, searching for its place in history. The immigrant came out of the mud-hut poverty that gave him birth, reaching for his share of the American dream. As Houston threw off its small-town image, molding itself into a maelstrom of technology, culture, and finances, the immigrant laid out a plan for his future, calculating every move.

Bill Morgan forged ahead, putting his full energy and mind into his work, especially after Shirley told him they were expecting. He worked hard to make ends meet, and if that was not enough to support his family, would they have to suffer as he had in Europe? It was a formidable thought, one to which he refused to surrender.

When he edged into the meat business, he prudently bought a few items at a time and stopped anywhere a Coca-Cola sign hung out front, assuming it would be an eating establishment. Soon the adventure became a brisk business that led him to buy a refrigerator truck. He named it Allstate, using the house he and Shirley rented on Bassoon as his address.

In those moments when Bill reflected on the values his family had given him, he wondered if he followed in his mother's footsteps, for she slaved to feed the family, walking to market with her chickens and other goods, planning her children's apprenticeships. Like her, he was diligent, finishing what he started, not taking a "no" for an answer.

With his undivided attention to business, his customer base expanded. Though he was moderately successful as a peddler, that was not his dream. If it were possible, he worked even harder. The birth of two sons born within fourteen months of each other encouraged him to augment his growing meat business by constructing a building from which to run the company.

He planned every move—mental blueprints that took him from one step to another systematically. He had the meat truck. It was making money, and he gained confidence. He accepted the fact he had to have customers in order for the business to grow enough to support a family. He knew that prestige and identification were important, that he would prosper faster if people did not see him as a peddler. He decided to build a place for his meat business, one with a name where customers could telephone in their orders.

Every extra penny went into the coffers. The hard work paid off. Finally Bill was comfortable with his knowledge of the meat business and the money he saved. He had enough money to help him buy the land and begin the building design. He was in a hurry, seeking security and acceptance.

Bill hired a young architect just beginning his profession. The two had a new career in common.

The architect learned quickly that Bill questioned every decision. Bill's "hands-on," industrious attitude was part of his unconventional education, and he was frugal to the last penny, making him "street smart." It would be a learning experience for both. Later the young architect compared Bill to his own father, who came to America poor and uneducated.

The expansion program embodied two phases—a three thousand-square-foot packing plant with a loading dock and parking facilities and later construction of a three thousand-square-foot space for coolers and freezers. The structure was to occupy land adjoining St. Augustine and Porter Streets in east Houston.

At first Bill worked from a small customer base, his old customers. Realizing he needed to expand and bring in more, he hired salesmen, butchers, and cutters, and Shirley worked in the office. But he continued to do much of the work himself, even delivering meat or working in the freezer. If he had not dealt in perishable and time-consuming goods, Bill would still have put in long, hard hours. It was a part of his life experience, even more important now that he had family.

In seven short years Bill Morgan had bought and sold the Kwik Snak Cafe and experimented with door-to-door and used car sales as well as the meat business. First he peddled meat out of his car, then a truck, finally owning his own building. He married and had two children. He was a driven man.

In 1960 he knew he was at the point where he had to expand his meat packing business, shrink, or sell it. Expansion was costly, requiring money he did not have. Going into debt was not a part of Bill's plan. He always kept a little comfort money, just in case.

He did not have long to wait for a buyer to offer him a price he could not refuse. The deal, which included paying Bill rent on the building, helped feed his family, and the profit he gleaned gave him the comfort of safety.

Now he had the capital to choose another profession. Finding a business where he used his hands was a plausible decision. He was good with them, having learned as a farm boy how to repair things and do carpentry.

Even while he peddled meat, Bill dabbled in real estate, building a couple of small rent houses in a low-income area. From these he collected rent weekly. Some land tracts he purchased in the same area made a profit when he sold them, the easy money surprising him.

Bill's and Shirley's first home after their wedding
—they rented one room with kitchen privileges.

First purchased home owned by Bill and Shirley on Bassoon Street, '56-'65.

Bill's metamorphosis from making money by the sweat of his back to surviving using his brains created dollars, and he turned those dollars into a nice income. The wise investing of that money made life easier, and he and Shirley moved into a larger home. It was 1960 and their third child, Mindy, had just been born.

Bill Morgan was on the right track, and he never allowed himself to be derailed. Determined to succeed, he analyzed and calculated each move. Borrowing money was not a part of his plan unless he could pay it back. He never bought what he could not pay for.

After extensive, hands-on research, he decided on his profession—construction of warehouses and multi-unit apartments. Bill Morgan's timing was perfect. Since the 1950s construction of major buildings in Houston had been brisk. Suburban communities had annexation fever, adding one hundred square miles to Harris County in a short time. Houston was coming into its own as a national city, even featuring a downtown parade for President Dwight D. Eisenhower.

An oil and petrochemical industry worth three billion dollars and a multimillion dollar Ship Channel business defined the city's commercial future. The business and political environment, along with a lack of zoning laws, allowed easy access into the building business or any form of real estate because it was not difficult to acquire a site.

Money was readily available in varying cycles. Banks wanted to lend during those times when money was not tight. They were fairly generous with loans, open to new customers.

The city of Houston demanded housing. The population had reached 1.3 million by the late 1960s and the land area 450 square miles. By 1975 it would be one of the fastest growing cities in the nation. Spurred by the Space Center and the Ship Channel, Houston ranked among the top major cities in construction dollar volume. Available housing was in short supply; none had been created since 1929 and everything was outdated.

A 1954 tax law aided the up-cycle by giving tax benefits to developers and apartment owners. This made construction attractive because the fast rates of depreciation enabled a person to shelter income, allowing more investment.

Houston was a young city with a very young population, many of them single. Numerous young marrieds either did not have the down payment for a house or were not interested in getting into a house. This helped strengthen the demand for apartments in Houston. The idea of young singles living in apartments was something very new to the apartment world. Up until the post-World War II period, everyone lived at home because that was all they could afford. However, a long, good up-cycle opened up in the mid-1950s.

Because of no zoning regulations, the fast-growing Houston market was open to competition. Insurance companies and banks liked to lend in Houston, builders liked to build there, and people liked to live there. This created more competition in the Houston market than almost anywhere else.

Much of Bill's research concerning the construction business was first-hand experience. He found a building under construction and observed the activity, from its conception to completion. He questioned builders, subcontractors, electricians, plumbers—all those who could teach him the trade and economics of building.

Finally he garnered the faith that, if he were to build, people would move in. He moved slowly at first, managing his money on a weekly basis, then monthly. When he constructed the buildings, he produced income. Then and only then he went to the bank for a loan.

Bankers took the income and worked it into a loan package. The loan gave Bill all the money back plus a few more dollars for construction. Basically he was risking nothing in that next project.

When he built his first little apartment complex, his sister-in-law teased him as she watched him on a job site.

"Are you crazy?" she asked. "Why are you going around picking up nails from the floor?"

"In order to be the president, you have to be janitor," he answered as he put the nails in the carpenter's apron he wore around his waist.

How could his helpers understand how hard he had to work to get the money for a project? When they spilled the nails, they left them on the floor. If that nail had a life, Bill was going to use it.

Some would refer to him as tight. Tight, he believed, was a matter of degree.

"What you see is what you get."

Bill learned to compensate by saying this to others. He was never a person to improvise. If he did not know something, he simply did not know. He did the best he could to find the correct answer. He knew how to make that tenacity work for him.

Certainly Bill was intelligent in managing his money. This surprised him. He often wondered where he learned the skills he suddenly discovered in himself.

He was his own superintendent, bookkeeper, and contractor. He conducted himself in the building business just as he had in the other business—hands on. At first the trunk of his car was his office just as it had been with Allstate. He called his new trunk-office Globe Construction.

One of the things he learned from watching others build, especially on bigger jobs, was the waste of materials and the overabundance of supervisors. He did not have the means to hire, and he could not delegate. Very conservative by nature, he wanted to know what he signed for when he signed checks. Did he get his value?

Bill's frugal philosophy of making all the decisions himself and guarding every piece of material resulted in less monies spent on the product than he witnessed others spending. This provided extra income that bankers could interpret into a greater value, allowing Bill to "mortgage-out" the project. If he spent a hundred thousand dollars on twenty houses, the loan officer gave him a hundred and thirty thousand dollars. The rent from the first twenty houses provided an income from which to service the loan. With each project he followed this system and accumulated his cash.

He built first in a low-income area, later in higher rent areas; first houses, then small-unit apartments and warehouses. He made sure each deal stood on its own feet with some margin for numerical error. This philosophy buffered him in case the arrangement was weak or interest rates increased, forcing him to get concessions from the bank. The fact he had a lot of equity in a deal could affect the economics of it but would not put him out of business. The more he built, the larger his business grew and he found he could no longer act as superintendent.

Before long Bill began building larger apartment units in more visible areas. Ten years after he began his development business, he rented an office in Meyerland Plaza and hired office personnel. He had always used subcontractors when he worked out of his car.

Realizing that leasing properties meant needing someone to manage them, Bill established Globe Management. He hired a manager for a project and gave that person half the rent to collect it. Again he devised a system, hiring a district manager for his four or five projects. Usually the manager's husband was the maintenance man. The other managers received a stipend for delivering the rent monies to the district manager. All business was conducted in cash. A Brinks truck picked up the money for safekeeping.

Until then he personally ran a "tight ship," overseeing acquisition and feasibility of sites, layouts, loan packages, economics, and cost takeoffs. He used progress sheets and each item was budgeted. He knew the actual construction costs to the nail. Never leverage-oriented, he always had substantial equity in his deals, never building on a volume basis. Sometimes he built one project a year or every eighteen months, often with his own money. He

*Bill's first construction project–apartments
on Los Angeles and Horace streets.*

Early duplex project on E. Lockwood and Collinsworth.

Kashmere Royal #1, Lockwood and Crane.

Warehouse built for rental purposes and his own use.

saved enough money before buying a piece of land to pay cash for it and started the project with his own money. When that ran out, he borrowed the remainder. This earned him a reputation among bankers for being frugal. Sometimes he would not draw on their loans for four or five months after a project was started.

While he was in the Meyerland office, Bill sometimes worked with a partner as a separate entity. When they did something together, they called the business M&G Investments or MG&P Investments. Otherwise Bill owned and managed Globe Construction and Globe Management.

Texas lawmakers retained the tax law in 1969 that first passed in 1954 benefiting developers and apartment owners. The construction business, especially multi-unit apartment building, was brisk, competition keen. The market became very innovative and encouraged more competition. Owners offered special features including central air, swimming pools, recreational packages, and other enticements to the potential apartment dweller. Most apartment developers tended to develop on major thoroughfares that gave them visibility. Each builder tried to outdo the others.

Throughout the 1970s and at the peak of Houston's building boom, more than thirty thousand apartments were built yearly as well as thirty thousand houses.

In the 1970s Bill further expanded his business, constructing his own office building on Bellaire Boulevard. Later he sold that building and the company moved to Gulfton, where he had a warehouse. By the time he moved to the Gulfton site, Bill employed a number of people. He had weathered the slight construction slump in the 1960s and 1970s. By the late 1970s Houston was the fastest growing major city in the nation with a population of 2.5 million and covering 521 square miles. His business flourished.

Michael, Bill's second son, came into the business in 1979 bringing with him a degree in construction and business. In the early 1980s, Globe Construction moved from Gulfton to Gessner into a building Bill bought with some partners. They occupied an entire wing, and their employees increased in number.

By 1980 the city attracted a thousand new families a month, but a shock wave rocked Houston's economy in the late 1980s. The city had been in an upswing in construction with occasional slight recessions since World War II. If one was fortunate enough to be in the construction market in that period—between the growth of the city and the late 1970s—the economic climate was forgiving of mistakes. Generally during that period there were business cycles with some years of overbuilding, the property eventually occupied.

He survived the building slump in 1973 with his conservative theory of building with his own money. In 1981 interest rates rose to nineteen and twenty percent. No one could foresee the significance of the price of oil dropping from forty to thirty dollars per barrel in 1982. It worked its way back up to thirty-two dollars and stayed in that range for several years before it started edging up a little.

Bill Morgan "pulled in his horns," cautiously calculating a plan. Always the learner, he talked to consultants and economists, trying to judge what was happening. The comparative advice suggested that the economy was changing rapidly. Bill's general sense about building had always been "I build it, I keep it." Michael lovingly referred to this theory as "old European mentality."

The consultants with whom Bill and his son conversed confirmed Bill's general sense of playing it safe when they sold their apartment investments and put the cash into the stock market. As property values dropped, Bill joked, "There's another office building going up just in case somebody might need some space."

He built his last property with cash. That was his safety net. Times were tough, and it was important to make the correct decisions. His hard work and his family's future depended on it. Once again he drew on survival skills from the strength of his own experiences. Quickly he liquidated half his building assets, keeping his warehouses and living on the income. The properties he kept had very little leverage on them, very little debt. He sold his least favorite first. By 1984 he was no longer active in the building business.

The earlier tax laws that benefited apartment owners were revised in 1986, disallowing the taxpayer to deduct interest against other ordinary income, not even losses from apartments. This created something called passive income that negated tax benefits on real estate holdings. People found it no longer advantageous to hold on to property. Many gave it back to the lender, dumping the entire product on the market.

The tax law took away depreciation and deductibility of interest. If a person had apartments doing poorly or land declining in value, one was left with no reason to keep the property. Losing tax benefits caused many people to pay money into their project without getting any benefit out. Because they could not deduct the losses from their apartments, many people lost income and simply walked away.

Then oil prices fell drastically, dropping from twenty-eight to ten dollars a barrel in 1987. Many independent oil companies went broke. No one needed equipment because it was not necessary to drill wells when oil was abundant. All companies started cutting back and laying off people. As a result Houston lost population. People walked away from two hundred houses a month. Banks foreclosed on as many as thirteen hundred houses per month. The crisis was worse than even the 1973 oil crunch, and it cast a gigantic dark cloud over the 1973 to 1981 boom. The dilemma became a vicious circle.

From the peak to the trough—1982 to 1987—approximately two hundred thousand jobs in Houston were abolished. Very few people saw it coming. Once the crisis hit, it was a matter of being able to cope, to weather the storm. Some got out early because apartments could no longer be seen as a cash flow vehicle. At one point people had taken tax losses and had not been interested in cash flow, but the economy did not allow that luxury now. Rent and occupancy dropped perceptively. Loans to apartment owners and operators ceased and assets became almost worthless. Some found themselves owning properties that did not have enough income to pay operating expenses, let alone pay interest expenses or principal reduction.

Some forty-five thousand units had been built a year, many times with savings and loan associations as partners. Ironically multimillion dollar savings and loans did not survive when their equal-partner apartment builder did.

The building recession of 1986 finished the builders who survived the '70s depression and who did not accumulate a nest egg. Less than twenty percent of Houston builders survived both recessions.

Many compared the devastating crash to the Great Depression. A whole generation of young people had not faced adversity and did not know how to cope. Most people thought it was another dip and they could just ride it through.

When the building market crashed in 1986-87, Bill Morgan was liquid, again surviving on his instincts and common sense.

Fred

Bill was a hell of a negotiator and an excellent teacher. I still use some of the skills I learned from him. He taught me everything I know about real estate.

I joined him in the apartment business in 1977 after knowing him briefly. I was a CPA with an accounting background and I knew he was a hard-working, fairly successful real estate developer. I had no experience in real estate, but I was looking to make a change.

Bill took his construction company and added the dimension of property management. He named the subsidiary Globe Management after he saw a globe sitting in the office at the courthouse where he had gone to get a name for the company.

When I joined him, he already had a fair-size operation, but at the executive level, he was doing it almost exclusively by himself. He had property managers but not a controller or bookkeeper. After I worked for him two weeks, his warehouse manager quit, and the next thing I knew, he pushed me into property management. I fell in love with it.

He taught himself everything. When he started out, he was selling meats in the food business and on weekends he built apartments on the east side of town, a low-rent area. He was out there with the guys who were doing the construction, smashing his thumbs. He told me he was collecting his "stomach money."

He apparently built apartments as a sideline while he was doing the meat business, and as he made money, he invested into expanding. He created quite a bit of stress for himself though. I know he had stomach problems at one time.

By the time I started with him, he already had the Meyerland Court Apartments and most of his warehouses, but he was over-stressed as far as managing them.

At the same time he could be very patient as well as very demanding. He let me make my own mistakes. I messed up a lease one time, real big. He let me do my own thing, knowing I was going in the wrong direction. Of course with Bill you didn't make the same mistake a second time.

As years went by, he eventually turned almost all the property management over to me. Bill wasn't the kind who says, "Fred, you've done a great job. Here's a raise." You had to ask him for it. He would always listen. He told me when you are negotiating with somebody, let the other person do all the talking. He was a perfect example of that. When you were sitting down negotiating with him, he could sit there like a stone. It would drive you crazy until he'd say something. Unfortunately you would finally blurt out something, and that's what he wanted you to do. Now he knew what you wanted, and it was easier for him to negotiate.

"Kill them with kindness" was another one of his phrases. I never heard him use a real curse word. No "S" or "F" or "SOB" words. You could tell when he was upset, but he would just turn the other cheek. If he were doing a business deal with a bank or an employee, he generally would not say anything negative. He would just kill them with kindness. I still use some of the phrases he taught me.

There's a big turnover in this business with apartment managers. We used to hire all the time. When I first started with Bill, he did the interviewing. After awhile I made him stop because he was so straightforward in his reactions. One lady came out of his office almost in tears because he wanted to look at her teeth, literally. I said, "Bill, you can't do that." It was before hiring laws were passed.

Sometimes he wasn't too diplomatic about some of the people who worked for him, especially the apartment managers. Often he told them to their face how he felt. He didn't consider if it hurt feelings. He said it as he saw it, just being honest. I guess his success came from straight talk and with learning to deal with sometimes tactless people.

Bill Morgan was probably as fine a builder as you could find—of apartments in particular—in Houston. If everyone built the way he did, there probably wouldn't be as many problems in real estate. He knew where every board, every nail was going to go. He would waste nothing usable. He took the boards you used to pour concrete for the sidewalks and washed them off, perfectly good boards he could use in the attic or someplace they couldn't be seen. Other people would have thrown them away.

He watched the construction budgets meticulously, keeping track of them himself. You had to be a brave subcontractor to bid on a Bill Morgan job. He would look you in the face and get every detail, get the three best bids, decide the best, and get that guy back in.

He'd say, "Joe, I would really like to do business with you again. You have done a great job in the past, but there's another bid lower than yours. If you can't do it, I understand, but can you lower your price a little bit so I can give you the job?"

Nine times out of ten, it worked. Bill would say to me, "All I'm doing is seeing if the guy has any fat in his deal. He's not going to do it if he's going to lose money."

I was on the inside for ten years. Bill Morgan never took advantage of anybody. He was never dishonest. He built his products not for profit but for income, quality products that even to this day are maintained and generate income. His locations were good, visible locations though he usually paid more for the land to put in an above-average product.

Hard work was the key to his success. By the time I started with him, I think he had done his heaviest work. In fact, he told me he would like to start having a little bit more time with the family and recreation. Ironically he said this as he was starting one of the biggest projects he ever had. It was the transition period between Globe Management and the Morgan Group.

Bill had a very good business sense. He stopped at the right time because of the bad times in the '80s. He knew when to cut back, including salaries.

If I had more sense, I would have ridden it out. Ten years wasn't easy to throw away. Someone else made an offer, more money, and I left with Bill's blessings.

Bill was successful because he was focused on getting the job done, extremely knowledgeable. He knew every nook and cranny of the properties he was building, knew how to market them. He was an extremely good negotiator, not only with subcontractors but also with financiers—getting better terms than anybody else was because, with each success, he earned their respect.

I never beat Bill Morgan in a tennis set. It was so frustrating. He completely controlled the game, getting into position—center court—and making his opponent run. Discipline made him successful on both the tennis court and in the building business.

Vangy

He's human but shrewd. Mr. Morgan is not like most business people I've dealt with. He's sympathetic and listens. Most people don't have time. He makes you think that what you're saying and what you're doing is the most important thing right now. He has a kind attitude, not nasty and arrogant like some business people I came in contact with.

That's not to say he couldn't be a pest. I will tell you, his voice was mellower when it wasn't bill time. That's when he was real firm, like I was an adversary.

I was a property manager, one of the six. After the monthly bills were paid, he would call and talk all together in a different tone. I learned never to ask him for anything when it was time to pay bills.

He was so serious back then, not a very humorous person. He worked very hard, personally looking at the entire business.

I never will forget when I met Mr. Morgan. It was in May 1965. I was a frightened country girl who never had a job. When he interviewed me, he asked such questions as "Did you work in the fields?" I think he was trying to see if I was a genuinely honest person. I had worked in the fields, and I told him so.

He asked me why I wanted to become a manager, and I told him one of the benefits was having my little daughter, Theresa, with me on the property. I could tell from his expression that he liked that answer.

When he offered me the job, he pointed out my lack of experience. That was very shrewd. It meant there weren't many dollars for me. I realized I was going to have a place to stay, rent free, and not have to send my daughter to a sitter. I was excited and happy about it.

After I came on board, he sort of held my hand. Everything he'd do, he'd share with me. For instance, one time Mr. Morgan was in another part of the office when an angry resident, a cab driver, came in. Usually a resident would get angry about repairs not done in a certain length of time. They all wanted them done yesterday. Anyway this big guy came in the office, pointing his finger at me, telling me I'd better get it done. I'm standing there trying to listen but frightened to death by the expression on his face.

Mr. Morgan came out and said, "How do you do, sir?" He shook his hand, got him to feeling at ease, and then he said, "You must remember she's a lady."

So he talked to this cab driver and before that man left the office, he was fine. Then Mr. Morgan turned to me.

"Sometimes we all can be mean. When you go in a store to buy a pair of shoes, Mrs. Mathis, do you pick the first pair that you see?"

"No, I don't," I said.

"So the salesperson has to put up with you just as you have to put up with these people."

He was always there for me with a lesson, firm but kind. He never told you anything in a demanding-type way. He was forceful but in a way that made you want to do it. We're talking about a real mentor.

I used his techniques, like listening attentively, because they worked. I wondered if Mr. Morgan took that Dale Carnegie course because he sent me to it, thirteen weeks of it. It only enhanced what he taught me. He paid for it too and sent me to all kinds of seminars. Whenever I needed anything to work with, I always had it. I never had to hassle with him.

I know he appreciated me, even if he didn't always tell me. One time I was ready to quit for some silly reason, and I wrote him a letter. He called me in, reviewed my salary, looked at the vacancy rate and looked at everything I did at Kashmere. When he finished, he told me he knew I had a hard job serving in a capacity where men had to take instructions from a woman, some not liking it. He told me I had his support. And then he said, "You have been doing a magnificent job."

I was surprised. He didn't often give compliments. Then he looked at my salary and said, "For one thing, you're not making any money." He really said that. I never asked for a raise. My work was gratifying, and I didn't think about stuff like that.

"You're not making any money, and we're going to change that."

I couldn't speak. I just watched him making notations as he talked, telling me not to worry about things, just to hang on. We even had lunch together.

A couple of days later I received a letter from him saying that it was good to see me and to keep up the good work. It went on to say I would receive an increase in salary. Believe me, it was enough to notice. From that point on, like every year, I would be evaluated and I would get myself a raise.

Every Christmas I got a bonus of a thousand dollars. This was every Christmas! There was a time he would give a little bonus to all the on-site managers, but my bonus was always more.

And along the way he would do little things. I remember he had a little rent house on Los Angeles Street, in the Kashmere area, and his resident brought the rent to the office, fifteen dollars a month. Sometimes it would accumulate to over a hundred dollars. Mr.

Morgan would come to the office and I would say, "Here's the rent for the house on Los Angeles."

Sometimes he'd leave me some of it. After I proved myself to him, showed that I was a loyal, trustworthy employee, from that point on it was no problem. He realized that, even though I enjoyed my work, I needed to be compensated fairly too. I can't think of a time that he refused me anything I asked for.

One time I called him and asked him to help with this organization called Christian Rescue Mission.

"You think the Lord will bless me if I do it?"

He wasn't joking. He cared. He gave enough to take care of four families for a while. All of those things tend to put him in a category by himself.

And that wasn't all. He knew my daughter, Theresa, from the time she was a little girl. When she finished high school and was off to college at the University of Houston, Mr. Morgan paid her tuition. Yes, he did; he did that. And all through the time he would ask how she was doing. He knew that Theresa was important to me.

I remember when my baby's father and I separated, it was a week or so before I even told Mr. Morgan about it.

"You and your daughter need to just get away and just forget about everything. You're a businesswoman now. You can be independent. Go and enjoy yourself and forget things."

Mr. Morgan wrote me a check for four hundred dollars, just like that, and my daughter and I went to Dallas to my sister's.

My father was two hundred miles away. Here's this business-man—an honest, decent person—giving me fatherly advice.

"When you leave the office, forget about it. Go home and fix yourself a good meal and just enjoy yourself. I learned things like that add a lot to your life. You can't just have all work and no play; makes anybody dull."

I wasn't so sure he followed his own advice.

I don't know how he got like that and still was shrewd enough to brave the building business environment.

Things got pretty rough in the real estate business in the '80s. My vacancy rate was low, about eighty-five percent occupied. Things were just getting tough. I was sort of burned out, and I think Mr. Morgan was too. He was telling me about some changes he was getting ready to make and I didn't want to be left in the hands of someone else.

After I left in 1985, I went to a bank, but I didn't stay long. Mr. Morgan had spoiled me, sheltered me. I didn't know things happened out in this world like they do.

I got back into management, but it wasn't the same. Nobody conducted business like Mr. Morgan. People were haphazard, didn't stick with things, no follow-up, and I had a hard time following their lead.

I wanted to come back to Mr. Morgan, but I was embarrassed. I knew, even if he did not have a spot for me, he would have created one. I believe that. But my pride sort of took over, and I just stuck it out.

Somehow he survived the building crisis in the '80s. I wasn't too surprised. I never knew he was a survivor from World War II, but he used to say things like "people have it so good here. Where I came from, it wasn't so good." I think that was why he always wanted to treat people fairly and I think that's how he outlived the '80s building problems.

Looking back, that was the best job I ever had. I'd go back into the business in a minute if I could find another Mr. Morgan.

Gary

There's no word to describe Mr. Morgan. He's more than a father figure to me.

I was real close to my father. He died when I was fifteen years old. I'm fifty-one now. Like Mr. Morgan, he was a real hard, hard-working man. He used to work for Southern Pacific Railroad in Louisiana.

My father, he stayed on my back all the time. Whatever he gave me to do, I would do it. If I couldn't do it, I would tell him.

At the time my father died, I was the youngest boy and still in high school. I had to quit to go to work because my mother wasn't well. My brother and I had to work and bring money home and do a lot of chores around the house.

Then I made up my mind to come to Houston, and I started working at the Astrodome. Then I heard they were hiring at Globe Construction, and I went to talk to them.

I spoke to Mr. Morgan and told him my education wasn't great, but I'm willing to work.

"You're hired!" he said without hesitating.

I've been here twenty-three years. I hope to be here another ten to fifteen years before I retire. I've been told several times that I'm crazy to be working for the same company, but I respect this company. They treat me right.

One reason I'm still here is because Mr. Morgan did a lot for me, and I won't walk away. I couldn't find that anywhere else. He's a good man, and as of today, anything he says he wants from me, I try my best to give it to him.

Several times I got mad at him though. On construction we were working beside each other and, well, nobody is perfect, and you do make mistakes when you're working among a lot of other people.

He stopped me and said, "Gary, take your time and do the work right. The best way you learn is from your mistakes."

I wanted to walk away because I didn't like to be criticized. But I said to myself, "No, that man knows more than me and I need to respect him. He gave me a job, he wants me to do it and do it right, and that's what I'm getting paid for."

After that day if I made a mistake, I assured him I would get it done the right way.

"Good. That's what I want you to do," he'd say. "If you don't know what you're doing, ask somebody who does."

Many times over the years he reminds me of this.

He's a man who is always doing something with his hands, wants it done right, and draws sketches to give it direction.

I respect Mr. Morgan because he showed me a lot through the years. He was real professional, like he'd been in business for a long time. He knew what he was doing. You need to look up to folks who know more than you. That's what I told my son.

Around the holidays he always got a bike for my son when he was small. He's fifteen now and still talks about Mr. Morgan. He knows he's a hard-working man who started from the bottom. He knows he helps other people and that means he helps himself. That's a good model for my son.

Sometimes nobody else goes out of his way to help you, but Mr. Morgan does. The whole time I worked for Mr. Morgan, he treated me like part of the family and he treated the rest of my family the same. I respect him for treating me like that. I guess the reason he does is because he wants respect too.

Mr. Morgan started from scratch and he accomplished all this. If you don't get to know him, you don't get to know the company. He has come a long way to accomplish what he has now, and his kids should be moved for what he did and what he accomplished. I am.

Steve

You can't help but admire stories of people who had nothing when so many of us have so much and don't accomplish in business nearly the sort of things Bill has accomplished. It's remarkable.

He doesn't have an education, but he has a level of direct experience of seeing things happen, "where the rubber meets the road" type thing. That kind of experience is not found in a textbook. He has the know-how that comes from seeing things work in the real world. I think he has an insight into human nature from going through the experiences in Europe and the United States.

There's just something unique about him. He has a tremendous amount of energy. His mind is always working. Someone said one of the keys to his success is to look at any apartment building in the city of Houston and Bill Morgan could have done the same thing for less money. Somehow he has an uncanny level of judgment.

I asked him once how he avoided the "belly-up" crisis in Houston's building industry.

"I guess I was so dumb, I was smart," he said.

He's not dumb at all. He relied on common sense. He told me how he got into the real estate business. While he had the meat packing business, he bought two corner lots somewhere in Houston. They were just dirt, and two years later he sold the lots, making more in two years holding on to them than he made in two years in the meat packing business. That's when he decided he was going to get into the real estate business.

Bill once said when he was building apartments, he would watch the construction and learn the right ways, always asking a lot of questions.

A ploy he used that was pretty shrewd was putting an option on a piece of property close to where a successful developer was constructing apartment units. If it leased quickly, Bill knew it was a good location. While the developer probably spent a hundred thousand dollars on demographics and took all the risks, Bill waited it out for much less.

You know the funny thing about Bill is when he does or says something, he is usually ninety-nine percent of the time right.

8 THE THIRD MIRACLE

"FAMILY MEANS EVERYTHING, YOSSELA. WHAT YOU DO AS MY CHILD is what I am. Everybody has three names—the one I give you, the second you give yourself, and the third the community gives you."

Whenever his father told him this, Bill had felt such a sense of responsibility and had tried even harder at whatever task faced him.

After the war he made every effort to find information concerning his family. The news of massive murders brought him to a state of near despair though he still continued his inquiries. In Bill's mind he held the hope of returning home and resuming a normal life with his loved ones. Once he reached the States, he accepted the realization it was a dream long since anesthetized.

He, the lone member of his family, had survived. That was the first miracle. The second was the chance to live in a free country and have the opportunity to build his own economic future.

At one time the fear of whether or not he could cope in the "real world" nearly overtook his exultation of being alive, and he questioned, "How can I learn to function?" He battled the incessant nightmares that threatened his ability to show the happiness he felt. The struggle continued throughout his marriage and with the birth of his children.

When his first son was born two years after he and Shirley married, he stood at her bedside and looked down at the small bundle she held. His heart stopped. He thought it would burst. Love for the child welled in him like a storm thrusting its wind force, pushing, pushing. This small being was a part of him—the hungry, barefoot kid getting beat up for being a Jew, running for his life, losing all he loved.

Tears clouded his eyes. He choked them back.

The baby gurgled and he stared at him. Shirley offered him his son, but he hesitated. She encouraged him, and he finally reached for the tiny creature.

As he took the baby, holding it out from his body, he stared into its face, and he could not believe what he saw.

My God! It was his brother! Here comes a son that looks like his brother Solomon. Truly, he thought, this is a gift from God.

He brought the baby close to his body, cradling him, loving him. The moment rendered him speechless. How could he express what he felt?

When the nurse came for the baby, Bill hesitated giving him to her. Foreboding threatened to overtake his gladness, eroding the joyous moment.

How can I keep him safe? he thought. I cannot let him go through the same thing I did.

For years Bill harbored guilt over his lost family. He vowed he would not lose this one.

Silently he promised, "This child will have everything because I had nothing. I will work even harder and make sure it happens. Dear God, keep him safe!"

He and Shirley named their firstborn Ronald Isaac. Somewhere in the dark recesses of his inner being Bill knew Yitzhak Margulies would be pleased Yossela named his firstborn son Isaac even if it was an American version of Yitzhak's name.

The same year Ronnie was born, Bill became an American citizen. The naturalization process was a happy day for him. Now he could vote. What pride he felt in becoming a citizen in a country that gave him safety and opportunity.

The next year Michael Solomon was born, followed by Melinda Etta, named Etta after his mother. His fourth child, Wendy, was born in 1964. Auburn hair crowned her small head, hair the color of his mother's.

By 1968 his fifth child, Scott, completed Bill's plan for five children. As he held Scott in his arms, he saw his youngest brother. Time had erased the names of the two youngest siblings but not their faces as he last saw them, nor the pain haunting Bill. Overwhelmed by the moment, he pledged silently to protect this child, as he had the others, from the pain his lost family felt.

Being born a peasant in a mud hut gave Bill little understanding, or the luxury, of growing up in the American society. He was not always tactful when dealing with people, not even his own family. Though he did not understand the complexities of receiving and giving love, he knew what he wanted and would not stop until he got it. If actions express love, then he would pour out affection. In business and his personal life he was diligent, finishing whatever he started.

The children grew up, each trying to find his or her direction in life, but never straying far from the firm hand of Bill, the father to whom family meant everything. It was to be preserved above all else. To be able to claim a new family was the third miracle in Bill's life and he would protect it at all costs.

Shirley hinted he should hug the kids more. He wanted to be closer to them and it felt good to give and receive the embraces, but still he feared risking his emotions.

Inside he was full of love, happiness, elation, but the joyous expressions did not always show on his face. They were lost to the past. Unable to show his feelings outwardly imprisoned him, the wall stopping him from becoming a "normal person." How could he suddenly—after so many years of abuse, danger, and pain— show the joy he finally began to feel?

So much happiness had been taken from him, his ability to show his feelings had vanished too. He could not openly distinguish between his misfortune and his fortune.

Most of the time he was misunderstood. Bill knew people did not understand the lack of smiles. He had survived, but sometimes he felt like a cripple. This he could tell no one. How would he explain it? He had hands and feet and a mind, but he was not normal. How could anyone understand? When people talked to him, they were not talking to a typical person. Nineteen years in the States had taught him nothing about expressing joy or communicating feelings with others. He brought with him only pain. How could he know how to express glad feelings?

Bill was a model citizen, working and paying his taxes. It would have made things easier if he had finesse or appropriate conversational skills. He did not. Inside he was only as normal as his background would allow.

Just as he planned his future, he directed the lives of his children, refusing to follow certain patterns of American family life. The family would have meals together. They would go places together, leaving no need for the American babysitter.

Most of his efforts went to providing for his family's financial future. He wanted them to have the things he did not have as a child. To Bill, securing their future necessitated long hours in pursuit of that dream. He spent as much time as he could with his children— even rushing home to prepare meals, one of the few pleasures he allowed himself.

Not knowing the American way hindered him somewhat. He did not know baseball nor understand the tradition of going to school and meeting with teachers. When the children were little, they did not understand that he was different, but when they grew up, they knew he had an accent, not like the other fathers who went to school on Father's Day Out.

From an early age he took the boys with him on the job, teaching them. Too quickly the years slipped by and the older children of the five were off to college.

When both Mindy and Wendy showed signs of a serious relationship with a boy, Bill stepped in.

Steve, Mindy's young man and future husband, would later refer to his talks with Bill as "powwows."

As he had done with Steve, Bill grilled Howard, Wendy's beau.

"Howard, what are your intentions toward my daughter?"

Bill was noted for going straight to the point.

The young man should not have been surprised by Bill's direct question. It was obvious that Howard's first impression of Wendy's father was that he seemed stern, difficult to get to know. Bill would have been surprised that he frightened the young man.

"Well, have you thought about doing something with your life?"

It was obvious Wendy's dad did not look favorably on Howard's job with a telephone equipment company nor on the fact that the young man came from a divorced family. Bill had definite feelings about what divorce did to children and how that might carry to the next generation. At the same time he recognized Howard's good traits.

Bill sensed Howard loved Wendy but that he hesitated approaching the subject of marriage because he had few finances and lacked the college education needed to become an attorney, something he had contemplated for some time.

To Bill, it was important that the two take the obviously serious relationship to the appropriate position of marriage, and to do that, the young man needed stability in his future earnings. Bill decided he would help in any way he could, especially with the college tuition.

Whether Bill's "talks" with Howard and Steve pushed the marriages forward or not, the weddings did take place.

Bill gave his daughters gala weddings, all a bride and groom could wish for. Bill took pleasure in being able to provide for the girls. And as the boys married, Bill acted as the proper father of the groom. Only the thoughts of his parents' absence diminished Bill's joy.

When Michael joined his father in the business in 1979 and Ronnie in the early '80s, Bill was overjoyed. Sons or not, Bill would not let his boys slack off. Michael liked construction and would be out at the site at dawn. He worked hard alongside the others. Ronnie was interested in a career in law and could not spend as much time in the summer working on the site.

Bill passed on to his sons a work ethic and a philosophy of business that would serve them well—hard work causes staying power, enjoying what you are doing stimulates creativity, and being efficient and cost-conscious provides the best product for the dollar spent.

He taught them the importance of hands-on management and how to train their instincts to recognize opportunities in markets which could result in potential profit. They learned from him to rely on feedback from residents and managers, understanding that keeping a positive relationship with the customer is a primary necessity. Satisfying their needs was a key to success.

He showed them the importance of operating on facts and fundamentals, that income comes before expense, and not to believe your own fanfare.

Their first venture alone was the building of some townhouses. Ronnie was still working at the law firm and Mike was working for his father, but business was slow. Mike went out and found some land and Ronnie and he joint ventured. Bill was not financially a part of it though he was there with advice. Bill was good for ideas, for direction.

Bill sold the majority of his holdings in 1983-84 to the highest bidder, keeping only his favorite and most profitable investments. For the first time in his life he was liquid, and he liked that feeling. He was also sixty years old. There was something in the back of his mind that said, "Why take further chances? You've created a secure future for your family."

Mike wanted to follow in his father's footsteps with the same kind of business. In 1985 he spent a year going back and forth to Atlanta looking for land on which to build townhouses, but he could not find the right site or the right price.

When the boys faltered, discouraged at the slow turnaround in the building business, Bill met Mike in New York where he and Patti were honeymooning.

"It's great you're gallivanting around the country," remarked Bill, "but you're newly married. You need to come home and settle down. Wait. Things will turn around. Take my properties and use them as a base. You and Ronnie form a partnership."

Thus Bill's investments secured the founding of the Morgan Group. It was a gift he gave gladly. The building business was still slow in 1987, but in 1988 the Morgan boys hired an acquisitions person and began contracting for deals—office buildings, warehouses, and small apartments.

Using their dad's financial statement, they easily received bank loans, and Bill loaned them the earnest money they needed. Their second deal was an office building on Richmond and Gessner to which they moved their offices. The "boys" designated Bill the company consultant.

They learned it was not efficient to build small projects in the 1990s. Choices for borrowing were broad—banks, insurance companies, partners, mortgage lenders, pension funds, investment companies and private investors were contacts for equity money.

The Morgan Group set a record for new construction resale in Houston in early 1993 when the Memorial Apartments sold for a

*The Memorial apartments in Houston sold for a
record fifty-five thousand dollars per unit in 1994.*

record $55,000 per unit. In 1994 the company earned national recognition for the sale of the Greenwood Apartments in Denver, Colorado. The $23.25 million deal at $79,897 per unit set a market record, a welcome benchmark for appraisers and investors.

The Morgan Group was among the few builders that prevailed in business after the building crisis of 1986. As they thrived in Houston, they invested in an expansion market, creating offices in Florida and Colorado. By 1995 they had expanded further and moved to a penthouse office on Westheimer in Houston.

Bill's "boys" were successful businessmen, managing a record-setting company involved in the acquisition or development and management of almost four thousand multi-family units and about one million square feet of office and industrial space.

Bill could not have been more proud of his children. His hard work had paid off. Ronnie, who handled property management, was elected president of the nation's largest apartment association at thirty-eight. A leader in the community and active in the fight against racism and intolerance, he also became an award-winning photographer. Michael successfully headed development in the Morgan Group, and Scott, who joined his brothers in the business in the '90s, became project manager and vice president of construction. All three married lovely, well-educated young women, which pleased their dad.

Mindy and Wendy attended college, married long-time sweethearts, and gave up anticipated careers to stay home and raise their children. Dad's philosophy of family was firmly embedded in their lifestyles.

It was Mindy and Steve who gave Bill his first grandchild. Erin was born in 1985. It was like heaven met him on earth when Bill looked at his granddaughter. At last the fruits of his labor were coming to fruition, and happiness filled his heart. He actually lived in a normal country as a normal human being. He longed for his

The Morgan Family, 1994

Back Row: Jayme, Scott, Michael, Ronnie, Bill, Steve, Howard
Middle Row: Patti, Marci and Laura, Shirley, Mindy, Wendy
and Becca
Front Row: Russ, Philip, Ryan, Blake, Erin, David, Stephanie,
Kimberly

Lilly Morgan, 1996

Hannah Cohen, 1995

father's words: "Yossela, you have done well and we are proud of you."

Though he always felt the joy of holding his own little children in his arms, he did not have the tools to show outwardly what he felt inside. The hardships in Europe had taken the human feelings out of him. He was afraid to express what he felt.

Whether Bill Morgan realized it or not, a gradual change came over him. Fear of failure no longer dogged him. As he grew older, he proved he could survive in many ways and his confidence soared.

Not having to concentrate on the financial aspect of his life allowed him to analyze his own vulnerability and to focus on expanding the good feelings, like hugging the grandchildren and spending playtime with them. He could not bring back his lost family, but he was blessed with another, and he referred to his beautiful family as the third miracle in his life. He was more than happy. He had everything to live for.

By 1996 Bill and Shirley had twelve grandchildren, five boys and seven girls. To Bill they were like owning IBM stock.

Bill consummated the American dream, a dream that began as a nightmare in Europe. He secured a future for his children and their children. Still, questions remained unanswered.

Bill D.

"Survival of the fittest" has to do with ability on one hand and the desire for survival on the other. I'm of the opinion when I talk about survival of the fittest, I'm thinking about people who have an instinct for business.

You really have to remember the survival syndrome with Bill Morgan. His background was terrible. I'm not sure very many of us could do what he was able to do. As far as I am concerned, the building recessions were just a setback for him. He saved his money while everybody who was making a lot of money was spending a lot of money. Bill made money and saved it.

His ability to deal with the building industry comes from the gut. I don't believe this is something taught in college. What Bill acquired over the years was through blood, sweat, tears, and getting his fingernails dirty.

I knew Bill as a competitor. This is a very small industry. It employs thousands and thousands of people, and it involves billions of dollars in Houston, but the number of developers is small comparatively.

When you talk about instincts, you talk about the ability to transfer the authority in your company to other people. I can relate very closely here with Bill Morgan in that I have a son in the business today. Bill has three sons in the business. Having the ability to turn his business over to his sons and stay on in some sort of a supervisory capacity—knowing when to advise and when not to, when to walk away—takes wisdom.

You really have to analyze the man at this point. If you take into consideration the amount he has accumulated and what he has done with it since, then you realize what kind of a guy he really is. Most people would not be as charitable as he is. If you call on him for a charity, you can bank that money. You know it's coming.

He needs to do this for himself, but the main thing is he has instilled this quality in his children, who are charitable people and do a lot of community work. When you start talking about people devoting their time, which is as important as the money, then you realize that the parents did a hell of a good job in raising their kids.

He is a family man. He is absolutely crazy about his family, his grandchildren. In some cases he can be a little obnoxious about it too. This comes from a good person.

Ronnie *

"You know, last night I spent several fretful hours leaning on the keyboard of my computer, thinking of what I could say that would keep all of you interested for at least one of the five minutes I have been allotted to speak to you tonight.

"I thought I could talk about the success that we anticipate and expect with our tort reform agenda and our success in electing more pro-business, pro-tort reform legislators and balancing the Texas Supreme Court.

"I thought too of talking about property tax reform, about outrageous property tax rates, and valuation assessments in Houston and Harris County that are killing the economics of our properties and discouraging further construction and investment. Most of you are aware that several Houston apartment developers have already abandoned further local development efforts in favor of those out-of-state opportunities where the property tax system is fair and evenly applied.

"But even though I could dwell on both tort reform and the need for property tax reform, I thought that, to keep your interest, I would simply tell you a story.

"The most important reason that I am here tonight is because of the inspiration and lessons taught me by my father, Bill Morgan.

"My dad came to this country in 1949 after living through the horrors of the Holocaust, horrors that you or I could not even come close to imagining. He came to this country as an orphan, without friends, without any family, and not speaking a word of English. He might as well have landed on the planet Mars.

"But despite these unfortunate facts and the tremendous odds my dad confronted in making something out of his life, he succeeded. And boy, did he succeed! Utilizing his gifts of common sense and his ambition and willingness to work hard and learn, no matter what it took, he went from being a non-English-speaking immigrant janitor in a shoe store to one of the most successful real estate developers in the city of Houston. My dad proved to me that if you want something bad enough, there is absolutely no reason that you cannot get it.

"Not only that, but he created with my mother, Shirley, a new family—a family of five children, who grew up in a house abounding with love, with now five spouses and, as an added bonus, ten grandchildren (and, as I know my Mom is now thinking, hopefully more to come).

"When I think about the odds that my dad conquered to be successful and create a new life for himself, I also wonder if anyone could have ever been in any worse situation or circumstance. It could not have gotten any worse for my dad. If he made a dollar, he spent a dime and saved ninety cents. If he didn't understand any particular English word, he would paste it on his mirror and look at it while he shaved and brushed his teeth. With all of this self-taught word learning, there is one word that he never did understand, and that was the word 'no.'

"When he believed he was capable of moving up in his position at the shoe store and he heard the word 'no,' he didn't accept it or understand it, so he moved on. When he worked at Foley's basement selling shoes and making one hundred fifty dollars per week and he was ready to move up in his position and he heard the word 'no,' he didn't accept it or understand it. He moved on. When he was peddling meat to restaurants out of the trunk of his car, if the owner said 'no' when he walked in the front door, he simply left and returned through the back door. The word 'no' was just not in his vocabulary, and he would not take 'no' for an answer. He was guided by the belief that hard work and perseverance, in a positive and productive direction, beget opportunity and, with opportunity, success.

"There is no way I can imagine being in my dad's position and overcoming the odds that he did. He traveled the infinite distance from his beginnings in a poor farming village in eastern Poland over sixty years ago to sitting here tonight watching his son become president of the Houston Apartment Association.

"For the lessons you have taught me and the inspiration you have given me, thanks, Dad."

*Edited from Ronnie's acceptance speech at the Holiday Dinner Dance December 9, 1994. Reprinted by permission from *Abode Magazine*, copyright, January 1995, Houston Apartment Association.

Michael

My dream has always been to do what my dad did, create something on my own, with my own hands, prove to myself that I can do it. What I have to thank my father for is pointing me in the right direction.

Bill Morgan came to this country with nothing. He decided he wanted a piece of the American pie, and he went out and got it. When I think of how he did it, I think of discipline and being willing to sacrifice. Add to those principles hard work and common sense. To this day he can't spell, can't work a calculator. He just knows where the decimal points should be. Commitment is a very good word to use to explain his success. He sets his mind out do to something, and he does it.

Where did he get this from—genes maybe? People are born a certain way with different personalities. I think my dad is impressionable. He is ambitious. So, in a sense, I think he sees what others have done, by observation, reading or hearing a story. He grew up in a small village where the reputation of your family was everything. It wasn't based on how successful you were in business because everybody was poor. It was based on how loyal you were to your family, how well educated you were in the Torah. Back then, they were very religious. Maybe that's just the European way, but I think his father emphasized these points to him. He pointed out the success of others to his son, and I think that was the foundation for my father's being impressionable.

I grew up with that too. He was always making comparisons. He would say, "Come meet this young man. See how successful he is, how well educated." If an authority figure or a father figure is telling you this guy is okay, you want to please your father. Even today when I meet successful people, I get excited. It motivates me. I see a successful person and want to learn more, use them as mentors.

You know, Dad has been criticized for not being tactful or saying the right things at the right times, but, with his background, where could that have come from? He says he is going to shoot that duck, and he shoots that duck. Sometimes his methods aren't as diplomatic as others more polished and educated, but by the end of the day, I would bet that seven to eight times out of ten, my dad would beat a Harvard or a Yale grad.

The older I get and the more people I meet, the more I realize what an amazing guy he is. At the same time he's human and very vulnerable. My father believes what people tell him. Sometimes he's ended up losing money based on those beliefs, and so have I, but it's a trait I wouldn't trade.

There's no question. He saw my personality and pushed me in one direction. He saw Ronnie's personality and pushed him in another. He was very involved in our lives, perhaps to a fault. We would have meetings once a month, and he would record them and we would talk about what's on our minds. He probably still has those tapes.

When I look around and see other families and how the kids strayed, I realize there's a very delicate balance of controlling your kids' lives and giving them independence at the same time.

He never showed us affection in the sense of hugs and kisses, but liked us to follow him around. I remember going to his packing house and wearing the white coats that were always too big, going in the freezers and touching the meat hanging on the hooks. That was a big thrill.

When he was in the meat business, Dad would barbecue on the grill outside on the driveway. That was on Sundays and we used to love that.

I remember when he went into the building business, he bought a black pickup truck. It had the tool compartments on the side and a rack that reached over the flatbed to put lumber on. Ronnie and I used to love riding around the block in the back of that truck, hanging on to the rack.

We would only see him an hour or so at night, at dinnertime. He would be gone early in the morning and come home late at night. He used to come home and make his own dinner. I loved his cooking more than my mom's. I would wait for him to cook the meal, then I could eat with him. When I think about it, Ronnie and I did a lot of things with Dad. I remember, early on, we used to go with him to collect rent. He used to take us to get haircuts every Saturday. I remember him playing racquetball at the Jewish Community Center. He was a very good player. He actually took us to a tournament with him, and he ended up winning. I think it was in Wharton, Texas. We stayed at a hotel with him. That was pretty neat!

Ronnie and I used to play horsey with him in the living room. We couldn't wait for him to come home from work so we could jump on his back like the Lone Ranger or the Cisco Kid on television. My dad was the perfect size for that when he was on all fours. I couldn't understand why he always said, "Ugh" when I jumped on his back. Now I know why.

I remember the excitement of moving into a new house, and Ronnie and I had a room upstairs. That was a big deal, going up the stairs. That's when I started to meet more kids and play in the neighborhood more.

When I was in third grade, we moved to Meyerland. At that point he was really working hard. I think he was forty or forty-one years old and he got sick with an ulcer. I never really knew what was going on as a little kid, but I did know he went to the hospital. After that he started taking better care of himself, going into sports and being a little more disciplined at leaving the office at five o'clock.

I didn't realize it then, but he was a good athlete as a child. I sort of attached myself to that because I loved sports and was pretty good. Dad was always too busy to go to our games. Sometimes my mom would go or just drop us off. I don't know if I did or didn't miss him being there.

As a teenager it got tough. Maybe it was adolescence, or he just got more firm with us. There was a part of me that was very afraid of him. He was definitely the disciplinarian. If we did something wrong, we got spanked. Ronnie and I were just typical kids. They would tell us to do something, and we would let it go in one ear and out the other Dad's patience was very thin, and now I can see why. He was under a lot of pressure at work, just trying to survive.

In high school he was very tough on us, very aware who we were hanging out with. I was getting speeches all the time. His big thing was he didn't want us running the streets. He wanted us busy. He wanted us working. His work ethic was very big. It was always dinner table talk. He would bring home building plans to work on. I took an interest in that. I would sit and watch him work.

In a sense I created my own social life, either through Hebrew school or elementary school. Dad wasn't that much a part of it. I just remember we played basketball on the driveway and I would see him come home.

As I grew older, it was more his trying to instill some responsibility in me and Ronnie and the kids in the neighborhood. He would have us do odd jobs here and there.

As a father he had a big influence on us. It was sort of monkey see, monkey do. I would always see him work around the house and would try to help even though I was too little to do anything—just holding a screwdriver and that sort of thing. And I think as we got older, sixth or seventh grade, it was sweeping the garage or sweeping the shed in the back or even going to work with him.

There were days I resented it. I think he never related to our childhood. That was probably the most difficult thing. He knew what we were going through, but to him that wasn't the most important thing. The important thing was becoming a responsible person, getting an education, getting into college, getting a good job, and getting ahead in life—probably because he missed his childhood and couldn't relate to it. We were just American kids spoiled rotten in an affluent society that didn't know what life's all about.

I think I have a special relationship with my father when it comes to work. I'm better able to express myself when it comes to personal feelings, goals, and aspirations. Ronnie and I grew up pretty much like twins in a sense. We went through everything together. And the girls were the girls and there was definitely that separation because of gender. But the first son has a special place in his heart. It's the Jewish or European way, I guess.

He was a very controlling father. Just the fact that he forced Ronnie and me together in business is typical of his personality. It was like a shotgun wedding. He wanted to keep the family together. He wanted to keep the family together.

"You'll be better off financially and in your career if you stick with Ronnie," he told me.

Ronnie and I wanted to be independent. We didn't want to depend on our father. There's no question about it. My dad likes to see what's real. And what he saw was what would be best for us. This is the beauty about Bill Morgan.

I think he is misunderstood. The man is very wise. It wasn't hard for him to turn the business over to us. He turned it over with open arms. He said, "The business is yours, guys." It was more important for him to see us together than it was for him to make another buck. He said, "Here's the ball. It's yours. Run with it."

He was right. He always let me hang myself first. If I could do that with my kids, that would be the greatest gift I could give them. It's not that you're giving it to them and they don't appreciate it. It's like, if you're really interested in business and you want to do something, I'll give you a head start to a point, but you can blow it or make it. He had faith in us.

He is controlling, likes to keep things on track, but only from the standpoint that it makes sense. He's not doing it from an ego stance or because it makes him feel good. It's just two times two equals four.

He always told me growing up that it's easier to do a big deal than it is a small one—same amount of effort—yet he would build only say forty units when everyone else was building two hundred. He never wanted to risk the money he put into the project. He always told me to stick with quality real estate. He dropped hints here and there. It was the way he raised us—good and bad—but definitely more good than bad.

Even when my dad started to make money, it was still a struggle. He never wanted to part with a dollar because he always wanted that security for his family. His first charity was to his family. He's a finisher. People could always rely on him. Ronnie and I are where we are because of Dad.

Ronnie and I have a responsibility to my father. He started with nothing. He went from point A to point B. Ronnie and I will take it from point B to point C, and our kids, point C to point D.

Teresa

You must get to know Bill Morgan quite deeply before you can really feel his love because obviously sometimes he does have a barrier. He is protective, protects himself easily. But the essence of this individual is profound and wonderful.

I admire his mental capacity. I admire the fact that he was able to do what he did. You know I put myself in his position because I came here alone from a very good background with a lot of love, feedback, and support.

Sometimes the only thing lacking in Bill Morgan is a little finesse. Where would he have learned it, alone in Europe as a youngster from a poor family, from the country that was emotionally cold, from his fellowman who shared no love or giving? What support did he get for life, for carrying him through devastating life situations? He had to learn it on his own—how to fight for life. It was a struggle. There wasn't much time or training in the way of finesse or sharing his deepest convictions or personal feelings.

I think Shirley and Bill have a very good understanding. They complement each other's personality. She gives him what he really needs—caring and moral support, social graciousness, access to friends. She's a natural to have friends and to be liked. While he was the disciplinarian in the family, she gave the hugs and kisses, yet when I think of Bill and his children, I think of a devoted father in so many ways, from coming home to cook their meals to giving them purpose in life.

9 TEST OF FAITH

"I'LL GET YOU, DIRTY, CHRIST-KILLER JEW."

The boy ran as fast as he could, trying to outdistance both the words and the large hand reaching for him. His heart, in cadence with his pace, beat so rapidly he thought it would stop, breath coming in short, rapid spurts, filling his throat and crushing his chest. He feared falling, so exhausted he was. Just as he thought he was out of range of the man who chased him, his fears came true. He staggered, stumbling and falling to the ground, knocking the last breath from his body. As he lay gasping, the man stood over him, his face warped with anger, screeching his foul words and holding the shiny, sharp instrument above the boy. The assailant lifted the ax high above his head and hurled it toward the figure on the ground.

A scream pierced the night.

"Bill, wake up! You're dreaming again. Wake up!"

It was always the same—the nightmares that raided his sleep, that haunted him for years. Would he ever be rid of them?

The demon dreams came less often, but when they did, they were intense, controlling. In each of them, Ukrainians or Nazi SS chased him, laughing, brandishing their sticks or axes. Or he hunted the Jews in the woods with an ax. Many times the faces he chased were those of his family members—Solomon hanging by the neck from the post or his little starving brother, vacant eyes staring at him.

Why had God let it happen? It was a question that possessed Bill.

"God will take care of you. You need not worry."

Those were his father's and grandfather's words.

Over and over Bill questioned the existence of God, his struggle always hovering over total belief, the childhood teachings imprinted in his soul.

Bill certainly had good reason early in his life to be confused. But as much as he tried to be angry or to exclude God from his life, he could not do so. Bill reviewed his life, step by step, and realized that there had to be some kind of guidance that led the uneducated farm boy to the destiny he achieved.

He believed the teaching and guidance of his father left him with purpose. It was that purpose that gave him the means with which to structure his life from the moment he walked out of the ghetto. Something, someone had to have guided him in surviving, obtaining American citizenship, marrying the right girl, succeeding in the business world, and having beautiful children and grandchildren.

He came to believe that each of us should take inventory of our life. He came here with nothing. God had to have led him to the gifts he now shared with his family and others. With sweat and hard work and God's guidance he succeeded, believing it was his duty to leave a better world than when he entered.

Bill realized it was important to believe in something, especially when you have children. A parent must give them moral guidance.

Even as Bill recognized his success and basked in his children's accomplishments, he still had the haunting dreams and unanswered questions about his lost family and the tormentors of his youth as well as God's presence in his family's time of need.

He disallowed God's existence, yet he welcomed the bits of faith that crept into his thoughts. God had always been a mystery in Bill's mind. If he asked himself one question, he got a dozen answers. His strongest senses held on to the belief that a "Being" created this world and gave life, sustenance, and the necessary things for the human species to survive. He felt he must recognize that.

He realized a human being's life span included a time when he would say goodbye to worldly things and there was nothing he could do about it. He was brought up to believe that a person lives for God, prays to God, thanks God, and that He is present no matter where you are, looking over you. But when he saw what happened to his family and the families of other Jews, he had doubts. At one point in his life he doubted he would ever return to the Jewish religion or even believe in God again.

Having been raised in Europe, Bill felt that European religion was very strict, old fashioned, and irritating to the Christian community. In reflection he realized that European Jews separated themselves in every way—dress, talk, prayer. Furthermore, he saw this separation from neighbors and suspected that was one of the main causes of anti-Semitism.

He experienced strict orthodoxy and, instead of having been blessed by it, he had been cursed. In order to avoid past mistakes, he adapted as quickly as he could to the American culture. He did not wish to go back to the strict atmosphere and did the best he could to maintain his Jewishness, a halfway mark between conservatism and liberalism. Giving credit to a real religion was not a part of his belief system.

When he lived for four years in the Ukraine, he often wondered why it was such a big deal about being Jewish, especially when others treated you poorly. As he matured, he looked for faults in the Jewish religion and could not see any as it was described in the Holy Book. He believed the Ten Commandments offered everything a human being needs to live by. Nowhere in those teachings could he find that, as a Jew, he was a Christ killer, a cheater, lazy—

accusations he had lived with as a youth. Even as he hid on the Ukrainian farm, disguised as a Christian, he knew in his heart he could not become steeped in the Jewishness that was his youth.

Bill saw God as a soul cleanser. In time of distress this belief gave him Someone to talk to and Something to be afraid of if he did not order his life according to the law. Could he do this without being a part of the orthodox community?

He questioned the reality of formal devotion giving a person extra years, additional comfort, or a bounty of blessings. He saw a difference between orthodox Jews in Europe and American orthodoxy. There was no other religion in Europe except the real orthodox. He perceived that fewer Jews practiced orthodoxy in the States than in Europe.

He attended synagogue on high holidays and maintained the same rituals—bris ceremonies and babynamings—but he did so with less zeal and lengthiness than prescribed. He observed all the main holidays—Yom Kippur, Rosh Hashanah, and Passover. The children went through Hebrew school and all bar mitzvah and bat mitzvah activities. He was involved in several synagogues, serving on boards and committees. Always the same question followed him. "Why couldn't my parents be here to enjoy the fruits of my labor?" He wanted to hear them say, "Yossela, you've done well and we're proud of you."

The continuing nightmares plagued Bill's attempt to reconcile with his Maker. He sensed the rebuilding of his family was totally on his shoulders. For a long while he believed that miracles do not just happen, that each person creates his or her own miracles. They are planned and there is no guarantee of fulfillment.

No matter how many times he made his deals, lived in the world of reality, the unanswered questions of why he survived and his family did not still crept into his body and mind, no matter how much he resisted it.

The guilt lived with him; the pain ate at him. He questioned whether or not it could ever be erased from his mind. Would he ever erase from his memory someone coming to the door to kill you, the shouted slurs, leaving his family starving in the ghetto? If he could just cry, letting go of the pain that saturated his body, his mind, stole his heart! He longed for tears to flood his entire body, washing away the pain, the guilt, and the questions.

Torn between the nightmares, forgiveness, and understanding, Bill finally realized what he must do.

Josef K.

I asked God a jillion times, "What did my father do? What did my sisters do to deserve this?"

You just swallow the hurt. You keep it to yourself. I don't know how to describe it. I would not change religions nor deny being Jewish, though deeply religious I am not. I always learned to obey what God said. I still feel that way at times. At night I still wake up in a sweat, bitter about losing my family. I do not feel guilty, but it does cross my mind why I survived and they didn't. I have nightmares, even now. The Gestapo is chasing me. The Poles are chasing me. They will kill me. For five dollars, for a pack of sugar, they would kill a Jew. The Germans would kill you because you were a Jew. So I'm running and they're chasing me.

Max

You can question God all you want, but He doesn't answer. Either you believe or you don't believe. We were not orthodox, perhaps my mother a little. She was very religious, lighting candles on Friday night. My father was more conservative, shaved. We were raised to observe the holidays.

I believe in God, but how do you believe in a miracle when something like that happens? Where are the miracles when you saw what you saw there—the atrocities? I know unbelievable stories. It was not a miracle that I survived. It was pure luck.

Morris

I was in the concentration camp where they have the ovens. They brought in ten thousand people every day and killed them.

I sorted the clothes from the people who came and were gassed and put them in the ovens to burn.

I never lost my faith. A lot of people killed themselves after the war because they were by themselves. But you establish yourself, you get married, raise children. You don't lose faith. I started out being Jewish and I'll finish being Jewish.

Josef M.

You always knew and were aware of the fact that you were a Jew. I believe in God. That was the way I was brought up, very religiously. We always looked up to God. All the Jewish people I knew did, whether in happy or tragic times.

During the Holocaust everybody was beseeching God, but the answer did not come; however, it never crossed my mind to say I was not a Jew. I was born a Jew, stayed a Jew, and will pass from this world as a Jew.

We now know there are no answers to the Holocaust—only questions.

Bolek

At the end of '45 when we were liberated, I became an atheist.

We were a conservative family, not extreme orthodox. We observed Jewish holidays, and my father wouldn't turn on the lights on a Saturday. He dressed modern—no beard or ear locks.

"Where was He?" That's what I said when this happened to the Jews, but I changed my mind before the arrival of my first child in 1949.

I was taking an inventory. I felt, with a child coming, it was a good idea for the child to have some crutch, some belief. It would not be helpful to have children grow up without faith.

Before, I would not let the name of God into my mind, for about four years. I even watched myself in conversation saying, "Thank God." I was rebelling in a big way, challenging the being of God. I asked, "So who are You? You weren't there."

I did not have any feelings of guilt of surviving. I'll tell you why. During the war my dad used to say," If they take everybody, don't run after them. Try to save your life. You will be someone who can tell the story."

He was a wise man. He did this for my benefit, so I could handle things.

There is something left. One strong generation creates ten strong generations.

Celina

During that time I didn't think about religion. I was too young. Now I think God had nothing to do with it. I think people did this. God gives people a brain to make choices, and that's the choice some of the German people made.

There was a mixture of guilt feeling that I survived and my family did not. But there was a feeling of great victory, of being able to survive despite the Germans. By the same token, I felt that I had to do something with my life, that this gift of life I received has to be compensated in some way. I have to do something important in my life to deserve this gift. Just think—six million people didn't survive, and to be one of so many family members to live—this cannot be for the purpose of eating and sleeping and living just an ordinary life.

In all my speeches and teaching of children, I say there is goodness and evil. I believe there are enough good people to fight the evil. It's just a matter of being involved. If you just sit there, evil may win.

I never wished that I wasn't Jewish. I just felt it was such an injustice to the Jewish people. Even if I die, I don't want to be anybody else. The Jewish are not so easy to be destroyed.

Walter

I suffered a crisis of faith myself. When you go through the horrible things, you lose faith in God. When you see people digging their own graves and praying to God while somebody is blowing out their brains. . . .

I was in Auschwitz, where thousands of people every single day were gassed and cremated.

We have a saying in our religion that on high holidays, God decides who's going to die by fire, by water, by other means. And I asked my father, "What did we do for all of us to be dying by fire?" It was beyond his comprehension. My father told me that God abandoned us. Survival was strictly a toss of the dice.

When we went from the ghetto to the forced labor camp, they took all the elderly people and the children under the age of fourteen and put them up against the fence and shot them with machine guns in front of all of us. I was only twelve years old then. I had a sister seven years younger than myself who was shot in front of all of us. My father saved my life. He had me standing on some bricks that made me taller and this is how I survived this particular selection.

Thanks to my dad, I survived many selections. When we arrived in Auschwitz in 1943, I was thirteen years old. My father always tried to have me with him because he felt that without him I wouldn't have a chance. When we arrived in Auschwitz, we were told to strip naked and stand six abreast. After about two minutes you could notice that all the healthy young people were going to the left. Everybody else, older, bad skin, or anything, was going to the right, so you immediately wanted to be with the healthy-looking group. My father arranged for me to be in that group. He was on one end, and he wasn't healthy. Between us were older men, a man with a hernia, and a guy with bad skin. So when I was standing there on the end, I looked healthy in comparison to them. This is how I survived.

I stayed in Auschwitz for eight weeks. I had a very bad job. We cleaned and folded all the clothing that was taken away from the crematoriums. Also sometimes if you were unlucky, you were chosen on the detail when they used to take out the people who were gassed. You had to remove their jewelry and the gold from their teeth. You had to knock it out. It was a nightmare. For about twenty years after I was liberated, I would have dreams about it. Every day you dealt with corpses, with dead people.

On the fiftieth anniversary of liberation, the rabbi asked me to make a speech about what Judaism means to me. One of the things I said in my speech is that most people when they think about life—normal people—they think about life as childhood, young adulthood, and old age. Survivors don't think that way. Survivors think about life as before, during, and after the Holocaust. The Holocaust made such a tremendous impact on all of us that everything we do is related to this time in our life.

Howard

Shirley says the nightmares are continual, nightly. He sleeps very little.

I really didn't have an appreciation for how he has to deal with it on a daily basis until I learned about his background, how he left his parents.

We think of problems in our own life, and those problems, no matter how traumatic we think they are, seem to subside over time. We learn to cope with it.

It seems to me most people who go through something like that end up unable to deal with the world on a normal level. He was an adolescent without the same reasoning ability and foundation as an adult to deal with those kinds of problems.

Bill is coping with them, but I don't think any of them have really let up. The guilt haunts him the most. He is in America and successful. Why? Because he left his parents and his situation, and now they're dead. I think he feels responsible, but that doesn't mean his actions weren't justified. Perhaps, to a certain extent, he has vindicated his actions to himself because there's nothing he could have done. He would have died too, but it doesn't help the guilt.

Rabbi

When anything bad happens, we blame God. For example, lightning hits one's home, and we go to sue the insurance company. What do they tell you? It's an act of God. Where was God? When I get a raise in salary, nobody says it was an act of God. They say I sweated and I perspired.

Where was God during the Holocaust? God was crying together with everybody else. God was in Auschwitz being burned together with everybody else in the crematorium, and He was holding our hands as we walked into the concentration camps and into the crematoria.

It was Hitler who actually caused the destruction of the Jewish people. God gave us freedom of choice, to be good or to be bad, to be moral or immoral, to be ethical or nonethical. Otherwise, what do we have in this world? A bunch of puppets with a master puppeteer.

Hitler chose to be a terrible individual, the devil on earth. The only devils we have are the physiological devils within us. What happened during the Holocaust was the choice of human beings. It was a choice of Hitler and of millions of people who did not criticize him.

The survivors' nightmares are a part of the experience. Many are under psychiatric care for this. Most of them are not. They live with it. It's like a lot of people live with headaches. The aspirin does not help. If they involve themselves with some activities and try to do away with hatred, maybe it will help, but it's always below the surface. It's one question I have no real solution for.

Bill does live with guilt, as do many of the other survivors. I tell them, "Your families wanted you to do this because they were physically unable to save themselves. If you had stayed with them, it would have been the end of your family, the end of your people, and the end of your religion. Hitler's victory would have been more extensive if you would have stayed with them. Somebody had to live on."

Unfortunately those who could not go forth had to be left behind. It was a terrible blow. It was a trauma that nobody could understand. I've said this many times. Somebody had to live on. Somebody had to tell the story. "Thou shalt choose life."

In a sense Bill is the essence of what the United States is about. *B'ze'at ah-pecha Tochal lechem* "By the sweat of thy brow shalt thou eat bread" (Genesis 3:19). When he came to the United States, he saw in New York Harbor a lady with a hand sticking all the way up into the sky with a flame on it, "give me your tired, your poor, your hungry." He said, "I'm tired, I'm poor, and I'm hungry." And he said, "If you want me, I'm going to do what you said." What she, the Statue of Liberty, gave him was opportunity.

I know Bill as a fellow who pulled himself up by his own bootstraps. He is a success story. Every person has the opportunity to go ahead, but it's not going to be handed to you on a silver platter. You have to work for it and you have to sweat for it.

He wants his children to have what he did not have. All his children were my students. I've done all their bar mitzvahs and babynamings.

Bill and I shared a lot. He has been very active in our synagogue, very generous in regard to the Holocaust survivors because he understands what they went through. He financed my program called TNT on television for years. The Bible says, "Thou shalt put phylacteries on your arm and your head for a sign." TNT means tallit, the prayer shawl, and 'tephillin is Hebrew for phylacteries. Our goal is to reach young kids and young parents. And we do. We would have anywhere from 125 to 250 every single Sunday for breakfast. Bill sponsored this program for years and years.

He's been generous in regard to everything—TNT, the Jewish Federation, Israel bonds, United Jewish Appeal, and Jewish National Fund as well as non-Jewish organizations.

One of his goals has been to infiltrate his children with the same spirit—to realize they are Jewish and have been blessed to help, aid, and assist other people, not only Jews but non-Jewish people also. He's trying to correct an error, a misdeed, of the past. He's trying to develop a new spirit with his children and others.

Sheldon

With pure thought and pure attitude all that can be is yours. I believe that. A sense of charity, fairness, and even-handedness will allow you to go through life's adversities. As bad as they are, sometimes they're opportunities for growth.

I will always think of Bill Morgan in that way. He is a perfect example. He lost his whole family, came to America, worked hard, scrimped and saved, succeeded, and all the while gave to others.

I met Bill through his son Michael. We became good friends, both of us in Denver at the same time. His father came to visit and Mike introduced us.

Bill was interested in my background. My father was able to save my mother's family, but his family was tortured and murdered because he worked for the underground. I didn't know I had a brother who was gassed at the age of one and a half until I was thirteen or fourteen and was told by my godfather. My dad was never caught, perhaps because he was blue-eyed and blonde and had a German-sounding name.

He had a sixth-grade education and was a poor farm boy from a large family in Poland. When the war started, he joined the Polish cavalry, becoming an officer—something unheard of because he was Jewish. He joined the underground, working to rescue children from the ghettos and assassinating SS officers, doing what he could to help the resistance. He was lucky to survive the war. He came to America, worked in a shoe factory, working constantly. It was his way of coping with his guilt and pain.

Dad passed away when I was thirteen, leaving me without a lot of direction in my life or a male figure to look up to. It was Bill Morgan who found me a job in his organization in Texas. He provided me with opportunity, genuinely caring about my welfare, almost as if I was one of his kids.

I subsequently opened my own company and owe much of my real work experience and business acumen and ethics to Bill Morgan. I knew him as a tough, shrewd businessman with an enormous heart, a high sense of values, and the ability to care deeply. I sense he genuinely wants to give back the same opportunities he received when he came to this country.

I truly believe in God, that there aren't coincidences. Fate took me to Denver and I met not only my friend Mike, but also his father whose values I've brought to my own community.

Michael

Organized religion really didn't have much to do with my life in the Morgan family. My parents had everything to do with my life. My mom sees the world through rose-colored glasses. If there is anything my dad ever needed, it was that. For us growing up it was the best balance we could ever have.

I grew up to respect and be nice to people, to recognize the importance of family, and to try to do the right thing all the time. I went through the motions of Hebrew school. Not much sank in. I couldn't recite the verses of the Torah or anything else.

It's interesting that, within the past five years, I have met and socialized with people who are not Jewish. I'm finding they have the same values. You know you always hear of Christian family values. As a Jewish person you really don't know what that means. Actually some Jewish people take offense to that. But you know what? It's the same. It's just growing up and being a good person, helping people, being nice to other people, appreciating life. That to me is a really important thing.

I have a philosophy. If you live your life by both the Bible and the Torah, you can get good things out of your existence. I remember I wrote a letter to my parents on my honeymoon telling them how much they had influenced my life. Because I am the way I am, I attracted the woman of my dreams. If I could have painted a picture of the woman that I wanted to marry, it would be Patti. She is incredibly intelligent and has the same set of values. And I see it in my kids.

I feel my parents were a positive influence on how to live your life. Now I have to do that for my kids. I see the growth, where my dad came from, where Ronnie and I are headed. And I see my kids' future. The key is to keep it together. Life is precious. Time passes quickly. The meaning you bring into your life influences the meaning it has.

10 Going Home

Continuous stretches of field, interspersed with forest, flew by.
Bill stared out the window of the minivan, lost in thought. He felt
alone, even with the others nearby. As his mind carried him into the
recesses of his memory, their conversation was lost to him.

Was it centuries ago he sat as a sixteen-year-old on a train,
traveling the same countryside? How easy it was to remember the
experience. Melancholy swept over him, threatening to bring tears.
The young boy of his memory fought to hide the trembling, so alone
and scared was he. No one could come to his rescue, most of all the
parents he left behind. He could not, would not cry. So ominous
was the moment, he felt as though his body would act of its own
accord and cause him to leap from the train and accept the conse-
quences.

Suddenly laughter interrupted Bill's focus, jarring him into the
present. Ronnie and Scott exchanged a story with the interpreters
as though they were old friends.

How incongruous, thought Bill. I am casually traveling where
once so much harm and pain existed. What can I gain from reliving
the old hurts?

Bill could not quite associate himself with the present Ukraine, so mixed were his past and present emotions. Young Yossela's shadow hovered over him.

Over the last few years he had come to realize that he could do nothing about his past, and as he grew older, maturer, more confident, he began gradually telling his family what happened. He knew he was not exonerated nor made whole, but he sensed some relief from the guilt and pain.

The five-hour layover in Amsterdam provided Bill the opportunity to meet other survivors who were on a special trek back to their homeland. Each shared his or her story of hiding in caves or forests or of being hidden by Gentiles.

Bill found their stories interesting, but the emotion of reclaiming the past as well as the long flight tired him. Even after they reached Amsterdam, they waited another five hours to board the plane for Budapest, followed by another two-hour delay. He wondered if he had made the right decision to return to his past.

In Budapest they left behind modern conveniences. Buses transported them out to the runway where the plane, a Russian-made TV-134, waited, its windows made like portholes, hung with curtains. After an hour the plane landed in Lvov. By now Bill and his sons, Ronnie and Scott, had been traveling twenty-one hours.

It was difficult to believe Lvov—once a thriving, dynamic business and cultural center, its French-style architecture standing beautiful in the stark landscape—now seemed uninteresting. From there Bill and his sons traveled by car to Stanisławów, renamed Ivano-Frankovsk after the war.

The reasonably new hotel into which they registered was dark and dilapidated, emphasizing the lack of change between the old and the new Ukraine. The elevator did not work and air conditioning was nonexistent.

With a hired driver, three interpreters, and Michnik, self-appointed head of the local Jewish community, Bill and his sons began their search. Their first stop was at a local government office. They would need further permission for their research.

Dealing with government officials in Ivano-Frankovsk distracted the travelers from their itinerary. Bill's financial success preceded him for the Russian city planner met him with open arms, suggesting Bill could be very helpful in building a hotel there. Obviously Michnik backed the proposal. Politely Bill disengaged from both men's enthusiasm for investment money and turned the conversation toward his own goals.

Finally, and reluctantly, Michnik took Bill to the area once designated as the Stanislawów ghetto. A large building and surrounding grounds now housed an insane asylum where once the Nazis imprisoned Jews. Still standing was a building built in 1897 that served as a synagogue, used now as a Russian club, a disco.

Bill finally faced seeing the ghetto. Nothing looked the same. He could hardly remember the faces of his family as he stood on the ground where they were hostages to Nazi cruelty. What had he hoped to see, to feel? Had he hoped for closure? He found none.

From there the guide took them to the Jewish cemetery where Bill witnessed as a youth the people gunned down by the German SS. He was shocked at what he saw. Vandalized tombstones, broken or dug up, lay among tall weeds in a field the size of two or three baseball stadiums. No longer a formal burial ground, the area was now an unkempt field.

Bill learned that the section, where there were no tombstones and where mass graves were dug, was shifting, pushing chalk to the surface. When local authorities tried to improve the plot plane, they dug up some human bones.

As Bill stood looking at the very spot where he helped dig the mass grave, shivers raced through his body. Here he witnessed the slaughter of his fellows. From here the sixteen-year-old Yossela fled, escaping the carnage. This very place and the events that occurred here were the catalyst for the decision he made. The memories flooded him, threatening to overpower him.

The other travelers forgotten, he walked into the weeds. Alone he stood in silence.

And then he heard it.

"Yossela."

Startled, Bill looked around him. There was no one. Was it the breeze blowing through the nearby trees or noises in the distance? Was it his imagination or the echo of the gut feelings deep inside?

Suddenly it came to him clearly, so clearly no longer was there doubt that they, his family, were in this particular cemetery. He would not be able to explain the sureness of it, but reasoning would tell him his family was here beneath where he stood, their earthly remains lying here in the mass grave.

When he had left the ghetto, they were extremely weak. It was just a matter of time before the people with the wagons came to collect their bodies and deposit them in the nearest burial place. If they survived the starvation and disease, the Nazis would have marched or trucked them to the cemetery for execution. No one else would have accepted their bodies. It would be here, at the Jewish cemetery, they were dumped and covered in order to disguise their murder.

Bill could not find words to utter, not at this moment, but he heard his mother's voice as though it were yesteryear. "You can't leave. You are the only one who brings us food." Did she speak those words or had her eyes done so? Bill's memory failed him, and guilt taunted him into believing she said the words.

Then he felt it once more, his father placing his hand on top of Yossela's head and saying, "Go with my blessings until we meet in heaven. Say a kaddish for us."

Bill could no longer hold back the tears. The past rushed to meet him—the parting at the ghetto, watching their faces, running away, the guilt of leaving them and saving his own skin.

He lost track of time, standing there in the field where the bones of more than a hundred thousand of the annihilated lay. After a while the weeping abated. He knew that, even as he might stand over the bones of his family, they were in heaven with the angels. The Jewish religion says a righteous soul departs for heaven as soon as it is buried, and his family was certainly worthy of heaven.

"Someday I will meet you there," he whispered, and he turned and walked out of the field.

Later Bill and his sons would return with a rabbi and an elder for a prayer service. There among the buried, Bill and his sons would hold kaddish, lighting candles and saying their prayers.

The day after the visit to the cemetery, Bill's efforts centered on finding his hometown, Czerniejow, as well as Jezierzany, the town where he hid as a Polish Catholic.

In Czerniejow they met the mayor and talked with two old people who remembered the Jews who lived in the town. He even recollected some of their names.

They also met a man, an old drunken man, who named not only Bill's father and mother, but his uncle and aunt as well. He also remembered seven children in the family, but he was too drunk to give details. Bill told him he would return the next day to talk and asked the man's wife not to give her husband anything to drink before their meeting.

They met another man who used to play with Bill's younger brothers and sisters, and further down the street they saw Bill's school. Bill marveled at how serene the classrooms and playground appeared, a contrast to his memory of taunts and thrown sticks. When they reached the corner where his house once stood, they found a vacant lot, but standing next to it was his aunt's house, now the home of a Ukrainian. How incongruous it seemed to Bill to stand where he once lived in dire poverty. Now a free and wealthy man, he was still destitute, burdened with the weight of his guilt.

Exhausted emotionally, Bill prepared to leave. They had spent five hours searching for clues to his past. As they prepared to depart, the mayor gave Bill a book as a gift and answered his request to talk

Cemetery where Yossela dug graves—now overgrown with weeds. Bill feels that his parents were dumped in the unmarked mass graves.

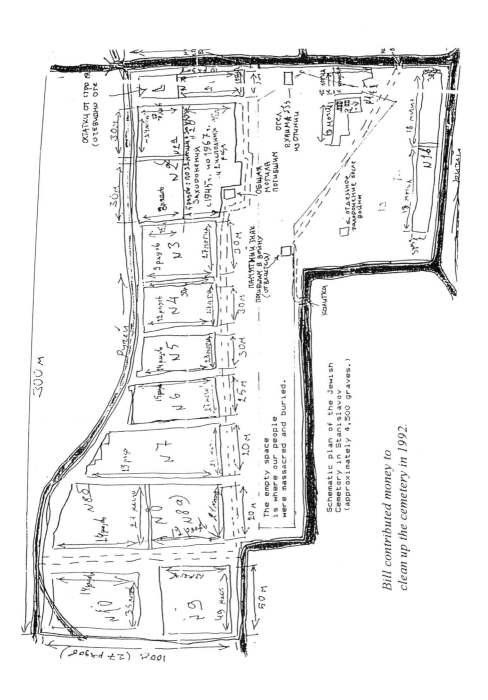

Schematic plan of the Jewish
Cemetery in Stanislavov
(approximately 4,500 graves.)

The empty space
is where our people
were massacred and buried.

Bill contributed money to
clean up the cemetery in 1992.

to the community. She would make arrangements for him to speak in a town meeting in three days.

After lunch the group began their search for Jezierzany, the small village where Bill lived in disguise as a Polish farm boy. Soon they learned there were three towns with the same name, but they refused to give up until they found the correct one. Around six in the evening Bill recognized a large church on the main street of the third Jezierzany.

He continued the routine of asking elderly citizens questions concerning a boy named "Stefan" and the farmer for whom he worked, but soon frustration set in. No one could remember any names.

Bill kept the group moving, looking for familiar territory. It was then they came across an old man who remembered the name of the farmer Bill had worked for. Everyone was excited. They followed the man down a dirt path, where suddenly Bill recognized the water well and the farmhouse.

The occupants of the farmhouse were the farmer's son and his wife. The son knew of "Stefan" and so did some neighbors. They brought out pictures of the farmer that Bill recognized immediately.

He was very excited, showing his sons the farmer's house and barn where he slept and worked. He even cranked the water well one more time. They spent three hours before they had to leave for the hotel. All agreed Bill would return in a couple of days.

The following day they went back to Czerniejow to visit with the drunken old man, meeting him as he drove his horse and cart back to his house. Inside his house, one of the better homes in the neighborhood, he spoke again about Bill's parents and his uncle and aunt. He said that Bill's mother was fat and his father short and skinny. He noted that Bill resembled his father.

Bill wanted more, for he had recognized the old man's house. As a child he had passed it many times. At the opportune moment, he tried to get the old man and his wife to acknowledge that the

A view of the area near the village of Czerniejow.

A typical road in the village of Czerniejow.

An aunt's house in the Ukraine–one of the three family structures left standing. Yossela's house was under the oak tree.

A neighbor's yard looks today much as it did in 1941.

*The school house Bill attended
–first through seventh grade
in the Ukraine. His classroom
is pictured to the right.*

Bill's former neighbors in Czerniejow.

"The biggest revelation to me was watching my dad as he realized, by modern standards, that the people and land he once knew were geographically lightyears from what we know, a land forgotten. This stirred emotion in him, but he tried to remain detached."

Ukrainians were not the angels the villagers reported them to be. They did admit some Ukrainians were bad, some had mistreated the Jews, but basically the Ukrainians liked the Jews and lived well with them. They said they were sorry to see them go.

Bill was amazed at their poor memory. Clearly he remembered this particular old man chasing him and his brothers down the alley, yelling to get off his property, shouting the slurs.

Outside a crowd of villagers had gathered. When questioned, one man remembered playing with Bill's brother, Bunya, and his sister, Byla. Bill had not been able to remember her name until the man said it. Now he felt as though he had found a prize, his youngest sister's name. He longed to find out the names of the two younger brothers. No one could remember them.

After lunch Michnik took them to a place in the forest where twenty-six thousand bones of Jews had been recently discovered. He read an explanation of who was killed at this spot, and the group lit candles, placing them on the ground and leaving them to burn.

The following day in Ivano-Frankovsk, Bill, Ronnie, and Scott visited a local synagogue where they participated in the service. From there they walked to the "square" between the new and old synagogue, arriving at the auditorium where they were surprised to find around sixty people wanting to ask him questions. They were interested in how he succeeded in business, whether there was anti-Semitism in the United States, and the prospects for peace in the Middle East.

Bill welcomed their interests and answered as best he could. He found it interesting, their thirst for knowledge of the States. It was widely known that most Jews from the area had emigrated or were in the process of emigrating to Israel or the United States. A few of the old timers remained, unsure of a move in this period of their lives.

The next day as they prepared to return to Czerniejow, news that Gorbachev was dismissed greeted them. A perceptible air of nervousness clouded the response of their guides. No one seemed to have any idea what would happen in the country with this change of power. The lead interpreter told them that a state of emergency had been declared in certain republics, and when a music program is on television—as it was—the people know something negative has happened.

Rumors spread that Gorbachev got what Kruschev received. Government officials called him to a meeting, told him he was in ill health, and said he should retire. The wildest rumor heard was that Gorbachev was arrested and that there were tanks on the streets of Moscow.

Their friends advised Bill and sons not to venture out of the hotel.

Fear swept over Bill. How could this be happening in 1991? Was he doomed to have the past repeated? He and the boys talked of heading straight to the Hungarian border, but it was a six-hour trip by car. Should they give up their research efforts?

Further television news reports indicated that Gorbachev was sick and incapable of governing. At first Professor Fishuk, whom they met when they arrived, said the news was just "chicken feed." An emergency committee had been formed including the head of the KGB, and states of emergency were declared in Moscow and other areas.

By now Fishuk had changed his mind. The situation was grave, and the BBC reported many stories, one of which was that Gorbachev was killed. The professor had come to believe the incident was a military junta and advised them to stay in the hotel, not to venture out. It was possible the roads might not be safe. He was afraid blood would be shed. On television they saw tanks in Moscow and the people setting up makeshift barricades.

Finally Bill and his entourage decided to continue their trip. They were due in Czerniejow for the town meeting. A crowd of townspeople greeted them at the auditorium where the mayor had arranged the event.

Along with an interpreter, Bill moved to the stage. He watched as more people arrived, school children and their teachers, old and young men and women. Soon the room was filled to capacity, causing latecomers to remain standing.

After a short introduction Bill moved to the mike. He had not prepared a speech, but he thought a long time about what he wanted, needed to say. Would he be able to reach them, to make them understand his feelings?

All eyes stared at him as he stood before the crowd. He had their full attention. He told how it felt to be a small Jew boy in a Ukrainian village. He spoke to them of taunts and sticks and stones. He told them about his grandfather's untimely death. He talked of the fear as he and his family marched to the orders of the Nazis, leaving their belongings as they were herded into a designated imprisonment. His voice caught as he remembered and told them of the jeers shouted at the Jews as they marched from the village to the ghetto.

"Why did I suffer so much?" he asked. "American school children ask me, 'Who is a Jew and what's wrong with a Jew? Why did they want to kill you? Aren't you mad? How can you tell us to love and forgive?'"

Pausing, Bill looked at his audience. "I answer them. My mind tells me one thing, but my heart tells me not to hate. I would like to have the answers for my own children, the reason why I am a product of hate and an orphan. All I can tell them is that I am Jewish."

No one stirred. Bill continued, "We're all God's children. A little child cannot help to whom he is born and only God has the right to take us away. I came here with a heavy heart and an open mind. I ask many times, 'Why did your grandfathers and fathers hate me so much?' I cannot answer, but I have a mission. That mission is to talk to young people, all people who will listen, and spread love, not hate."

He spoke to them for more than thirty minutes with the interpreter repeating his statements word for word. As he finished,

Before returning to the U.S., Bill held a town meeting with the residents of Czerniejow, his birthplace. He said to them: "We're all God's children. A little child cannot help to whom he is born and only God has the right to take us away."

Tears were shed as these Ukrainians listened to stories about his childhood as a Jew in their country.

After Bill spoke with the townspeople, the children sang songs and brought fruit.

After his talk, the people gathered around the emotional Bill, offering hugs and asking questions.

he pleaded that little children learn to be tolerant of each other, that all welcome the differences between people and cultures, and to consider working as a group to aid peace and friendship between all nations.

He stood quietly for a moment, then raised his arms as if to embrace his listeners. "May God bless you," he said.

No one stirred. The silence screamed at him. He looked at their faces, some with tears streaming down their cheeks, the older children wide-eyed. He descended into the audience and took his seat on the front row. It seemed an eternity before anyone moved.

Finally the noise of children, ushered to the stage by a teacher, broke the silence. On the stage, dressed in their Sunday best, children held baskets of fruit and flowers as they sang a song.

When they finished, they laid the baskets of "holy fruit" on the stage. Then they descended the stairs and took the flowers to Bill, who sat quietly, tears streaming down his face. One and then the other reached over and put an arm around his neck. He hugged them back.

When the children returned to their seats, individual adults came to the front and to Bill, responding to him with outstretched arms and smiles. Many had stories to tell him. Several elderly people said they knew Bill's family well. One remembered playing with young Yossela and his brothers. They used to take buttons off their clothes and play a game with them. They remembered Yitzhak had a grocery store and that he was very kind to the townspeople.

Much later and exhausted, Bill and his sons returned to Ivano-Frankovsk. They rode in silence, emotionally drained.

When they returned to the hotel, the tour company manager assured them there was nothing to worry about concerning the Gorbachev situation. He promised personally to guaranty their safety. They had no idea what news was broadcast to the United States. Yeltsen gave an ultimatum to the governing committee to produce Gorbachev within twenty-four hours and asked the best doctors in the USSR to examine him for a diagnosis. He also demanded that, if Gorbachev were produced in good health, then all of the governing committee would be tried as criminals.

The coup was over, and Bill and his sons' lives had not changed because of the events in Moscow. The Ukraine had not been placed under a state of emergency after all.

Their search continued with a return to the farmhouse where the farmer's son and his wife prepared a feast for them. A woman acquainted with Bill during his years in Jezierzany was there. Bill asked her what she thought when she heard he was Jewish. She said she had always known or suspected he was Jewish but never told anyone. She said "Stefan" betrayed himself one night when the educated son of the farmer was telling a joke. The punch line was in Yiddish and "Stefan" was the only one who laughed. They agreed between them that they would tell no one.

Bill sat calmly as the interpreter recounted the story told by the woman. As she finished, he looked at the woman and smiled, but inside he did not believe the story. Even after all these years the derogatory remarks rung in his ears. Why would they have protected his identity at the same time they cursed it? Even so, Bill decided to accept the story. What would be the purpose of insisting it was a lie? What would it accomplish? Perhaps accepting these people as they are now could create a balance of understanding between the two cultures and lead Bill not only to a sense of closure, but to discovering other information.

The revelation of the story changed the complexity of the lunch. The mood changed from anxiety and impatience to displays of both emotion and laughter. They sat together for another two hours, toasting cognac and eating.

Before he left, Bill visited the dying older brother and a niece where he saw more pictures of the family. Old memories rushed back as he saw a picture of the farmer with whom he had lived for four years in disguise.

Bill revisits the farmer's living room where he slept the last days before he fled.

The yard around the barn was much as it was when he lived there as "Stefan."

Descendants of the farmer with whom he lived as "Stefan." The man standing to Bill's left is the farmer's son—the niece is on the right.

Stefan carried water to the cows and horses— also to the farmer's house from this well.

Bill left Jezierzany with some sense of closure, but none from Czerniejow. He had seen the places and showed his sons they were real—both Czerniejow and Jezierzany. He found the same poverty, and at the same time, improvements such as electricity. He confronted the Czerniejow villagers, asking why they drowned his grandfather. They said it was not they. It was somebody else.

His disadvantage in finding information lay in the fact he did not remember names or birth dates of neighbors or even some family members. He knew Yitzhak Margulies and Etta Gabirer Margulies and that there were seven children, but he could not remember his grandfather's name or his aunt or uncle's names nor his younger siblings. How would he ever find records on them?

Bill always dreamed of going back and walking down the streets where he went to synagogue and school. He wanted badly to get the hurt out of his system, to find an answer to why his parents managed to end up in a place where they lived a miserable life and met a grim death.

Bill went to his homeland to clear his conscience, to make sure every stone was turned. He knew time was not in his favor. He returned also to reclaim his memory of the area and his childhood in order to pass it on to his children.

Going home again was far more difficult than Bill realized it would be. He found a confused landscape of poverty and memories embedded with the hurt that did not give up.

Scott

There's one specific and remarkable moment I truly remember about our trip to the Ukraine. Dad and I were at dinner one night. He never talked much about his past or the Holocaust. He never brought it up. The only thing I ever heard was that he had one brother, one sister, and his parents.

Just the two of us were at dinner, and I asked him again. "How many brothers and sisters do you have?"

He said, "Scott, I've never told this to anybody, not even your mother, that there were seven of us."

My mouth just dropped. I could not believe that he never told anybody. I was the first one, and I'm the youngest, and I'm here with him in Poland and he's telling me these things. That was amazing. I think that's what really started him thinking and wanting to talk about it more.

I felt so close to him. Dad had never told us this. You have to believe it's been in the back of his mind all this time, for the last forty years. Not even to tell your own wife that you had that many brothers and sisters is surprising.

He never wanted people feeling sorry for him. I think at that time, because I'm the youngest, he realized it was important to tell me the truth, so I can pass it on.

He told me I resembled his brother, and that's got to be tough, looking at me, reminding him of that. I think he saw his younger brother die of starvation in the ghetto, and his brother Solomon was a police officer and he was hung. It was such a bad memory; he couldn't remember his younger sister or his two little brothers' names.

This talk between us, just the two of us, was a humbling experience for me. I have a journal where I wrote four or five pages, just about that one night. Being the first one to know this information was stirring, amazing.

Irene

In the winter of 1991 Michnik, head of the local Jewish community, invited me to translate a letter. It was Mr. Morgan's, describing his life during the cruel years of World War II. I was so greatly impressed that, when asked to translate an answer into English, I did it without delay.

Michnik called me in August wanting me to help him communicate with some Americans who came on a visit. It was Mr. Morgan and two of his sons.

I joined the group consisting of the Morgans; Martha, the official interpreter; Lyana, the tourist company representative; and Michnik.

The first place we visited was the village of Cherneyuv (Czerniejow), not far from Stanislawów—sometimes spelled Stanislav—now named Ivano-Frankovsk. After World War II almost the whole village was sent to the liberation camps.

It's rather hard to explain what was happening in these parts in the '40s and '50s. It was not easy to find people who remembered the Margulieses, Mr. Morgan's family. One by one the farmers told the whole story. There were many Jews in the village before World War II, the Margulieses being one of the families. They had a store, a very small one, and as they were very kind and understanding, they often lent food and money to the villagers if asked.

Everybody agreed that the family was very nice. People also remembered Bill's other relatives. Unfortunately all of them were killed during the war.

August 19, 1991 was a very special day. It was Spar, a religious holiday when fruit is blessed in the church. That very day was appointed for the requested meeting in the village with the residents, Bill Morgan's former neighbors. All villagers, young and old, gathered in the club to listen to the American guest.

In my opinion, they came out of interest. Americans were not often visitors to the villages.

There was a misunderstanding at first. The head of the Village Soviet had put an advertisement on the board concerning a meeting with Mr. Morgan, but the villagers decided to ignore it as the head belonged to another church. It was the time when different churches were in opposition.

So our team, so to speak, had to stop people on their way home from the church after the service and to explain things and invite them to the club. In half an hour the hall was full.

Bill Morgan stood in front of the people and told his story. Oh, it really was a distressing story, for my jaw was trembling while I was interpreting things.

Then came the questions and presents to Bill Morgan. You see, it was a great holiday—blessed fruit, apples and pears. The embarrassing moment was after Mr. Morgan mentioned a rather unpleasant memory he had from childhood. He had been stoned, haunted, and beaten by children at school just because he was a Jew, and he often complained to his wise father about those children. He was told not to take it close to his heart because those children didn't realize what they were doing, that he had to forgive those poor creatures and never be angry, for "we all are children of one God."

Certainly no villager remembered that incident. After being driven out of the village to the ghetto, the Jews starved. Nor did they remember that at night Bill and his brothers tried to get to their village and dig out some potatoes they had had in the plot. But somebody occupied their house and sent dogs to drive them out. No doubt, nobody remembered that and no one knew who occupied their house and grabbed their belongings.

The villagers agreed that there had been some bad people among the residents but those present at the meeting . . . oh, never!

I didn't notice any shame on their faces. Nevertheless, the meeting was a success. I mean, everybody was impressed. I was glad the villagers heard the whole truth, for the Jews had experienced an unpleasant attitude, to put it mildly, on the part of the local population.

It was not very easy to find the place where he hid in disguise during the war for there are several villages in the region with this name. We had to travel for long hours looking for Yezhezhany (Jezierzany). Finally we got to the Ternopol region and Bill Morgan recognized the street leading to the church, the central square.

Another adventure began when we asked the residents about the house and the farmer, for Bill Morgan didn't remember the farmer's name. We walked along the village streets, among the stones and dust, accompanied by some drunken old villager who said he knew the place we looked for but each time failed to find it.

When at last we lost any patience and decided to leave, I addressed a teacher who seemed sober and clever and told him what and who we were looking for.

"There was a farmer," said the teacher, "who had two sons who were killed in the war. He had a daughter and son-in-law, and there was a guy working for them during the war."

While we were talking, an ancient, lame, and ugly old man was standing near and exclaimed, "I know the house!"

He brought us to the very house, and Bill Morgan recognized it, the street, and the *krinitsya*, a well. A couple who appeared to be the farmer's son and his wife met us. They looked shabby—if this word can describe people. Everything in the house looked dull, ancient, like some abandoned place.

Mr. Morgan remarked it was just like it was in the early '40s when he was staying there, even the beds. The bucket and the chain in the well were rusty, but the people still used it.

I can't say for sure what Bill Morgan experienced at that moment. It is hard to say. On one hand, it was there where he survived, and thanks to those people, remained alive. He was standing there in front of them—a well-to-do happy person, his two sons beside him. On the other hand, they, I mean the farmers, were so old and miserable that you were tempted to help them, give them money, and protect them from further misery.

Then the farmer's daughter came, a middle-aged woman whose husband was suffering in bed, dying of cancer. The villagers invited Bill Morgan and his sons to have dinner together, but it was too late to go back to Ivano-Frankovsk after dinner, so we promised to come in a couple of days, and we left.

So many strange things happened while the Morgans stayed here. When we crossed the bridge going to Yezhezhany in the morning, everything was OK. On our way back we saw a sign: "The bridge is damaged." We had to beg the guards to let us go. The Morgans kept asking me why they had locked the bridge, but all I could answer was, "God knows."

They finally let us cross.

A sign on a restaurant's door read, "The restaurant is closed for sanitary reasons. No alcohol available."

When they finally opened the door for us, the hall was full of people who were drinking, dancing, and singing, and again I found it hard to answer the question, "Why?"

We came to the village again and were treated well, all hospitality and smiles, but I felt some tension on both sides. The daughter mentioned they had known Bill was a Jew, or rather suspected him to be, but never told anyone.

Bill Morgan didn't believe that. He said if they really had, they would have informed the Germans or just sent him away. He remembered his former co-villagers in Cherneyuv jumping for joy and clapping their hands while the Jews were being driven to the ghetto in 1941.

I may tell you that Jews are not stoned, haunted, or beaten anymore, but there are cases when children are teasing because of someone's Jewish origin. I myself have experienced such an attitude. Now the local nationalist organizations call the people to fight Russians and Jews. Not long ago there was a leaflet on the buildings of the synagogue—"Jews, get out of here!"

But where can I get out? It's the place where I was born, brought up, buried my parents. It is here that I have taught English to so many students, and now I teach methods of teaching, doing good for the country like my parents did.

I proved my love to the Ukraine. Instead of staying in the USA forever like all Ukrainians do when they go to visit relatives, I returned to my country.

Ronnie

I was touched because Dad was touched. He was definitely affected by the town meeting. He was crying. But I knew that he knew that these people really hadn't changed. The hate was still there. You couldn't help but be emotional by it, but you were also separated from it.

The biggest revelation to me was watching my dad as he realized, by modern standards, that the people and land he once knew were geographically lightyears from what we know, a land forgotten. This stirred emotion in him, but he tried to remain detached.

My dad had talked some about these places, but they were never real to us. It was like any other story. Now we were able to see exactly where he came from. He made it real to us, yet in a certain sense it was unreal. It was hard to imagine that these people over the last fifty years have probably gone backward more than forward. I'm talking about toothless peasants who were essentially his neighbors. And they were by no means his peers. These are the people who subjected him and his family to misery. Even though they denied it, it was obvious that they were the ones. Knowing that, it wasn't difficult to be detached from them. The emotional part from my dad's perspective, I guess, was knowing he was reliving the misery. I don't think he has any pleasant memories at all from his village or the Ukraine.

He hoped to find some connection with somebody who was still around, but he didn't. He did accomplish most of what he set out to. He found his village.

His biggest goal was to show us where he came from. He found villagers who knew his family before the war, who said he looked like his father, villagers who knew the name of one of his sisters.

We found the farm where he hid out during the war, a big accomplishment in our search. He showed us where he hid. We met the farmer's son and niece and neighbors who knew him under his alias.

It was a good full circle for him even though he would have loved to have found some survivors of his family. He didn't. If he thought he would locate any family member, I didn't.

We were there when the Gorbachev coup happened. When our local contact expressed some concern, my dad was ready to take the next car to the Hungarian border because, in his words, he knew how miserable these people could be and he didn't want to experience that again.

There was a farmer who still lived across the street from where his house was. When we first met him, he was drunk. When we came back and he was sober, my dad finally got him to say he and the others might have jeered the Jews when they were younger, but they were just making fun.

I don't think there was any regret. I don't think any of them has lost sleep over it.

There were a lot of tears in the audience when he made his speech. I would bet most of them came from people who didn't experience World War II, the second generation. But the first generation didn't show much emotion.

It was a feeling of hopelessness because I knew he was really drilling these people. "What did we do? What did I do wrong?"

He asked all of these people that question, and of course they couldn't answer. He kept asking it and wasn't getting the answer he wanted. He essentially was cramming it down their throats, to make them realize what they did to him and all the other Jews. I don't know if he was trying to get some kind of just deserts from them or what. It was a continuing question on his part that they never answered satisfactorily.

I think his speech did have an impact. It was very emotional. When my dad spoke, he was all substance, all from the heart.

Growing up, we never realized what a Holocaust survivor was or what he went through, that is, until recently. He started talking about it about ten years ago. The problem I find is that he lives with this every day although he's good at disguising it.

Lenny*

At age fifty-eight my father died of cancer. Twenty-six years later, in the summer of 1989, my wife and I set out for Stanislav (Stanislawów). Like many of our generation, we were embarking on a journey to seek our roots. My sister and I were the children of the sole family member from Stanislav to escape the Holocaust. My essential aim was not to trace the lives of these victims of Nazi terror but to reach for my father, to touch his life, so that now, after twenty-six years, I could say goodbye.

Left behind in Stanislav after my father's departure were his parents, four brothers, and two married sisters. Left behind as well was a bit of my father's soul.

Among the many sorrows weighing on my father's heart was the story of his youngest brother. In 1938 letters arrived from Isaac, age 17, and his parents imploring my father to arrange for his emigration to the United States. Whether his motive was solely to avoid conscription into the Polish army or whether he also had a premonition of what would soon befall his people was not clear. But Isaac's letters took on increased urgency: "Please rush the papers so they'll get to the consulate as soon as possible," he pleaded in June. And in November: "I beg you to get me out of here." Letters sent to Isaac after early 1939 met with no response. Had my father done enough? The question troubled his soul.

During my father's lifetime I had failed to move toward him. During these years I ended a prolonged adolescent rebellion against my Jewish upbringing. I set about the task of reexamining my heritage. As I did so, I began to feel keenly the loss of my father and the world of East European Jewish life which had nurtured him. Two decades after my father's death, I was ready to draw near.

Few events in the days to come would seem ordinary. We traveled in a sacramentalized space. We awoke to the sound of heavy rain accompanied by thunder and lightning. As we were about to leave, our hostess placed three exquisite roses in my hands. My heart raced. How had she anticipated my plan? We set out for the old ghetto streets.

The corner house at 41 Halicka Street was still standing! The large stucco dwelling was at least one hundred years old. In wonderment I moved my hand along its rough surface. These were the walls which had housed my father. These were the walls violated by Nazi storm troopers. Trembling, I placed a yellow rose on a windowsill. A memorial paper was attached, naming the dead of my family.

After walking around the outside of the house and gazing dreamily up and down the narrow cobblestone street, we drove to the site of the Jewish cemetery, following a route familiar to me from the many descriptions by Stanislav survivors. This was the route of the infamous forced march of Jews on October 12, 1941. In the back seat of the car and with my head pressed against my wife's shoulder, I could weep.

I had endeavored to feel my father's feelings and think my father's thoughts during a journey of six months. I had left memorials of flowers to his family. I had left a living memorial of newly created friendships with residents of his birthplace. I had realized his dream of weeping on the soil of his city. I had finally heard my father's tales of Stanislav. I can say goodbye.

*Edited excerpts from "Good-bye Father: A Journey to the USSR." by Leonard M. Grob, Ph.D., reprinted by permission from *Judaism,* vol. 39, no. 2, copyright, spring 1990, American Jewish Congress.

11 House of Love

THE SUN SHONE AGAINST THE WINDOWS OF THE DISTANT OFFICE BUILDINGS, causing the new spring leaves on nearby trees to glisten a vibrant green. The weather was unseasonably warm for March—and humid, which was not totally unusual for Texas, especially Houston.

A sense of anticipation filled Bill's mind as he sat with the others on the platform, looking at the crowd gathered for the occasion. The parking lot was full, the thousand seats filled, many occupants arriving two hours early. Now people stood on the sidewalks and in the street, blocked off for the opening. Bill guessed that at least two thousand people waited for the ceremony. "Standing room only" would sound good as the public read about the event.

Bill's thoughts muffled the voice of the speaker. He had risen earlier than usual, unable to ease the memories that rushed at him. From the twentieth floor of the high-rise he and Shirley had occupied since the 1980s, he watched as the city of Houston came awake, the lights of the sprawling metropolis reaching out to the horizon.

This place in time seemed surreal as he remembered his humble beginnings in the countryside of the Ukraine and the day his grandfather died. He had risen early, folding the pallet that served as his bed, the musty stench of poverty all around him. He saw clearly his mother and father stooping to enter the mud hut in which they lived.

As his mind yielded to the memory, he shuddered, the old hurts rushing back.

"Grandfather is dead," said Yitzhak, "killed at the hands of the Ukrainians."

Fifty-five years later, Bill could still taste the fear even as he had at sixteen. Would he forever be haunted by his past?

He did not have a problem with forgiveness on an intellectual basis. He knew that a hater was not a happy human being and hating something that cannot be brought back did not make sense. He knew all of that. The conflict lay between his heart and his mind.

His heart told him he would live a happier life if he were a decent human being, kind, forgiving. Logically it was time to let go of old grudges, yet his mind told him it was not he who should ask for forgiveness. What wrong had he done? Someone else killed his parents, his family, in cold blood. Should they not be the ones asking for forgiveness?

It was in moments like this he knew he needed God. Only God would save him. When he returned from the trip to the Ukraine, his thoughts dwelled on the reality that he was the only survivor of Czerniejow, the only survivor of his family. Could God have had anything to do with this phenomenon, letting one member of the village survive so he could tell others?

It was at that moment of truth, based on fact, that Bill knew his life would take a different direction. When Ronnie asked him to get involved with the proposed building of a Holocaust museum in Houston, he found the direction he was seeking—a new purpose.

At the point Bill made his decision to become involved in the museum project, it had already become the dream of a few. In 1989 the incoming president of the Houston Jewish Federation approached a Houston real estate developer by the name of Martin Fein and shared with him an idea that had taken various shapes and forms while floating around the Jewish Federation for about ten years.

An ad hoc committee was formed to study the feasibility and desirability of building a Holocaust museum in Houston, but the idea had not gotten far. The chair of the Houston Survivors' Committee served on that committee, which concluded its work with the resolution and recommendation to the Jewish Federation that a Holocaust museum be built in Houston, a living memorial to the Holocaust with education as its main purpose.

After a period of reticence because he had always believed in gearing his life toward the positive and the living, the developer agreed to chair the Jewish Federation committee and put together a museum committee of about seventy or eighty people. The idea of playing a meaningful role in educating future generations about the lessons of the Holocaust had struck a chord with him just as it would with Bill.

The committee hired an executive director, and the focus centered on the mission of the museum. If education was to be its purpose, how would this fulfill its mission? The conclusions led to making the proposed museum committee an independent organization, separate from the Jewish Federation that had demands on its money and staff.

A belief that the board had to represent the entire Houston community—and not be strictly Jewish—permeated the committee. In addition, the opinion was that emphasis should not be placed just on the victims, but also on the perpetrators and bystanders. It took all three components to comprise the Holocaust. That meant, by extension, that this was not going to be a museum for the Jewish community but one for the community at large. With this in mind, the committee sought a location central in the city and symbolic of the city's cultural heart and soul.

In the Jewish community some people felt that a museum to espouse Jewish culture and tradition was a worthwhile subject for a museum but that it portrayed Jews as victims. Some believed it would be too difficult to raise the money needed while others felt a museum in Washington was enough. In the general community, there were many who felt the project was too secular, too Jewish, but the committee continued to explain to both the Jewish and general community that the Holocaust was a unique event with universal lessons. The Holocaust represented the first time the full weight of a mighty industrial nation was targeted toward the extermination of a single people—not for territory or political reasons, but based on racial theory.

Committee members felt it was important that the project support the importance of being humanistic, Jew or not, American or of another culture. It was important to study the roots of evil rather than question which ethnic group had suffered the most in history. The idea was to study democracy, which offers choices, and the reasoning behind standing idle while evil erupts.

The fundraising as well as concept and scope committees had Jew and Gentile working together—a representative from the Catholic diocese, a Protestant teacher from the University of St. Thomas, and the head of the National Association for the Advancement of Colored People. The mission came into focus with all segments of the community represented. Fundraising was going to be the key to their success.

The group found a building and devised a support group to help with the fundraising. They named it the Circle of Tolerance with a goal of achieving a better understanding of how occurrences such as the Holocaust happen. The goal was to create a ripple effect of better understanding and sensitivity for each human being, respecting the differences among all.

Circle of Tolerance events as well as other fundraising events like an evening at the Museum of Fine Arts and a symposium carried the mission statement to the public. An exhibit by artist Peter Martsio depicting people who risked their lives to save Jews during the war highlighted one of the affairs.

Before long, impending success permeated the group activities. Gifts came in from banks, legal services, oil companies, and other large corporations.

As influential businesspeople joined the efforts, committee members were invited into many corporate and foundation boardrooms to explain the mission and the importance of educating the general public in order that history would not recur.

The roster of people supporting the project was impressive and encouraging, but donations trickled in. If the project was to be a success, much more was needed. It was important that donors believed that, whether they gave financially, emotionally, or with their time, they were giving not only to something worthwhile but to something that would attain success.

Bill Morgan was an initial six-figure contributor. His gift immediately influenced two more—one equaled his; the other raised the ante by fifty thousand dollars. The personal contributions would need to match or surpass the donations of corporations which to date equaled forty to fifty percent of the funds for the museum project.

It had been easy for Bill to give "seed money" to the project, once he knew that not only his money but also his talents could make a positive difference in the outcome of the project. His success had come from listening, learning by doing, and making constructive decisions for further goals. A museum needed to be built. He was a builder. He had the means, the contacts, and the heart to, as he would put it, "pull the wagon." He believed other survivors in the community would soon follow with their support of time and money.

He learned early on that a person can create his or her own miracles, his or her own future. If he could succeed with so little supportive background, survive when others did not, succeed in a new world with a new language and culture, then he must have created the miracle by sheer determination. Even as he took full responsibility for his success, he felt as though he must give God credit for giving him his thoughts, his resolve. He knew that, as a human being, he acted in whatever way he had to in order to save himself, but the "how," the intuition, had to come from Someone, Something of higher knowledge. He would more than likely carry this conflict to his grave.

His father would have been proud of his charitable nature, though Bill never considered giving to others as something unusual. He never felt sorry for himself and found himself thinking more and more of others and their needs, giving generously to those in need.

He smiled as he remembered his words as a child.

"Father, why do you invite others to our table when we have so little?"

"You don't have enough, and they don't have any."

It was a simple statement that remained in Bill's memory. Often as he collected rent on his rental property, he found the renter had little in the icebox. He would fill it and postpone the rent payment. He knew what hunger was. It was his duty to be charitable. That lesson he learned well from his father and he would teach his children the same. "If you know somebody less fortunate than you, do what you can for them."

Bill's good deeds were spontaneous, but in retrospect he realized those he helped had taken the initiative to help themselves, and he admired that attitude and rewarded it. He believed in the saying, "Necessity is the mother of invention." If you are really desperate, you think of all kinds of things to work your way out of a negative circumstance, and yet this philosophy was the source of a continuing debate within his own mind. Does God give the solutions or does a person invent them? The thought must enter from someplace. Survival was a contradiction in logic that Bill could not shake.

Perhaps God saved Bill, or gave him the means to save himself, to help with the museum project. He was the only survivor of not only his family but of the village of Czerniejow. He joined the museum project, believing that he and the other survivors had an obligation to tell the world what it is like to be hungry, hated, thrown in a ghetto or concentration camp, dehumanized. Though each of the survivors would never be able to describe the fear and sadness that could not be measured, they had a responsibility to help others recognize hatred and its results.

A shuffling of the crowd interrupted Bill's thoughts. Quickly he stood and placed his right hand over his heart. The swells of the familiar tune sent a warm tingling along his spine. He felt his lip quiver, and he remembered as though it were yesterday his arrival in New York. Standing on the deck of the ship, he asked God, "What can I do here, and where do I go? I have nothing to offer." This great country had given him so much, a miracle he could not explain.

Seated again, the speakers one by one gave their remarks. When the cantor began to sing "A Soul Saved," Bill's thoughts were of his mother and father who had given him life. Distracted from the events, he was startled when he heard his name.

"Now I would like to present Bill Morgan."

He did not hear the rest of the introduction. He looked at the crowd, wondering if this was finally real. The fruits of his labor were coming to fruition, and his heart was filled. He lived in a normal country and lived a normal life. Confidence in himself had guided him to success. He had fulfilled a son's mission, but his parents would never enjoy the fruit of their labor. He honored them as the Bible said he should. Perhaps God saved him for this moment. He moved them from the ditches of Europe into the Holocaust Museum where their memories are preserved and they are introduced not only to the generations they seeded but also to the community where their son lived to carry on their legacy.

Bill stood at the microphone. He looked into the crowd and saw his children and his wife.

"Honored guests, ladies and gentlemen. This is a great day for me and all of the three hundred survivors who now live in Houston. Most of the survivors, including myself, arrived here in the late forties and early fifties. All of these survivors have spent an average of four years in concentration camps. If you multiply three hundred times four, it translates to twelve hundred years of incarceration. It boggles your mind. Would you please stand and be recognized?"

His fellow survivors stood, a moment impregnated with history, its best and its worst.

"Thank you. My friends, you can imagine how glad we were to leave those God-forsaken countries, full of haters and killers, which I do not wish to name. How happy we were to come to this paradise called the USA, our final destination that we now call home.

"Upon settling here in this great city called Houston, we had no time to waste. We went to work right away because we needed money. We accepted any kind of job that was offered to us since most of us had no skills and we didn't speak the language. We made perfect dishwashers, janitors, and construction workers, and boy, did we work! We all had the hunger to succeed and rebuild our lives as well as our families, but it didn't happen overnight. It took years of sweat and hard work and dedication to get where we are today and to achieve the American dream. We achieved everything else except peace of mind and relief from the pain in our hearts. Our memories kept haunting us and haunting us day in and day out. The questions were always in our minds—why did we survive and our families didn't? And I could never find the answer. Perhaps there is no answer.

"Most of us are senior citizens—now fathers, mothers, and even grandparents. Usually when you reach a certain age, you become forgetful, so why don't we forget? Why are the past memories still haunting us just like they happened yesterday?

"This Holocaust Museum may be an answer to our haunting questions and pain. It may even become a healer for the unanswered questions. I know it did me a lot of good by being involved. It removed some of the guilt just knowing that our loved ones' memories will be preserved and not forgotten.

"Friends, in the back of my mind I was thinking, 'Yes, we were liberated from camps and hiding places, but we were never really liberated from hate and anti-Semitism.' Maybe this Holocaust Museum in Houston, which I call the House of Love, will help us remove hate from people's hearts and replace it with love through education. This is my hope as well as my dream. This is also why I am so devoted and involved with this great institution.

"So today, ladies and gentlemen, we are turning over to the public in this great city of Houston a magnificent monument that we hope will heal and unite all races.

"Now, with your permission, I would like to conclude with some personal remarks.

"I always had it in my mind that, after I completed this building, I will move my family's souls out of the ditches where they died, bring them over here, and place them right in the entry where I have placed a plaque in their memory. My children and grandchildren can finally meet my parents and brothers and sisters whom I have been talking about for so long.

"Now, to my children—Ronnie, Michael, Wendy, Mindy, and Scott—I can now answer the question you always asked me when you were younger, 'Where are your parents, Dad? Why does Mom have parents and you don't?'

"Well, here they are. Here are my parents and your grandparents. Now for the first time you can meet them. They are over there in this building.

"Now, for the first time, I know that my family's souls are here. I never knew the date that they died and could not say the mourners' kaddish. Now I know that today's date, March 3, 1996, is the day that my family's souls have been moved and put to rest, and the date that I can use to say mourner's kaddish in their memory.

"Thank you very much for your support and for being here today."

Marty

Bill came into the museum project as a board member. I was partner with his two sons in real estate development, and I certainly wanted one of his sons involved, who was active in the community. Bill had seemed a very appropriate asset because he was a survivor.

I was trying to build a well-rounded board, meaning that the museum had to be meaningful for the general community and, therefore, different ethnic groups, religions, and backgrounds. It also had to be meaningful for the survivors. We made an early commitment to the survivors that we would try to do just that. We would have a memorial room for them because they have no cemeteries in which to say a prayer over their dead.

A key moment in the board's history, in terms of fundraising and the scope of the project, came when we interviewed for engagement Ralph Applebaum and Associates, who designed the core exhibit at the U.S. museum in Washington.

Ralph came down to Houston, looked at our plan, at our building, at our concept statement, and he said, "You might as well throw these plans away. You cannot achieve your admirable goals in this space." He quickly drew out a sketch, very similar to the wedge-shaped building that you see today.

We had a raw building, still in the thinking stage. The land that we bought was a full city block in the Binz area, that is

Opening day ceremony, Holocaust Museum, March 3, 1996. Bill Morgan at podium, (seated left to right) The Hon. Robert A. Eckels, Harris County Judge, Mayor Bob Lanier and Elyse Lanier.

Architectural views of the Holocaust Museum Houston.

becoming now an extension of the museum district. It had a building on it that had been used as an orthopedic clinic since 1969.

At first we attempted, with a smaller budget, to achieve our goals within that building—several components for a memorial room, a library, an archives, a classroom space, a 2,500-square-foot core exhibit hall, and a room for changing exhibits. Ralph Applebaum said you couldn't do that. You need a core exhibit that is much larger.

One of the first things we did when we started our existence, even before we had a building, was to take oral testimonies at Rice Media Center. There's a wonderful professor of video and television named Brian Huberman, who either donated his time or did it at cost. We did two to three hours of video testimony on each survivor or witness to the Holocaust, building a library of over a hundred such videotapes.

We also had major symposiums with school districts, with educators, social studies coordinators. So we were serving the community even before we had a building. With that wealth of material, with the background that we had, Ralph said we could not achieve what we wanted to in that building. We didn't have a theater, a larger core exhibit, among other things. It meant that we had to change our initial fundraising goal of three million dollars to seven or eight million dollars.

It was a gut-wrenching decision for a board to take on that kind of responsibility. Now here's where I remember Bill's courage and involvement. Bill was one of those who wanted to go first class, to say that we will raise more money. There's an expression in Hebrew, in the Bible, that says, "I step forward, and here I am to take responsibility." That's when Bill more than doubled his initial gift. He got a matching gift out of a friend, who at first was skeptical about whether or not the museum project could be a success.

At that point Bill became very invested in the success of the museum, became more active in all aspects of the museum—

fundraising, designing, building committee, working with the de-
signers. Bill was a bridge between the local architect and the
actual construction of the building.

Once he had given his larger gift, he began to take initiative on
fundraising. I would not describe Bill as a committee person
though. When he got it in his mind to do something, he would take
action himself, raising some very good money. He became very
dedicated to the project.

As various corporations and individuals signed on to the
project, we began to build momentum, and we had to achieve an
aura of success. Then we had people coming to us to become
involved in the project.

Momentum grew. Bill met with his family, whom he has
fought to keep together, something very difficult to do in America
today. I think that's very important to him. They made a family
decision to raise his gift to a substantial increase.

I think people were flabbergasted, extremely touched, very
moved. I believe it was announced at a board meeting. It was the
largest individual and corporate contribution and a celebrated
event.

In the beginning it was a lonely task for fifteen to twenty of us
on the building committee because the project was not universally
accepted within the Jewish community or in the community at
large. As a result, some of the board members were hesitant to
approach community members for donations. Not Bill. There was
an incidence where one member was reticent in asking a certain
philanthropist for money. Bill said, "What the heck, I don't know
him. I'm just going to go and ask him cold." He got one of the
largest gifts from him. Bill is used to success from his own shear
guts and force of personality. I feel that he has taken to this project
like nothing else he has ever done, other than business. I also
believe he looks at the museum in a similar way that I look at it—
as a "house of love." He calls it that.

Like Bill, I felt this was the best legacy I could leave for the past and for the future. My father was a survivor of several concentration camps and the sole survivor of five children. He had a niece die in his arms in a cattle car. He never got over the pain.

He was at a satellite camp of Bechow when the Allies approached as the Nazi guards scattered into the woods, not knowing if the camps were going to be bombed. The Allies found my father unconscious, weighing eighty pounds. He was unconscious for three days. He woke up in a Catholic hospital and gradually returned to some health.

I didn't care to remember my family with stone statues in parks. I felt I could do something meaningful to help prevent other families from suffering the same loss by leaving this building as a concrete symbol of tolerance and an understanding of hatred and prejudice.

The main reason I got involved with the museum was because of my three beautiful children. I fear the world we're leaving them. Like Bill, I wanted to leave them a better legacy. When you see a country like Yugoslavia reawaken old ethnic hatred, ethnic cleansing, and genocide, it says something to me about the basic human condition. It also says something to me about what good people must do where you have freedom as we do in America. It's like cancer we must try and fight. I don't think we'll ever cure cancer, but we must make the effort.

Jon

When Bill approached me about two to three years ago, saying he would like my involvement in the Holocaust Education Center, I did not hesitate. He convinced me that I needed to design and to budget the electrical job. With his encouragement, we did so as well as the wiring and we charged about half of what it was worth. I did this job and another for the Jewish Community Center because of Bill. His charitable attitude certainly influenced me.

I think the messages for charity were fixed at an early age. I remember a story that he told me about his own father. On holidays when his family barely had enough to eat, his father was forever inviting strangers into their home to share what meager food they had. Bill has always felt that he must continue that example in honor and memory of his own father.

What better example can you have of a person who came through a living hell, lost everything that he had loved and knew, and made a tremendous success out of himself? He did not turn bitter or cynical, but instead turned his entire life around. He came to a foreign country, learned a strange language, created a successful business, and raised a wonderful family.

Bill Morgan is the reason I am currently in business today. We began talking in 1982, exploring opportunities for us to work together. After several months a job came along involving a ten-story building. If I could get it, it would justify the start of my own electric company.

When I approached Bill with the opportunity, he thought it was an excellent idea and challenged me to get the job. I was fortunate to get it. Bill stood right by me, establishing a line of credit at the bank and cosigning to guarantee the bond that was required for the building. The business was formed November 8, 1983.

Bill said, "You're going to need a place to office. I have several office warehouse buildings and I want you to choose the one that is most convenient for you and we won't worry about you paying rent until you're able to generate enough money to do so."

That's exactly what happened. I moved into the office building that he owned on 34th Street. I think the Morgan boys helped construct it when they were kids. I stayed there for the first eight years we were in business.

With the business plan I outlined, and Mr. Morgan's continued support, we grew to where we are today. We have over two hundred employees, and we have done over eighty to ninety million dollars worth of work since then. I could not have done it without his backing, encouragement, and guidance.

What better mentor, guide, friend, father figure could any person have? You can't find that many generous people. Why would he pick a complete stranger to back in business, giving me such a wonderful opportunity? I will be forever indebted to him. His generosity and his loving kindness makes this world a better place.

Michael

Over the years Dad decided he wanted to learn how to speak publicly, so he went to Toastmasters. When he started to practice in front of us, we probably gave him too much grief for rambling on or saying the wrong things. At first he wrote his thoughts on paper, but then started to speak from his heart. Once he gets in that mode, he can go on forever, especially about the Holocaust, so we didn't know what was going to come out of his mouth at the museum opening.

The opening of the Holocaust Museum was overwhelming, for obvious personal reasons. I was a little nervous before Dad got started, but the speech he gave was one of the most intelligent, most articulate, most emotional, most heartwarming, I think I've ever heard. I think it was the icing on the cake. The way he delivered it couldn't have been a better written script. It "made" the opening.

He brought his family back to life, right there at that point in time. I never spent a lot of time thinking about that. I never knew them. He never talked much about his family, but when he said in his speech that he pulled them out of the ditches, brought them to the museum, buried them there, and now had a place to go to mourn, a place to introduce them to the family, it was incredible. He brought his family to life for me that day. I never expected that to happen.

I get emotional when he speaks about it. Part of me feels like we too have suffered some of what he has gone through, but it's not tangible. I wasn't there. I didn't see it. I've known since I was very young that I was different—not because I'm Jewish, but because I'm different from my Jewish friends.

I grew up with a sense of what life and death are. My father worked hard but taught us to enjoy life. Even though he came out of the ashes, he's so darn optimistic, believes nothing's impossible. For me, I like that. I'm pretty happy-go-lucky and like to have a good time. I think I have a different perspective on things that no one else has. I feel that comes from him.

Ronnie *

"Fifty years ago my father and many of our parents were liberated, liberated from places that can easily be described as worse than hell. They were physically liberated to be refugees, to search for lost loved ones, to search for the optimism to begin the rest of their lives. Metaphysically they remained imprisoned, imprisoned forever, imprisoned to live their lives bearing the horribly tragic memories of their Holocaust experience.

"I am here to speak to you tonight as a survivor—a second-generation Holocaust survivor. Recently, within the last few years,

I learned about my paternal family history, my father's background. The details were sketchy of the loss of his entire family. The specific and unforgiving details of my father's memory, memory of his early life experiences as an involuntary witness to the Holocaust, were not shared.

"Who could imagine, even remotely, that after suffering the unspeakable, suffering through the cruelest and most inhumane events of recorded human history, that my father, that our parents, as Holocaust survivors, as Jews, could not only rediscover optimism, but rebuild their lives to become the most caring, loving, compassionate, giving, and productive people in the world?

"Look around us tonight. Look at the survivors. Look at us, the second generation. Look at the love and the feelings that emanate, that radiate from each of us. Look at our families. Look at our children. Look at their grandchildren. Appreciate this miracle.

"We can cry. We can feel sorry for ourselves. We can ask God, 'Why, why did this happen to us? What did we do wrong to deserve our past?' But these questions are the wrong questions. We are beyond wondering, beyond asking questions and being burdened by forced guilt. We have passed beyond that road to nowhere. We no longer ask questions—we make statements.

"We are proud to have survived. We are proud to be second-generation Holocaust survivors. We are proud of our parents and the adversity that only they, as Jews, as respected individuals, have overcome. Who else could have accomplished what they have accomplished? No one, no one else, not me.

"Our parents did not become weaker; they became stronger. And their strength is our strength, to continue living their legacy— their proud legacy—and to make it our mission, as the second generation. Not only should we take up the duty and the obligation to preserve their history, the memory of the Holocaust, but to the extent necessary, help mentally free them from those still-imprisoned thoughts and refocus their minds toward their achievements.

As difficult as that may be, we must guide them to acknowledge their successes and accomplishments, their families, their miracles."

*Edited from Yom Hashoah message, Beth Israel Synagogue, Houston, Texas, April 26, 1995.

Wendy

We always wondered why we didn't have grandparents on Dad's side. Then we used to say, "Do we look like your mother?" or "Do we look like your father or your brothers or sisters?"

I think he said Ronnie looks like his father. Now he says one of his sisters had red hair like mine. He said his parents were tall, but my mother says, "You were a little boy, so they looked tall."

He only talked about his past if we had a report to do on the Holocaust. We could ask questions, but he never gave details. He told us, at first, he had one brother and one sister. I think only three years ago we found out that wasn't true.

I would say when he had his first grandchild, we saw a big change in him. Until then he wasn't much of a warm, cuddly type person. I don't think he knew how. My mom has taught him how. She used to tell him, "Go hug the kids." It took him a long time to come out of his shell. Now he will come in the door and give me a kiss. It makes me feel good.

The grandchildren love him! They jump all over him and play with him. They call him Baba.

I think it's a great thing that he got into the museum, and I think it makes him feel better about himself, about his past. I feel honored—special, in a way—that he is a survivor.

He is special because he went through it and survived. I don't know how I could have done it.

Marci

My eyes weren't dry for very long at the opening of the Holocaust Museum. I was just very deeply touched by what Bill said. It was an incredible speech from beginning to end.

I think the part that really, really got me was when he said to his children—and he named all five of them—"I now have a place to bury my parents. This is where your grandparents are."

I just lost it. It was incredible, very emotional. It was fulfilling, yet draining because of the subject matter. Bill's speech got to me because it's a legacy for our children. Not only is it a place for Ronnie's grandparents, but it's a place for our children's great-grandparents. It affects all of our generations. We couldn't stop talking about the day.

I feel that it's very plain to say that what you see is what you get with Bill. "You may not agree with it, and you're entitled to your feelings, but this is how I feel about it."

I feel like he's a good person to talk to about a lot of things. If I really needed to talk to him about a very personal moment, I feel he would listen. He's a good listener.

I remember his speech to Ronnie and me at our rehearsal dinner. It was wonderful what he said to me. "I know you've lost your father. I want to do the best I can to be a father for you. I'm here for you."

It was really special because I felt the loss at that moment, not having a father at my wedding. Bill was really kind with those words.

Howard

We went to the dinner before the dedication of the project. This was several months before the opening. Bill made the comment, "I'm pulling my parents out of the grave with this museum."

I felt that the Holocaust Museum project was a real blessing for Bill, yet it also brought back difficult memories, probably better left alone. It was emotional for him to go back to the basic feelings he had as a little boy when he left his parents.

I think he carries around a tremendous amount of guilt—suppressed until certain things trigger it, causing trauma. It is probably more than any of us could ever bear and still be sane.

The weather was not good the evening of the dedication, and Bill had on his cowboy hat and trench coat. When we left the museum—it must have been after 10:00 p.m.—we saw him just walking around outside, looking at things. It's very much like him to go out and inspect things, from a building standpoint, but it wasn't that. It was almost like he was in a daze or just something wasn't right.

I thought he really needed to slow down and back away from this. I was pretty worried about him, emotionally, as was Wendy. I know Shirley had expressed concern that he's just way too involved, there every night, doing too much.

He's not a young man. To have something bring that kind of emotional upheaval in your life is probably very difficult at that age. I think the museum itself has been a blessing to him because he's gotten an outlet for the emotions, and yet it raises all kinds of evil spirits.

At the opening the speech he gave made you wonder. How does one walk around with that kind of guilt and emotion? I'm surprised he has the love left in him that he has. I mean, any human being who lives with the things that he lives with has got to be extraordinarily strong.

He said to his children and grandchildren, "If you want to meet your grandparents, then come here. Here they are."

How can you have a response to anything like that? I can't think of anything in my life that parallels that kind of emotion. It's traumatic.

I don't see how anything could erase his guilt because it's pervasive and probably the single most critical thing in his life that he's had the most difficult time with. I don't know how he lives with it. He tries to forgive, tries to educate and overcome it through education, in part as a lesson to his kids and grandchildren.

The grandchildren may be the key to helping him overcome any lasting prejudice against those who were the perpetrators of hate and murder. Much more important than holding on to the ire is his love for the kids. He loves being with them, observing them and watching them play. I think he gets a great deal of pleasure just knowing that from him sprang all of this.

Mindy

The Holocaust Museum is the best thing Dad has ever done, not only for his family, the loved ones left behind in Europe, but for his immediate family as well. I don't know if he realizes it, but he has left us a big part of himself that we will always have even when he is gone.

I think the museum, for him, was a tribute to his parents with the plaques inside and his words, "Now they're here with me." I realize that he, all of us, are still little girls and little boys in some respects. We all need our mommies and daddies. Here's this man who is so strong, though probably not as strong as I thought he was, because you think your parents are invincible and they can handle anything when you're a kid, and when you become a parent, you know otherwise. I realize that he loved them so much and felt guilty for what happened.

My dad has a lot of common sense and I think that is what helped him survive. I don't think he believed in God for a long time. I don't think a lot of survivors believe in God, yet Dad is extremely spiritual. We all are. We're not religious, but we have strong values and morals. We know we're Jewish and practice it, and I wouldn't want to be any other thing.

I understand my father and know him better now than I have in the past thirty-six years. I know my dad as the child longing for his mommy and daddy, brothers and sisters, aunts and uncles. I cry when I read and see about other survivors, always thinking of my father and the childhood he never had.

We are a product of our childhood. Parents who were very religious raised him, but then once the war started and he had to run, all he thought about was surviving. He had to work hard to do that, had to outsmart a lot of people. All that stuff carried over. He would not tolerate us watching television, not working hard at whatever we were doing. He actually was a bit of a perfectionist, not the most emotional father. I guess he felt it was a way for us to survive. I didn't understand it then, but I do now.

He changed when we started having kids, more and more as he's gotten older. He expresses himself more, maybe because he finally told us about his past. It's not something he has to protect from other people now.

Now I feel like I know what he is made of, what makes him tick. The light bulb finally came on as to what my father really is, and that it is a different picture than what it was when I grew up.

He didn't know how to give affection. My mom taught him. I feel closer to him now than I ever have, maybe because I'm grown up and no longer afraid to express myself to him. It's always been difficult for me to talk about my feelings so I understand his reluctance. He listens to my ideas and views now.

He is so full of affection now. He only knew survival and what he had to do for protection. He only knew hard work, smart work. I often wonder what would have happened if he would have finished college. He's a brilliant man.

I am educating my children on the museum and my daughter is doing a history fair project on the *Diary of Anne Frank.* We read *Jacob's Rescue* that is also a Holocaust book. I tell them all the time where their grandfather came from and what he had to do. They are really interested, which surprised me.

I know he loves us very much. He tells me all the time now.

I still put him on a pedestal, maybe because of the father-daughter thing or maybe because his life is so unbelievable. Yet he lived it and is here to tell about it. He has left us with something that we will always carry with us—the museum and him as a mentor.

We will tell his story when he is gone and hopefully our children will tell it when we are gone. And every generation thereafter will know of Baba, the human being who suffered, who turned his life into a success with family, love, business, but most of all with a museum of love, tolerance, and education. I love you, Dad.

Epilogue

Bill now speaks of the Houston Holocaust Memorial Museum as another miracle in his life, one which allowed him to move his lost family spiritually to a burial ground and one which educates against the hatred and abuse that caused their deaths as well as the deaths of millions of other people. The Morgan Family Center for Holocaust Studies was established in their memory as part of the museum.

Within the first year of the opening of the museum, one hundred thousand visitors toured the center. At least twenty percent or more were youth from four hundred schools in Texas and other states. Moviemaker Steven Spielberg brought his entire family to see the museum.

Bill Morgan was instrumental in creating a film catalog of student comments as they exited the museum. Some of the comments include: "I've seen things here today that you could never learn in a classroom or a textbook." A sixth grade student remarked, "I've learned where the path of hate can take us. I'm never going to stand by and not do anything again when I see hatred. If people had stood up for their friends and neighbors, maybe this wouldn't have happened."

THE
MORGAN FAMILY
CENTER FOR
HOLOCAUST
STUDIES

In loving memory of Yitzhak and Etta Margulies,
The parents of Yossel Margulies,
And in further memory of Yossel's siblings,
Sarah, Solomon, Bunya, Byla,
And two younger brothers,
Whose names have been lost to memory.

All perished during the Holocaust in the Stanistawów (Poland) ghetto
during or after 1941

זכר צדיק לברכה
MAY THE MEMORY OF THE RIGHTEOUS BE A BLESSING

Dedicated by Bill Morgan (Yossel Margulies), born in Czerniejow, Poland,
sole surviving member of the Margulies family,
together with his wife, Shirley, and their children and grandchildren.
March 1996

Even though running a museum can be problematic and frustrating at times, the museum staff continues to be amazed when they look at the student comments. All doubts as to whether the youth could make connections from the past to the modern-day world are dissipataed. The young people are getting the message.

Every week students send or bring to the museum things they've made—sculptures, poems, and art projects. Plans are underway to create an exhibit to display student contributions.

At least once a week the museum offers events on site, including monthly lectures open to the public. Seminars and workshops for teachers impact hundreds of students. A speakers' bureau sends survivors and historians to schools for presentations, and survivors are often present to answer student questions when they visit the museum.

University of Houston students have established a penny campaign to raise a contribution of 1.5 million pennies to repressent the children who perished in the Holocaust.

The Christian community continues to be involved. Of the visitors, more than half are non-Jewish. The first membership drive brought in eighteen hundred members and three hundred thousand dollars. Initially many were Jewish; however, non-Jewish membership is increasing.

The first annual benefit dinner brought half a million dollars to the organization, twice the amount raised in the past.

Lectures named for Ruth Lack, a former director of the museum who suffered a fatal accident, feature such noted speakers as Eli Wiesel, noted author and a survivor of the Holocaust. Presented annually, the lectures draw large crowds.

In March of 1996 the Christian and Jewish communities raised a half million dollars for the operation of the museum.

Bill Morgan now sits as chairman of the board.

The Morgan Group—which has expanded to Arizona, California, Colorado, Florida, Kansas, and Tennessee—has returned to the Houston market.* Plans are underway for a sixteen-acre site in west Houston where they will develop either a 322-unit luxury apartment complex or a 240,000-square-foot office building. Also they are one of several developers who are bringing about a renaissance in the inner loop of Houston.

Bill continues to work as a consultant for "the boys."

Regardless of any other accomplishments, Bill is most proud of his family. He is a mentor to his children and grandchildren, eager to teach them the importance of relationships and the significance of love that should never be taken for granted. He proudly proclaims, "A dollar is a dollar, but you can't buy the wealth of a family with a dollar."

Yosella, the poor farm boy who fled for his life and immigrated to a country which allowed him to prosper, created a legacy for the family he lost and the family he produced.

---

* "They're back: Morgan Group returns to home ground," by Tanya Rutledge, *Houston Business Journal,* January 10-16, 1997.

IN LOVING MEMORY

OF

GRANDFATHER MARGULIES
YITZHAK AND ETTA GABIRER MARGULIES
SARAH, SOLOMON, BUNYA, BYLA,
AND TWO SMALL BROTHERS
WHOSE NAMES ARE LOST IN THE PAIN

MARGULIES/MORGAN FAMILY TREE
(Key: B birth; D death; M married)

Grandfather Margulies
M: ?
B: ? D: 1941

(son)	(daughter)	(daughter)
	B: ? D: 1941–45?	B: ? D: 1941–45?
Yitzhak (Isaac) B: ? D: 1941–45		
M: Etta Gabirer B: ? D: 1941–45?	M: ? B: ? D: ?	M: Mordechay (Mordko) B: ? D:
	daughter B: ? D: ?	Moshko (son) B: ? D: ?
	daughter B: ? D: ?	daughter B: ? D: ?

Sarah (daughter) B: ?; D: 1941–45	Solomon (son) B: ?; D:1941	Bunya (son) B: ?; D:1941–45	Wolf "Yosseli" (son) B: 1925	Byla (daughter) B: ?; D: 1941–45	(Son)	(Son)

William Jacob "Bill" Morgan

M: Shirley Grace Fallas 1954
B: 1933

/
Ronald Issac
B: 1956

M: Marci Rosmarin 1986
B: 1959

/
Ryan Bradley
B: 1988

Blake Elliot
B: 1989

Lauren Brooke
B: 1993

/
Michael Solomon
B: 1957

M: Patty Blum 1984
B: 1962

/
Jeffrey Philip
B: 1987

Russ Daniel
B: 1990

Lillian Pearl
B: 1996

Melinda Etta
B: 1960

M: Steven Neil Finger 1983
B: 1959

/
Erin Kimberly
B: 1985

Stephanie Lynn
B: 19/87

David Michael
B: 1990

Wendy Paige
B: 1964

M: Howard M. Cohen 1988
B: 1963

/
Kimberly Rachael
B: 1990

Rebecca Grace
B: 1993

Hannah
B: 1995

Scott
B: 1968

M: Jayme Stein 1992
B: 1969

RESOURCES

Dawidowicz, Lucy S. *The War Against the Jews.* Bantam Books, 1975.

Galvin, Herman, and Stan Tamarkin. *The Yiddish Dictionary Sourcebook: A Transliterated Guide to the Yiddish Language.* Hoboken: KTAV Publishing House, Inc., 1986.

Gutman, Israel, editor in chief. *Encycopedia of the Holocaust,* Vol 4. New York: MacMillan Publishing Company, 1990.

Hilberg, Raul. *The Destruction of the European Jews.* New York: Holmes & Mier, 1985.

Hutton, Jim and Jim Henderson. *Houston: A History of a Giant.* Tulsa: Continental Heritage, Inc., 1976.

Landau, Ronnie S. *The Nazi Holocaust.* Chicago: Ivan R. Dee, 1994.

Pogonowski, Iwo Cyprian. *Polish-English, English-Polish Dictionary.* New York: Hippocrene Books, 1993.

Roehm, A. Wesley, et al. *The Record of Mankind.* Boston: DC Heath & Company, 1961.

Segal, Stanley E. *Houston: A Chronicle of the Super City on Buffalo Bayou.* Woodland Hills: Windsor Publications, Inc., 1983.